WILDCAT

A Romance of the West

Stephen L. Brooks

Doug,
Thanks for riding with Wildcat!
Steve Brooks

Digital Parchment Press

Copyright © 2014 Stephen L. Brooks
All rights reserved.
ISBN: 9781799225829

CONTENTS

CHAPTER ONE	1
CHAPTER TWO	8
CHAPTER THREE	16
CHAPTER FOUR	25
CHAPTER FIVE	29
CHAPTER SIX	39
CHAPTER SEVEN	48
CHAPTER EIGHT	58
CHAPTER NINE	69
CHAPTER TEN	80
CHAPTER ELEVEN	98
CHAPTER TWELVE	105
CHAPTER THIRTEEN	114
CHAPTER FOURTEEN	121
CHAPTER FIFTEEN	133
CHAPTER SIXTEEN	146
CHAPTER SEVENTEEN	158
CHAPTER EIGHTEEN	166
CHAPTER NINETEEN	173
CHAPTER TWENTY	181
CHAPTER TWENTY-ONE	189
EPILOGUE	202
AUTHOR'S NOTE	209

WILDCAT

CHAPTER ONE

The Crandall ranch spread across a couple hundred acres of prime grazing land. There were many in the territory who envied Tom Crandall for his range and the success he had on it, but there were none who didn't respect him as well. Tom Crandall had come out here with nothing but a wagon, a couple of horses, a handful of breeding stock, and a wife soon to deliver their first born.

Doctors back east had warned them about traveling along those dusty, barren, rock-strewn cuts that went by the name "roads," that it posed a danger to both his wife Molly and the child within her. But Tom and Molly were the type that if you warned 'em or forbid 'em them something, why they'd do it just to prove you wrong.

They had just gotten to the land Crandall had staked out in his previous trip a few months back when Molly started to groan and double with the pains of childbirth. They were surrounded by nothing but open land and water; not a living soul besides them within miles, except the horses and cattle; and they weren't much help in delivering a human child.

Tom eased Molly off the wagon and hauled himself inside it to root for some blankets. He made a rude bed for her, as soft as time allowed, and laid her on it.

Molly's cries by now were spooking the animals, but Tom couldn't take time to do anything about them. He knelt beside her, bathing her flaming forehead with a handkerchief he'd managed to soak in the nearby stream bed.

"It's all right, Molly," he said, "it'll be all right."

"The baby..." Molly gasped, "the baby's comin'!"

"Now you know it ain't time yet," he said, stroking her belly in hopes of convincing the baby it was too anxious to get out.

"No!" Molly insisted, grabbing Tom by the shirt front, "it's comin'! You gotta do somethin'!"

Tom didn't know just what he could do; but then no one

knows what they are capable of in a crisis. And this was a crisis.

Molly drew up her knees, clutching at each breath between words. "Lift — my — dress."

Tom needed the cool wet cloth on his own head now. The perspiration was staining his shirt, and he was burning up too, in spite of the cool breeze passing across them. "Now Molly, you know it just ain't right to expose yourself that way out here in the open."

Her grip was harder. "You weren't so shy about undressin' me about nine months back!" She pulled him closer. "Besides, who's gonna see anything out here except you and some dumb horses and cows? Now, lift my dress. Now!"

Tom and Molly had only been married about a year, but he knew better than to argue with her. He moved himself around until he was squatting by her feet and lifted the dress and petticoats underneath. Something was going on here, that was for sure.

Molly managed to raise herself a little on her elbows. "Now, I'm gonna push. You be ready. The baby's head'll come out first."

Tom wasn't sure about what he was supposed to do about it, but something told him the baby was coming no matter what he did or didn't do.

Molly gave a prolonged grunt and he saw something round and red with a suggestion of fuzz start to come out.

"Molly! It's — it's comin'!" Instinct kicked in and he realized his job was to catch the baby as it came out. He placed his hands just under the tiny head. "Do it again! C'mon!"

Another grunt, another push, and the head and shoulders were out. Tom held that head and shoulders as they emerged. "One more oughtta do it!"

Molly gave one more push and the baby was in Tom's arms.

"Cut — cut the cord," Molly gasped.

Tom lay the baby gently on the blanket, supporting the tiny head, and pulled out his pocket knife, opening the blade with his teeth, and cut the cord.

Land sakes, giving birth to babies was a messy business. But Tom Crandall couldn't care about that now. He grabbed a towel he'd brought out with the blankets and wrapped the baby in it. The baby cried its first breath, gurgled, and seemed to realize it was safe in the arms that held it.

Tom sidled back around and held the baby so Molly could see it. "Look, Molly! I did it! *We* did it!"

Molly whispered, "Boy or girl?"

In the excitement Tom hadn't taken time to notice. He'd been hoping for a boy of course, to help run the ranch. He opened the towel and took a peak. Then he managed a smile when he told her, "It's a girl."

Molly smiled on their baby daughter, and the smile was still on her lips when her last breath blessed the new-born. Her eyes, though they no longer saw, were still on her when Tom realized she was gone.

His tears washed his daughter's face.

He buried Molly right there, and used some spare lumber to make a cross with her name on it.

Years later, when his ranch had grown to be the most prosperous in the territory, he bought a stone marker and had it inscribed with her name, dates, and the words BELOVED WIFE AND MOTHER on them.

Almost two decades later, his daughter erected a second stone beside it for his grave.

* * *

All the ranchers around these parts and everybody in town turned out for Tom Crandall's funeral. The men dressed in dark, solemn "Sunday-go-to-meetin'" suits and the women in black dresses that covered everything from the neck down with hands concealed in black cloth gloves matched the somber mood around the grave site. Among the more prominent townspeople were Clem Grange, editor of the local newspaper, Doc Murray, and banker Morgan Hopkins and his wife and two grown sons. Even the children were dressed in black, their parents keeping a hand on a restless shoulder, squeezing occasionally to still a bout of the fidgets.

One figure stood out among this company in black. She was tall, a beat up Stetson turned back on the crown of her head, a tan suede jacket over a plaid flannel shirt, chaps tied over worn jeans, tucked into boots still dusty from the trail. This was the heir, Tom Crandall's daughter, Allison; though nobody called her that. She stood like a man, her thumbs tucked into her gunbelt and one knee slightly bent. A blade of grass protruded from between her lips as she chewed.

"Behold, I tell you a mystery," the minister said. "We shall not all sleep, but we shall be changed; in a moment, in the twinkling of an eye, at the sound of the last trump. For the trumpet shall sound, and the dead shall be raised incorruptible."

She listened just as closely as the others, and was just as solemn, though several of the women cast disapproving glances at her. She ignored them. He had been *her* father, not theirs. She had loved him, and he her, and now she was mourning his death the only way she knew how. If they didn't like the way she did it, that was their look-out.

The minister led them in the Twenty-Third Psalm, and she repeated the words just as the rest of them. Her father had encouraged her to read and educate herself, though the only books he owned were a Bible and a Shakespeare. And she knew much of both books by heart.

The minister concluded the service with a benediction and the crowd began to break up. Allison stood communing with the pine box that contained her father's remains as the others moved around her. Some came and offered their condolences, which she acknowledged with nods.

Clem, small and quiet mannered, took her hand and said a few words that echoed the minster's. The editor was a good man, who tried to live a good life; and Kat appreciated his warmth.

But Banker Hopkins was a bit different. "We're all so sorry to see your father go," he said, with the warmth of a winter wind. "But I'm sure you will follow through in his obligations, as he always did."

Kat frowned. "Just what do you mean, Mr. Hopkins?"

"Why, the mortgage on the ranch of course. There's another two years, I believe, payable monthly."

Kat wanted to suggest where he might place that mortgage

BOOK TITLE

but kept that to herself. "You'll get your money."

"Why Miss Crandall, I was just expressing my hopes that you will continue to honor your father's legacy of meeting all his responsibilities, that's all."

"Ahuh. Like I said, you'll get your money." She turned away from him to the next in line.

Two middle-aged housewives gave their sympathy but as they went their way she heard one of them say:

"Isn't it shameful? She won't even wear a dress to her own father's funeral, much less a black one. Standing there before the Lord in buckskin, dressed like a man instead of a lady."

She heard that and flame burned within her green eyes as she stalked after them, overtaking and confronting them, her hands balled into fists at her side, "Bet you don't think I heard you but I did. Not a lady? Maybe I ain't dressed like one, but I don't think a lady talks about somebody who just lost the best man she ever knew when they think she's not listenin'." The flame had reached her cheeks, reddening the freckles on them into a searing glow.

"Really, Miss Crandall, we really didn't mean anything by it," Mrs. Brody said. "I just meant..."

"What Mrs. Brody is trying to say," Mrs. Wheeler said, "is that..."

"That you didn't think I'd hear you. Or did you *want* me to hear you and shame me into wearing girlie frills to prove I'm a lady?"

"No, we don't mean that at all..." Mrs. Brody resumed her indignant tone.

Allison saw their husbands coming to their wives' rescue and cut the argument short. "Well, I'm gonna prove I'm a lady by not smacking the two of you right now 'cause it's my daddy's funeral and that would be disrespectful." Her fists remained tightly clenched at her sides. "So I'll thank you for your sympathy, and thank you again for keepin' your other opinions to yourselves." The bewildered husbands had reached their wives. She tugged at the brim of her hat so it shaded her eyes and she said to all four of them, "Thanks for coming and a good day to you."

She started away and turned back. "And calling me 'Miss

Crandall' ain't gonna make me more of a lady. You know my name: Allison Katherine Crandall. And if that's too much of a mouthful, just call me Kat."

The husbands were inquiring of their wives what this was all about as she strode away from them, down the slope of Boot Hill, to the tree where her horse was tied. She swung into the saddle and rode back to the ranch.

* * *

Allison Katherine Crandall. She told everyone to call her Kat; and some, due to the feisty reputation gained when she was a youngster, added a shorter version of her first name too forming the nickname Allie Kat. And that fit, because from childhood she was a scrapper. She took no lip off anyone, and could give it back as good or better than she got.

Her daddy had taught her well. She was a skilled horsewoman at five and a crack shot at seven. And when Billy Holcomb had tried to kiss her on her twelfth birthday, why the black eye she gave him cured him of any more of *that* foolishness.

When she turned fifteen she was riding herd with the best of the men. She was tall for a girl, and she purposely wore clothes that hid any softness in her body. The sun had bronzed her face and arms as though to match the hue of the long ponytail that grew uncut and untamed, flying like a copper banner from beneath her battered tan Stetson when she was in motion; which was most of the time.

And now at twenty she was owner of her father's lands, cattle, and other property. She'd never expected this to happen; the little girl inside her, the part she fought to deny, thought her daddy was going to be around forever; or at least a lot longer than this. But her daddy's men were good men, and they looked at her as one of their own. She could ride and rope and shoot as good as any of them. With their help there would be no trouble continuing on the Bar C.

Kat had reached the borders of her ranch. There was no fence; her daddy hadn't believed in them, but there were markers. Posts, driven into the ground at regular spots, bore rude planks with the Bar C brand burned into them. Kat saw that one of the posts was leaning and dismounted. She wrestled it upright and kicked some dirt around it, filling in the widened hole and shoving a rock or two to help brace it. Each sign also bore a number; the posts were numbered consecutively around the border of the ranch. This one was 475. That made it easy to identify when one needed repair. Kat noted the number and made a point of telling Larson the foreman as soon as she reached the ranch house.

She sat her horse and gazed at the land around her. Vast, wide, open, with woods at one horizon and mountains on another. Her father's land: rich grassland, fertile, healthy, with streams of fresh clear water partly aided by the hand-cut channels her father and his men and even she had helped dig. To the east she could see the smoke of the ranch house and another column of smoke from the bunkhouse. She gave a nudge to her horse and he knew to take her home.

CHAPTER TWO

Some of the cow hands were gathered outside the bunkhouse when she got there. All had been at the funeral, and those who owned Sunday suits and worn them now had changed back into their trail clothes. They lazied against the corral fence or sat on stumps or crates, smoking or chewing. The appetizing aroma of chili met her nostrils as she dismounted. Larson, the foreman, stood with some men Kat knew as Butch, Lefty, Grady, and Bennett. In the west a lot of men went by one-word handles, either a nick-name or whatever name they chose to give. Sometimes it meant the person had something to hide; but not always. It was just accepted for what it was. The hands all looked up when Kat started toward them with her man-like stride, but none took off their hats. They knew she didn't go for such foofraw.

"Kat," Larson said with a nod.

"Larson. And you other boys too; get everybody out here."

"Well Kat, we're jest about to eat..." Larson protested. "Yer welcome t' join us if you'd like."

"Not today. C'mon, Larson, get 'em out here. I got something to say an' it'll only take a minute. That chili smells good, an' I'm not gonna keep ya from it long." Her thumbs were in her belt again and her feet were apart like a man's.

Larson knew that was her brick wall stance; there was nothing doing against it. He went to the door of the bunkhouse and called out the three or four still inside. "Kat wants to talk to us before chow," he said.

The men came out. Besides the crew with Larson there were about a half dozen others. One still had his Sunday pants on, but the suspenders held them up over his underwear so he'd dispensed at least with the coat and starched shirt.

"I jest have something to say before you eat. I wanna thank you for showin' your respects to my daddy today."

"Why, we all thought right highly of your paw," Larson

said.

"We all respected him," Lefty agreed.

"Me and the boys thought the world of 'im," Dakota, one of the other hands, said. Nods and comments from the others showed the feeling was unanimous.

"Well I jest wanna say that things are gonna go on jest like they been," Kat continued. "We'll run this ranch jest like my daddy did, and I want you all to stay on and we'll do it together."

"We respected your paw all right," Larson said, "but I dunno about workin' for a female lady."

"I'm not a female lady," Kat said. "I think I've proved that to you all these years. I can ride and rope as good as any of you. In fact, I beat Slim there in the last rodeo." She pointed to the short, overweight hand who was snacking on a loaf of bread to curb his hunger pangs before lunch. Slim grinned but didn't try replying around the mouthful he had just bitten off.

""My daddy wanted a boy. Well, he got me instead. But you know he raised me like I was his boy; some of you have even been around most of that time."

There were some murmurs of agreement, except from the Larson bunch.

"So what do you say? Will you all stay on?"

Larson straightened. He was a good head taller than Kat, and corded muscle and hard bone were under the flannel and denim. "Not me. An' any of you who choose to work for a female might as well be puttin' on petticoats themselves."

Kat glared at him, but she saw that the men standing closest to him were with him on this. If he went, and they went with him, maybe it was just as well. "How about the rest of you? You know I don't wear no petticoats, and I sure won't ask you to. I've got no use for 'em; but I've got use for men who ain't afraid to ride herd, rope and brand like we always did."

Glances were exchanged, some questioning and some challenging. Two or three more moved over to Larson's side; a few stayed behind. When the imaginary line in the sand had been crossed only Hank, Rawhide, and Dakota remained on Kat's side.

Kat just nodded, her glare again fixing on Larson. "All right.

You men get your gear and get out."

"But you said you weren't gonna deprive us of lunch!" Larson said. His tone held obvious mockery.

"Lunch in this bunkhouse is for men who work here; not you. You all just quit; it was your choice, not mine. Stop by the ranch house and I'll have your pay ready before you ride out. And if I ever see any of you on Bar C land again, unless you want your job back, I'll shoot you on sight." She turned to the three who stayed. "That's my orders, boys; and if you see any of these 'em, shoot 'em down and leave be."

Larson looked like he was going to make a play but Kat's gun hand flexed impatiently while her thumb still hooked the belt.

"You don't really wanna try that, do ya Larson?" Kat said.

Three other gun hands stirred from the men who had stayed loyal.

"No, I reckon not." Larson gave a mocking tip to his hat and said, "C'mon boys; let's get the hell outta here."

Larson and his crew strode into the tack house to collect their gear. The remaining three gathered protectively around Kat.

"We were ready for 'im if you needed us, Kat," Rawhide said. "An' if he'd got you, even just a flesh wound, those hombres with him would have to make a stop at Boot Hill to drop his remains in a hole."

"Thanks. I coulda taken him, you know," Kat said.

"Sure Kat, we know," Hank said. "Jest lettin' ya know we're backin' any play you wanna make."

"Thanks, boys. I'm much obliged I can count on you."

* * *

A week had passed since Tom Crandall's funeral. Kat and Rawhide drove the buckboard on a supply run into town. She didn't like the idea of leaving only two hands back at the ranch but until she hired more men there wasn't much choice.

Clear Springs was a town that had been around long enough to grow a bit. Two things a western town before anything else were at least one saloon and one cemetery. But

BOOK TITLE

Clear Springs had a church, a newspaper office, a telegraph office, and even a bank.

Kat pulled the buckboard to a stop in front of the Brody's general store and handed Rawhide the list. "This is what we need. I've got an errand over to the newspaper office. I'll meet you back here in half an hour."

Rawhide had gotten his name from his looks: long and sinewy, dried up by the western sun like a strip of leather. His vest, chaps, and boots seemed made from the same uncured cowhide as his flesh. Straggly, wiry hair hung out in odd places from under his hat brim, and though he swore he'd shaved before setting out for town, his cheeks sure didn't look it. But then, they never did. Rawhide scanned over the list, scratching his head. "I dunno, Kat; I'm not sure what some o' this stuff is."

"Well, it's..." Kat looked over his shoulder to explain. "You dern fool; you've got it upside-down!"

Rawhide grinned sheepishly as he turned the paper around. "Shucks Kat, I don't go much in fer readin' writin' nohow. I reckon Brody'll know what it is, though."

"You just go ahead. And meet me here in a half hour. And don't go buyin' any o' that cinnamon candy that burns your mouth up, 'cause you'll just be drinkin' water the rest of the afternoon if you do."

"Yes'm Kat. I won't." He dismounted from his side and she from hers. The newspaper office was right across the street from the store.

Morgan Hopkins was coming out of the eating place which dared call itself a restaurant and saw Kat. "Miss Crandall!"

Kat stopped with a resigned sigh. "Hello, Mr. Hopkins."

"Don't forget what we talked about."

"I haven't forgotten. You'll have your money the end of next week."

Hopkins smiled. "It's not the money you understand; it's the principle of meeting your obligations on time."

"You'll get paid."

Hopkins tipped his hat. "Pleasure speaking with you, Miss Crandall." Swelled with self-importance he continued to his bank.

She didn't bother reminding him to call her Kat; her friends called her that, and he was nobody's friend far as she knew.

Kat entered the newspaper office. Clem Grange, the sole reporter, editor, typesetter, and printer of the paper was as usual composing his next edition. He was a small man of indeterminate age filled with nervous energy. Some claimed he was in his mid-sixties, but even if so he had more energy than some half that age. His sleeves were rolled up and held with bands, an eye-shade formed an awning over his brow, and his fingers were blackened with the ink that wouldn't wash off and was probably an ingredient in his blood anyway. He looked up as the little silver bell over the door jingled.

"Kat Crandall!" he said, carefully setting down the tray of type he'd set so far. "How are you making out?"

"Not so good, Clem. All I got left is three hands; the same three I had when I came by here last week."

"No one's answered the ad I placed for you?"

"No. How about the handbills I had you print up? Are they done?"

"Sure thing. I was waiting for you to call for them." He went to a table where he kept print for hire jobs. Her handbills were in a stack next to other similar work. "Here they are: a hundred of them. That'll be a half dollar."

Kat dug into her jeans and gave him the coin. "Thanks, Clem. Much obliged."

"Hope you get some takers soon."

"Have you seen Larson and any of his crew around town?"

Clem nodded. "Yes, I've seen a couple of them. I don't know if they're still with him or not, but they hang around. Especially that Butch and his pal Grady."

Kat frowned. "Hmph. Thought they'd lit out for the high country by now."

"They haven't given you any trouble, have they Kat?"

"No; and they'd better not."

"I'll tell Sheriff Stokes to be on the lookout for them."

"Stokes? What can he do? He just lounges around that office all day, collecting wages for doing nothing. Maybe he throws an occasional drunk in a cell to sleep it off, but only after somebody else has taken away the drunk's gun."

Clem chuckled. "That's law and order in the west for you."

BOOK TITLE

"You're right." Kat patted the butt of her six-shooter. "Sometimes this is the only law we got." Picking up the tied bundle of fliers Kat thanked him again and went out.

She took the bundle to the buckboard and with her pocket knife cut the twine that bound it. She took a handful off the top, tied the cord back together, and with a hammer and a small sack of nails she'd brought from the ranch started nailing the handbills around town. She'd gotten almost half of them up when she realized two pairs of heavy boots had been following her since she started. She hung one more and heard a voice snarl.

"Runnin' a ranch ain't no job for a woman."

She snapped her head around and saw the speaker, leaning against a post, a cigarette dangling from grinning lips.

"Butch. Hanging around town? Didn't your pard Larson find some work for you?"

"Oh, there's work comin'. Larson's got it all figgered out."

"Well, you can tell him for me that the Bar C is running fine without him; or you. Or your friend Grady." She nodded to the other mangy dawdler beside him.

"Really?" Butch pulled one of the handbills from his pocket, already crumpled into a ball. "Is that why yer putting up these?"

"We're short handed is all. Not that it's any of *your* business."

Some townspeople and passers-by were stopping now to listen. One of them was a tall man, burned by the sun until his twenty-five years nearly twice that. He took particular interest in the goings on.

Kat didn't have time to exchange the time of day with Butch and Grady so she turned about and down between two buildings.

She reached the other side. Butch and Grady were waiting for her.

"Oh no ya don't," Butch said, tearing the remaining handbills from her and grabbing her roughly, a coarse hand clamped over her mouth. There was a barn nearby, part of the livery stable but largely unused. "C'mon, sister." He dragged her to it and inside. "I'm gonna show ya the only thing a woman's good for."

Kat struggled, broke away enough to land a haymaker on Butch's jaw.

Butch only grinned as he rubbed it. "That's what I like; a gal with spunk." He lunged for her.

Kat was ready to fight, but screaming for help wasn't in her. She went for her gun but Butch quickly wrested it from her, tossing it onto the hay. Her flannel shirt tore open and her breasts peaked through.

Grady started to shut the door, knowing it was his turn next.

The door suddenly struck back at him, knocking Grady to the ground stunned.

The stranger who had been watching before stood in the doorway. "It takes a small man to beat up a woman," he said.

Butch looked up long enough for Kat to kick his shins. She was aiming for something higher but the shins would have to do. Butch stepped back and called Kat a certain name which at that time was reserved for female dogs.

His shirt was grabbed in a strong hand. "And calling a woman names. That's just not bein' a gentleman." A hard fist crashed into the same part of his maw that Kat had punched before. Butch wondered for an instant which was worse. The man's fist was poised now just in front of his face.

"I give you a choice," the stranger said. "Pick up the trash you left by the door and get out, or I'll make a mess of your ugly face."

Butch said, "I'll go." He was released with a shove. He almost went for his gun but didn't want to test this newcomer any more. At least not yet. His eyes on the stranger the whole time he went over to Grady who was just waking up. "C'mon, let's ride." As Grady gathered himself and found his fallen hat, Butch looked back at the stranger and Kat. "I'm not done yet." With that awesome threat he shoved Grady out the door and they went for their horses.

Kat had retrieved her gun and came to the stranger's side. She looked him up and down then nodded after the two. "I coulda handled him, you know," she said.

The stranger smiled down at her. "I'm bettin' you could. But everybody needs a little help now and then."

"Yeah; I guess. Thanks."

"Maybe I can help some more. I saw your flier and I wanna apply for the job."

"No thanks." Kat wondered if this was a setup and this stranger was part of the plans Butch said Larson was making. "I don't know you, and I want men I can trust." She started out the door."

"Trust? Well, looks to me like I just saved your life."

Kat stopped and turned back to him. "Maybe. Or maybe that's just what it looks like."

Kat strode away in that purposeful, manlike walk of hers.

The stranger grinned. Somehow he found that appealing. He walked to his horse and mounted, riding about a mile out of town to where his two friends were camped.

"Did you get the job?" one of them asked.

"Not yet; but I got a plan."

CHAPTER THREE

Kat drove the buckboard through the gate and pulled the horses to a stop near the corral. She jumped down and they unloaded the supplies. No one else was around, so the two other hands must have been out riding herd.

Kat and Rawhide got the supplies stored and Rawhide put the buckboard away and unhitched the draft horses. Kat hadn't said anything about Butch or the stranger who had come to her rescue, and Rawhide knew better than to ask about Kat's disheveled appearance.

While Rawhide tried his questionable skills at fixing something for them to eat Kat went to her room. It didn't look like a girl's room, and that's the way she wanted it. The one vestige of femininity was a small vanity and mirror which had been her mother's. It was the only thing from the mother she'd never known that she valued: the dresses and other pretty things were in a trunk which Kat never opened.

Kat's cheek was darkening to blue where Butch had struck her. She hoped his own jaw was showing where *she* had slugged him by now; *where* he *had slugged him too,* she thought. Who was that guy anyway, and what business was it of his to horn in? She refused to admit she was glad he did. Why, she was just ready to draw her Colt and let them both have it.

Kat took off the shirt Butch had tried to rip from her. The buttons had popped off and she was no seamstress. She'd find some way to mend it but not now. She tossed it aside and pulled a new one from a pile that served as her wardrobe.

She was finishing buttoning it as she came in the kitchen. After a couple of sniffs she said, "Hmph. That actually smells like it might be something edible."

Rawhide grinned and shuffled a foot. "Shucks, Miss Kat, it ain't nothin' but what us cowhands fix on the trail sometimes; you know that."

BOOK TITLE

Kat knew it; many a meal had been nothing but some canned beans, fatback, and a flapjack or two. And that's what Rawhide had fixed for them. She grabbed a couple of plates, squirted the pump on them a couple of times, grabbed a couple of spoons and did likewise. She dished out the vittles while Rawhide poured the coffee.

They sat down to their meal. No doubt Hand and Dakota were doing something similar out on the range. And it was anybody's guess as to which meal was better. The beans were cold, the fatback half raw, and the flapjacks burnt. At least the coffee was good: black as a tar pit and strong as lye; that's the way they liked it. Cowboy coffee; you don't drink it, it eats its way through you.

Kat was quiet, and Rawhide hadn't said anything about her change of attire or how the other shirt got torn. And Kat had no mind to tell him, either.

"Butch tried to rip it off me, OK?" she said. "That answer your question?"

Rawhide's brows climbed to his hairline. "I didn't ask nothin'."

"Good. See that you don't."

Lunch over, Kat started to the door. "I'm riding out to check on Hank and Dakota. If anybody comes about the handbills just hold 'em here 'till I get back." She got her horse from the corral, saddled him, and rode out. Her mount seemed to know where she was headed and all Kat did was give him a gentle nudge of spur once in a while to urge him along.

It was wide open land, and Kat drew in the air of it and drank it down like the gods' own nectar. The feel of her horse's muscles rolling beneath her, the chest swelling and shrinking with each breath between her legs, the easy rhythm of movement as she rode was life to her. The vast grassland where the cattle grazed was to her left and her horse carried her there as he had done since he was a colt.

There was the herd: a mass of moving, quarreling, stupid meat on the hoof. A couple thousand head it was, and all prime stock. She pulled to a stop just to look at them. They were quiet for now, but it didn't take much to turn the lazy herd into a crazed stampede blindly crushing anything in its way.

But something was different; somehow the herd looked smaller.

Kat stood in her stirrups and gazed over the herd, searching for her two hands. A herd like this needed more than two men to handle them; Kat made three, now that she was here, but that still was way shy of what was needed.

A beat up sombrero waved in an arc like some battle-scarred flag, and Kat waved her own hat in answer. Dakota had spotted her and was headed toward her. It was a long way round the herd and Kat met him as close to halfway as she could make it. Dakota's face was grim with urgency, but he knew better than to make a disturbance around cattle. He was medium height, broad in body but not fat, with always a day or two growth of beard whether he had shaved or not.

"What's up?" Kat asked.

"Don't know how to tell ya, Miss Kat," Dakota started and stopped.

"Just say it. I can take it."

Dakota swallowed then threw up his words in a rush. "We're missin' beef."

"What do you mean, missin' beef? You think somebody's cutting the herd?"

Dakota nodded. "Hank's makin' another count over yonder..." he pointed to where his pard sat down the other end, "but it looks like we're missin' some right bad." He waited for his boss' next words, which we needn't record here. We'll pick up after that first part of her tirade.

"It's that [characterization deleted] Larson. Butch said Larson had some work for 'em; looks like rustlin' was part of it."

"Yes'm. But we can't ride out after 'em; Hank an' Rawhide an' me ain't enough to handle that pack."

Kat knew Dakota wasn't talking from cowardice; just plain mule sense. But she knew something she *could* do, and made up her mind to start now.

"If rustlin' is what they got goin', they ain't gonna stop with us. I'm ridin' out to Sanders at the Lazy S and Peters at the Bar 50 and see if they're missin' any. You're right, the four of us ain't enough. But if they're hittin' other ranches we'll get some help; I'm countin' on it." She clucked to her horse and turned him back, headed for the worn trail that served as an open road.

* * *

Sanders and Peters were sympathetic, and offered help, but neither had been hit by the rustlers. Kat said the same thing to both:

"Thanks, but if you ain't been hit it ain't your fight. We'll take care of it. Much obliged."

And she rode off in spite of their efforts to stop her.

"Always was an independent cuss," Sanders said to his wife as Kat rode off.

Peters no doubt said something similar.

But this set Kat to thinking too. Sanders and Peters were two of the biggest ranchers around, along with her own spread. And if their cattle weren't being stolen then this was personal.

Whoever was rustling her beef was aiming at her and her alone. And Kat had a good idea who it was.

She pulled to a stop. A rider had joined the trail about a quarter mile up ahead, started her way, and stopped. *What was he after?* Kat stared across at him as he stared across at her.

He was big, and the horse he rode was big enough to suit his size. A wide brim hid his face, and dust decorated the worn clothes and boots. After a moment it was the big guy who broke the staring match and nudged his mount to her side.

"Howdy, ma'am," he said, tilting the hat brim back with a touch. "Are you Miss Crandall?"

"I might be." Her pause was a silent demand for identification from him.

"I'm called Bear Ketchum, Miss Crandall."

Kat nodded. "That 'cause you catch bears?"

Bear gave a gap-toothed grin. "Lotta folks say that, ma'am. Naw, it's 'cause o' my size."

Kat nodded again. "Oh? I hadn't noticed."

The grin widened and Bear took off his hat. "I know yer funnin' with me, ma'am, and that's all right. Folks been makin' fun o' me for quite a spell."

"Supposin' I am this Miss Crandall," Kat said. "What do you want her for?"

"Well, ma'am, I hear she's hirin' men for her ranch. I never met a steer I couldn't throw, or a rustler I couldn't out shoot."

"Rustler's, eh? Think there might be any rustlers about?" Kat's eyes tightened in suspicion.

"I dunno, ma'am, but you never kin tell."

"So you're itchin' for a job as a drover."

"Yes ma'am. Or any other work you might have. I just have one condition."

"And what's that?"

"Well, I got two pards who are lookin' for work too. And if you hire me, they come along. We're a matched set, you might say."

"Oh? They're all big men like you?"

"Well, no ma'am; one's kinda puny lookin, tell ya the truth. An' the other's not as big as me, but he's capable. Yep, we're all capable."

Kat sized him up. He seemed honest and sincere. "All right; I'll give you and your pals a chance. Come to the ranch and we'll talk about it."

"Thanks, ma'am. You won't regret it." He put his hat back on, touched it again in courtesy, and rode back the way he came.

Kat watched him go. So he mentioned rustlers; had word got around that fast?

She remembered something her pa told her: keep as close an eye on your enemies as you do your friends.

If these three were enemies, having them close by might not be a bad idea.

Kat brought her horse to a halt by the corral and called for Rawhide. Dakota came from the bunkhouse instead.

"Rawhide came out to spell me so I came back here to mind the ranch," he explained.

"See anything more of rustlers?" Kat asked as she unsaddled her horse.

"No. Seen one or two border posts leanin' over, but that's about all. Bull coulda done that."

"Yeah," Kat agreed, working her curry comb over her horse,

"but so can a man."

"They weren't completely over, an' yer pa never took to no fences nohow, so I left 'em alone."

"We'll get 'em straightened, don't worry." She continued with the curry comb silently for a while. Dakota waited, figuring his boss had more to say. "Saw a guy on the trail back," she said. Said his name was Ketchum; Bear Ketchum."

"Yes'm?"

"Big galoot; that's why he's called Bear, I reckon." She finished with the comb and gave her horse a smooth, affectionate rub. "Said he saw the handbills and wants to sign up. Says he has two saddle pals who want to sign on too."

"We can use all the help we can get," Dakota said.

"Sure; as long as it's help and not someone tryin' to work at us from inside."

"You mean like sabotage?"

Kat nodded and looked Dakota in the eye. "I'm grateful to you and Rawhide and Hank for staying on. And we need more men; that's a fact. So if they show up, I might have to hire them. But spread the word, I'm leavin' it to you and the other two to ride herd on 'em and make sure they're playin' for us."

"An' not for Larson, right?"

"Not for Larson or anybody else that might be workin' against us."

"I'll let 'em know."

* * *

Bear had to turn a little sideways to get through the wing doors into the saloon; that was nothing new to him. He sidled up to the bar, bought a beer, and took a gulp as he let his eyes roll over the denizens of the room. His two pals were at a table toward the back and he lumbered casually across to them and sat down.

"Sure that stool's gonna hold ya?" the smaller of the two men, Banty his handle was, kidded him.

Bear had heard that line from Banty and plenty of others most of his life and ignored it as he always did. "I saw Miss Crandall on the road," he said to the third man, a tall broad-shouldered man whose good looks showed the weathering of years in the western sun.

The man nodded. "What'd she say?"

"She said to come out to the ranch and we can talk about it."

The tall man grinned. "She's playin' it cautious; good for her. There's some good sense under that flamin' hair."

Banty grinned. "You kinda fell for her already, didn't ya?"

"That's OK," Bear said. "Laredo can have her; if he can tame her."

All three laughed.

"Who says I wanna tame her?" Laredo said.

And they laughed harder.

"I like ta laugh too," a voice said behind Bear. "What's the joke?"

Laredo leaned back in his chair until it touched the wall behind him. His hands rested casually on its arms as he braced a booted foot on the table edge. "Don't see as it's any business o' yours, Butch."

The big man scowled. "How'd you know my name?"

"I just asked around," Laredo said, "for the ugliest, smelliest skunk in town. They told me that was you." He bent and straightened his leg, rocking the chair easily as his eyes stayed on Butch.

Butch's hand hovered over his gun butt. "Maybe I'll take that as a complement. Maybe not."

Laredo shrugged.

"No need to get all hepped up about it," Banty said, waving a beckoning hand to the bartender. "Wet your whistle on us an' cool down a spell."

"I don't need you buttin' in," Butch said as he glowered at Banty. "This is between your buddy an' me."

"When you pick a fight with one of us," Bear said in a quiet, friendly drawl, "it's with all of us."

"That a warnin'?"

"Just friendly advice," Bear said, turning his grin on Butch. The bartender was taking his time coming over, sensing trouble brewing. "Tell you what: the barkeep ain't in a hurry so why don't I just go up and get that beer for you? Then we can all just sit and talk like old friends."

"We're not old friends. We're not new friends." Butch's hand closed on the gun butt.

That's as far as he got.

Bear's stool suddenly flew out from under him and tangled in Butch's leg, and Bear's mass followed, sending Butch flat on his seat. Bear stood facing him, his hands dangling loosely at his sides, the grin still splitting his lips but with a different cast to it.

Butch grabbed a nearby table and hauled himself to his feet. He'd stood up to bigger men than this and everyone in the saloon knew it. No way he was backing down; but his fight wasn't with him.

"What's the matter? Your friend afraid to fight me so he sics you on me?"

"No; I'm just closer, that's all" Bear told him. "An' like I said, you pick on one of us, you pick on all of us." Bear's grin widened. "Now personally, I got nothin' against you; but Laredo told me about you goin' after Miss Crandall, who I admit is a pretty good-looker. But there's ways a treatin' ladies an' ways not to treat 'em, an' maybe I kin teach you the difference."

Butch looked around. With the news of his attack on the Crandall gal some of the tide was going against him. "There's nothin' you can teach me."

"OK then," Bear said. "Why don't we just have that beer and agree to leave each other alone?" He started toward the bar.

Butch went for his gun again but Bear had been watching from a corner of his eye. He swung his left in a backhand blow that knocked Butch back on his hind parts again. The gun jarred loose and thunked to the dirt floor. Bear stood over him.

"If I were you I'd leave that gun be and fork me horse," he said. The grin was gone and his bright blue eyes had gone dark.

Butch turned away from his gun and pushed himself up from the floor. He knew all eyes were waiting for his next move. He glanced at the gun then started to back his way to the door.

Bear picked up the gun. "I'll just leave your gun here with the barkeep to hold for ya." He put the Colt on the counter and said barkeep looked at it like it might go off on its own.

Butch had reached the wing doors, and his back eased them open. Taking one last glare at the three he turned and went out. The sound of a horse galloping out of town followed.

Bear's grin was back and he directed at the bartender. "Sorry for the ruckus." He saw the beer that Butch had declined. "Guess I'll drink that," he said, dropping a coin to pay for it. "No sense lettin' good drink go to waste." He nodded to the gun. "An' you'll look out for Butch's gun for me, won't ya?"

The bartender's gaze was riveted to Bear as he nodded, felt blindly for the gun, and stowed it on a shelf under the bar.

Bear's grin stretched wide. "Thanks kindly." He touched his hat and returned to his friends. "That makes two of us to have a run-in with Butch."

"Jes' be sure t' give me a chance t' make it three," Banty said.

"I sure will."

The three struck their glasses together and drained their beers.

CHAPTER FOUR

Grady had witnessed his friend's defeat and followed him out. Butch was unhitching his horse and nursing his jaw when Grady came up to him.

"I wouldn't feel bad about bein' beaten up by that big hombre," Grady said.

Butch glared at him. "Yeah? He got in a coupla lucky punches. Next time'll be different."

"Ahuh," Grady said; though his agreement was only to placate Butch. "You'll get him next time." Grady doubted it, but knew better than to let on.

"C'mon," Butch said as he clenched his saddle horn, "let's fork these horses and go see the boss." He climbed into the saddle.

"Sure." Grady swung up too. "You tell him about them three."

Butch glowered even darker. Yeah, he'd have to tell Larson; and he wasn't looking forward to it.

* * *

Laredo, Banty and Bear left the saloon shortly after and rode out to the Bar C. When they reached the gate Laredo said, "You go ahead Bear and see if Miss Crandall is at home. Banty an' me will wait here."

"Sure, Laredo." Bear figured why Laredo chose to stay back and grinned as he guided his big horse through the gate and up to the ranch house.

Kat heard the approaching hoof beats; horse and rider pounded the ground like the beating of a kettle drum, so it was hard to miss them. She peered through the front window first, her rifle ready. When she saw Bear she chuckled at her own mistake. "Shoulda known," she told herself. Even so she strapped on her Colt before heading outside. Off by the front gate were two other riders; probably the saddle pals Bear had told her about.

"Hey," she said, her hand resting on the grip of her revolver.

"Hey, Miss Crandall," Bear said, freeing his ponderous bulk from the horse and touching his hat. "If the job's still open, my friends and me still wanna try for it."

Kat jerked her head toward the gate. "Those two the friends you're talking about?"

"Yes'm."

"Then call 'em down and let me have a look at 'em." She stepped in closer. "And the name's Kat, not Miss Crandall."

"Yes'm, Miss Crandall. I mean, Kat." He turned and waved his hat at the two and they rode down the slope into the front yard. They hadn't gotten too far before Kat started muttering something under her breath. Bear hadn't heard such talk from too many females, except maybe some saloon girls.

Her Colt had cleared leather and covered Bear. "You're tryin' to trick me, huh?"

"No ma'am — Miss Kat," Bear stumbled.

"I already told this hombre to clear out," she said, pointing at him with the gun barrel, "and if he's a pard of yours, he's not welcome."

"What about me?" Banty asked.

Kat sized him up. "You don't seem big enough "to handle a steer."

"Why Miss Kat," Bear started.

"Just Kat."

"All right. Kat." Bear resumed. "Banty don't look like much but he's roped more steers than any five men I know, including me. Don't know how he does it, but once he's got one in his lariat it don't get loose."

"All right. I'll give you a try, Banty. As for you — "

"The handle's Laredo, Kat."

"Laredo. As for you, I told you before to clear out. Do it." She trained the gun on him.

"Kat, if you don't take Laredo then you don't get me," Bear said. He started to haul himself back on his horse.

"Same goes for me," Banty said and turned his mount the way they came.

Laredo sat steadfast, his eyes challenging Kat.

"Go ahead; get outta here, all three of ya," she ordered. "I don't need hands that bad."

Hank and Dakota had come out of the bunkhouse to see what was going on. Hank was tall, lean and bony. His beard looked like he'd made it out of tumbleweeds and glued it around his jaw. Hank was the first man her father had hired, and he looked the same as he did twenty years before; and twenty years before he'd looked older than he probably was.

"Wait a minute, Kat," Hank said. "We *do* need 'em that bad."

"I'm boss here," Kat said. Green fire burned in her gaze, and her hair seemed to catch flame as well.

But Hank remained calm. "Kat, you know we need all the hands we can get. I don't know what you got against this one Laredo feller, but he looks like he'll do in a fight. And that's what we got on our hands now is a fight."

"I think I already proved that, Kat," Laredo said, "the other day in town."

Hank and Dakota exchanged glances. Kat had said nothing about seeing Laredo in town.

Kat released the cocked hammer slow and easy. "Looks like I'm outnumbered." She holstered the gun. "OK, Laredo; you and your pals have got jobs. Hank and Dakota here'll show you where to bunk. Just don't make me regret it."

Laredo swung down from the saddle and approached her, a grin cleaving deep lines in his cheeks. "Oh you won't, Kat. You won't." He took her chin between his finger and thumb and she swatted it away.

"Don't ever try that again," she warned.

Laredo grinned. "Feisty. I like that." He turned to his pards. "C'mon boys; we sleep in real beds tonight." He took his saddle bag and blanket and waited for the other two to do the same. They followed Hank and Dakota into the bunkhouse.

Kat watched through the window a few minutes later as the three newcomers unsaddled their horses and took them into the corral. She wasn't sure just what it was about this Laredo that set something going inside her. She had liked Bear from the start, and Banty seemed spry for an older man. But this Laredo might need watching. Somehow she just didn't trust him.

* * *

Larson, Butch and Grady sat at the rude table in the deserted cabin they used as their hide-out. Larson didn't like Butch's news. The fact that Butch had gotten beat up in public didn't bother him; but the fact that these three strangers might get jobs at the Bar C did.

"All right," he finally said. "So Kat Crandall has three new hands. That's not going to help her."

"What you mean, boss?"

Larson rose and leaned on the table, bearing down on them. "That means we step things up. We do more than just rustling her cattle a little at a time. She has six hands now; well, what if some of them get into little accidents, say getting some lead in them?"

Butch grinned. "Now you're talking, boss. I'm itchin' ta get that Bear guy in my sights." He pantomimed holding and aiming a rifle.

"And why don't you try it while they're riding herd? You know what happens when a gun goes off around cattle."

"A stampede?"

Larson nodded. "You know Crandall never put up fences. Those cattle'll stampede right off her range, and you and the boys can be there to pick up the strays."

"Sounds like a great plan, boss," Grady said.

"Of course it is, Grady," Larson complemented himself, "of course it is."

CHAPTER FIVE

A cowpoke sat on his bunk hopelessly trying to shine some of the trail dust from his boots. He looked up when the three entered.

"Howdy," Laredo said. "I'm Laredo, and this here's Banty and Bear."

Dakota looked them over one at a time before giving a nod and saying, "Dakota."

"Pleased to meet you," Laredo said. "Which of these bunks is spoken for? Don't wanna rustle into somebody else's claim."

Dakota pointed to three bunks with the boot in his hand. "Those is free. You the new hires?"

"Shore," Bear said. "Miss Kat hired me the other day. These varmints came along too."

"We can use all the men we can get." Dakota gave up the boot as a bad job and dropped it as he stood, hiking up his jeans. "More'n half of 'em went off with Larson."

"Was a skunk called Butch among 'em?" Laredo asked, testing the spring in his cot.

"Yeah," Dakota acknowledged. "Know 'im?"

"We've gotten acquainted," Laredo said.

"Can't say I was too kindly impressed," Banty volunteered.

"Me neither," Bear added.

"I say good riddance," Dakota said. "Kat's better off without him and that whole lot."

"How many went with him?" Laredo asked.

"Four or five of 'em. Don't know how the old man stomached 'em, myself."

"The old man? Crandall?"

"Yeah. Salt of the earth he was. Shame he had to die the way he did."

"How's Kat as a boss?"

"She's worth five men, she is," Dakota said. "Her pap

brought her up like a man, and she can ride and rope and wrestle steers with the best of 'em."

Laredo chuckled. "Sounds like you gotta crush on her, Dakota."

"Me? Guess all three of us do in a way. Don't none of us wanna see no harm come to her. But she don't want no frills or nothin' like most females. That's all nonsense to her."

Laredo sat on his bunk and rolled a cigarette. "I take it you gave it a try?"

"Me? Nope. I know better'n that. But Billy Holcomb — he run off after his folks died — he tried kissin' her when she was twelve. Let's just say nobody's tried that since."

"I can think of one who did," Laredo said, words and gaze darkening with the memory.

Dakota scratched his head. "Who you talkin' about? I don't know nobody that stupid."

"Butch was tryin' something like kissin', or maybe a little more," Laredo said.

Banty finished the story. "What my pard is too shy to tell you is he — well, he kinda talked him out of it."

Dakota put the puzzle pieces together. The names he called Butch needn't be repeated here. "I woulda killed him on the spot." His hand gripped the gun at his side. "I'll kill 'im next time I see 'im."

Bear's grin was unpleasant. "You gotta stand in line. Me and Laredo both got dibs on him first."

"Hey, I'd like a try at him myself," Banty said, drawing his gun and giving the cylinder a spin.

Dakota nodded sagely. "Yeah, Kat brings that protective side out in all of us, whether she wants it to or not. Guess we'll just have to see who gets to him first." He rubbed his belly. "Say, you boys et yet?"

"I could eat," Bear said.

"You can always eat," Banty joked.

"And you can always use some fattenin' up," Bear joked back, jabbing an elbow that nearly knocked the little guy over.

"We ain't had a meal since mornin'," Laredo said. "So if you're offerin', we're eatin'."

"It's settled then," Dakota said. "I'll rustle up some grub

then we'll ride out and see what's goin' on with the herd."

Dakota opened some cans and threw them in a pot, added some jerky, and once it started bubbling and calling to them with an appetizing aroma he doled it out in bowls which he set out with big hunks of sourdough and a brick of butter. They ate like cowboys, ravenous and fast. After the third helping each Dakota said it was time to head out.

Dakota led at first and soon the lowing of the cattle was a siren call guiding them on. Laredo saw two riders and Dakota waved his hat to them. The riders came over, taking their time to be sure not to startle the herd. The riders looked the newcomers over.

"Rawhide, Hank, this here's Laredo, Bear, and Banty. Kat just hired 'em to help ride herd."

Introductions in the west are rarely more than a nod and a word, which is all that passed here.

"We can spell ya if ya want," Dakota said.

"Sounds good to me," Rawhide said. "My belly and my backbone are becomin' right neighborly."

"Right neighborly?" Hank guffawed. "They been kissin' cousins as long as I've known ya. C'mon, let's see if these galoots left us anything."

As Rawhide and Hank rode back to the bunkhouse, the long lean cowhand was silent, his bony chin digging into his prominent Adam's apple. After a bit Hank broke the silence.

"What's got you more downcast than usual, Rawhide?"

"Hank, you think those three are here to help or are they more of Larson's gang?"

Hand was puzzled. "What, you think they're up to no good?"

"I dunno. Seems I've seen that one he called Laredo somewhere before."

"Yeah? Where?"

Rawhide shook his head. "Don't recollect. Mighta been in Abilene a ways back, or... I just don't know."

"You think we oughta warn Kat?"

Rawhide rubbed his grizzled chin with long, horny fingers. "I reckon not; not just yet. I might be wrong. I been known to be wrong, you know."

"You and about every man that's ever been born," Hank said. "We'll just keep our eye on him for Kat's sake. Yeah. An' we'll tell Dakota to do the same."

Rawhide nodded and the continued riding.

* * *

The sky was a black stretch of broadcloth, neither moon nor stars lending any light. Crickets chirped at the darkness and a coyote howled, trying to conjure the moon from that same darkness.

Three men huddled around a campfire on a ridge overlooking the Bar C. A coffeepot gurgled with its hot, powerful contents on a rude platform of stones around it. Each held a mug of it, steaming and black, and it burned its way down their throats.

"Nature's helpin' out," Butch said.

"Yeah," Grady agreed. "No light but our fire."

The ironically named Slim held his tin mug between his fat hands, his belly swelled out like a balloon as he squatted on his ample haunches. "Don't ya think it's a bad idea? The fire, I mean."

"Relax," Butch said. "Nothin' illegal about a fire."

"Yeah, but what if one of them Bar C guys see it?" Slim protested.

"What of it?" Butch countered. There's three of them an' three of us," Burch said. "An' I'm equal to two of 'em, so the odds is in our favor."

Grady chuckled. "Yeah. Besides, she can't have more'n two of 'em ridin' herd at a time."

Slim blew on his coffee. He hadn't so much as taken a sip, though the others were on their second mugs. He shook his head. "I still don't like it."

"What's with you, Slim? You yellow?" Butch's glare cut through the dark.

"No, I'm not yellow. Just don't like it. What's Larson got against the Crandall gal anyway?"

"That's his business and none o' yourn. We got orders to stampede the herd, an' that's what we're gonna do." Butch drew his sidearm. "An' if you can't take it, hit the trail."

Slim knew Butch's bullet would hit him before he even forked his horse. He wasn't yellow, but he wasn't stupid either. "OK, Butch; cool off. I'm with ya."

"You better be. Even all that fat won't stop a bullet, an' don't forget it."

"I won't." He took a long draft of his coffee to steady his nerves. Of course, coffee ain't made for that. He tightened his grip on the tin mug, though the rippling of its dark contents still betrayed his inner turmoil. He'd just have to ride it out.

* * *

Laredo tilted back and looked into the sky. Not a star nor a moon. He'd be grateful for even the tiniest sliver of moonlight, but he knew it wasn't happening. The only light was the soft glow from Banty's cigar, as it bobbed along toward him with Banty's approach.

"Great night for a murder," Banty said cheerily, the cigar clenched in his teeth.

Laredo only nodded as he scanned the unrelenting blackness about him. The herd was but a mass of dark within dark, sensed by their odor rather than any semblance of form. Some of the more distant hills were snow-capped, and the random blotches of white made vague smudges in the night. The nearer hills were there, though there was no way of spotting them for certain. Skyline merged into the night sky as though they were one and the same.

Wait; there was something. What Laredo thought might be just another smudge of distant snow drifted, floating. Snow frozen onto a mountaintop didn't move. And below this tiny cloud was a dim red glow, hinting at the edge of a horizon line.

"Look there," Laredo whispered, pointing to his discovery.

Banty squinted and the smoke and fire teased him like a desert mirage. "Somebody's made camp over yonder," he said. "Who ya suppose it is?"

"Somebody up to no good, I recon," Laredo answered.

"Wanna go over and take a look-see?"

Laredo shook his head. "If they're headed this way we'll

know soon enough. Just keep an eye out."

Banty nodded. "As you say. I'll jest mosey on a little closer jest the same."

"Be careful."

Laredo couldn't see Banty's answering grimace, loaded with 10,000 insulted epithets.

Banty made his way slowly toward the faint glow on the horizon. He eased up within a few hundred yards and sat his horse under a sheltering tree he had almost blundered into in the dark. The smoke cloud fattened briefly as the fire was put out. *They must be gettin' ready to ride.* The faint sound of creaking leather and the jingle of harness reached his ears.

Banty turned his horse back to the herd.

* * *

The fire was nearly out, but Butch wanted to make sure of it. Once he was satisfied he gave the order to mount up. He and Grady waited until Slim forced his bulk onto his long suffering horse, an animal better suited for hauling freight than carrying a man, but after long employment resigned to his fate.

They started down the ridge, slowly at first or as slowly as the steep hillside allowed. Butch had a sense of direction better than any compass, even in the dark. They followed his lead as they rode on their nocturnal business.

* * *

Bear and Laredo had both lit up while waiting for Banty's return, their fresh-rolled cigarettes tiny red lights which his keen eyes saw. They saw the glow of his cigar and met up a few score yards from the herd.

"Sounded like three of 'em," Banty said.

"Only three?" Bear complained. "Why, you can take care o' them by yourself, Banty. Yuh don't need us." He started to turn his horse.

"Sure I can, but even I can't rope all three of 'em without one gettin' loose. If we all cast at the same time, can't none of 'em get away."

"OK, we'll help ya," Laredo said, "if you insist."

Banty had an idea about how they'd approach the herd and the three placed themselves along the way he suggested. The dark deepened the stillness, and the distant sounds of the hoof beats of the three horses seemed deafening when they came.

Three ropes snaked out and each spinning loop found its mark. The lassos were jerked tight and the three captives came to a sudden halt.

Laredo and his friends surrounded their prisoners, each with one fist coiled tightly by a rope and the other gripping a gun. "Take yer irons outta yer holsters real gentle like," Laredo said, "and toss 'em as far as you can."

It was a hard job with their arms pinioned, but they did it.

Laredo rode closer to the leader. "Howdy, Butch. Thought we'd cross trails again."

"Caught ya red handed, you rustlers," Banty said. "We'd string ya up right now, if we could see enough to find a tree for each of ya."

"We ain't rustlin'," Butch said. "We were just out for a midnight ride."

"Oh, I get it," Banty said. "Like three buckskin Paul Reveres, huh?"

Butch's face contracted in ignorance. "Who?"

"I'll be glad to give you a history lesson," Laredo said, "just before we hang ya."

"You can't hang us!" Butch protested. "We ain't done nuthin'!"

Banty scratched his grizzled chin. "Seems my ol' school ma'arm told me somethin' about that not bein' grammatical; but I forget."

The three prisoners glanced at each other with the same unspoken question: "Who are these guys?"

Laredo gestured with his Colt. "All right, get down off your horses." When they hesitated he thumbed back the hammer on his gun.

Butch, only a couple feet from the .45 caliber bore, obliged and the other two followed suit. Banty and Bear also dismounted to tie the ropes tightly around their wrists, binding them behind their backs.

"Banty, Bear, you take care of the herd while I march these three hombres to the ranch house."

"Then, you're not gonna hang us?" Grady said.

"No; not until after the trial, anyway," Laredo answered. "Seems there's a judge comes through town in a week or so an' my daddy always taught me to do things right and proper. But don't worry, you'll get hanged sure enough."

The three prisoners were obviously not relived at the news.

"Of course if he's delayed, we can always see that you're shot while tryin' to escape." He tied the three ropes into one and made them fast on his saddle horn. "Now get movin'. An' that little bit I said about tryin' to escape goes for right now, too. An' it'll be all that harder for the other two to go on foot while draggin' their dead pard." He gave the ropes a jerk. wink of sleep.

This was the first night the three newcomers had ridden herd without one of her regular hands riding with them. What if they were part of Larson's gang, and drove the herd off somewhere? What if the rest of Larson's bunch was meeting up with them and it was all part of Larson's plot?

What did Larson want of her ranch, anyway? He said it was because he didn't want to work for a woman, but what hold did he have over the others that mutinied along with him?

She sat up. No sense trying to sleep when sleep didn't come. Never a one for frilly truck she pulled on jeans and a plaid flannel shirt and went out to the kitchen. She lit an oil lamp, and welcomed its yellow glow. Might as well start a pot of coffee; if she was going to be awake, she might as well stay awake.

The coffee was just about ready when she heard a single set of hoof beats and some scuffling feet outside. She opened a shutter and saw a tall rider coming, preceded by three weary men on foot. Their sizes matched her three new hands; especially the big one. What the hell was going on? Was the tall rider Rawhide, and had he gone to check on the new hands and caught them at something?

Kat stepped outside, carrying the oil lamp with her. No, it wasn't Rawhide; this man's shoulders were broader. And she saw Rawhide and her other two hands coming from the bunkhouse on hearing the same ruckuss.

The rider touched his hat. "Sorry to wake you, Miss Kat," he said, "but my pards an' me caught these three rattlers tryin' to do some evil with the herd. I thought we could put 'em up in the old barn until first light, when I'll take 'em into the sheriff."

Kat came closer with the lamp and recognized the faces of Butch, Grady, and Slim.

"Just what the hell is this?" she demanded of whoever would answer.

"It's all a mistake, Miss Kat," Slim said. "We were just out ridin' an' this hombre..."

"Shut up, fool!" Butch growled.

"My pards an' me figgered they'd come to cut off more of the herd," Laredo said. "So we' lassoed 'em an' I brought 'em back here."

"We'll help ya, Laredo," Dakota said. He'd run back to the bunkhouse and returned with a couple of shotguns and sidearms.

"Go back to bed," Kat ordered. "You three are goin' out first light an' need your sleep." She took two of the sidearms and thrust one into the waistband of her jeans and covered the captives with the other. "I'll help tie these three up." She glared at Butch. "In your case, it'll be a pleasure." She thumbed back the hammer. "And don't get any idea of running off. We shoot runaways."

Slim gulped. "That Laredo guy said the same thing," he said to Grady.

Kat glared first at him then at Laredo, who grinned back at her chagrin at being caught thinking along the same lines as him.

Laredo dismounted and Dakota followed just to back their play as they hustled the three into the barn. It didn't take long before all three were securely tied.

"I've gotta admire yer skill with a rope, Miss Kat," Laredo said.

"It's Kat. Just Kat." My daddy taught me a lotta things. He wanted a boy, but he got me."

Laredo said, "Well, I for one am glad you're a girl."

"What do you mean by *that* remark?" The fire was back in Kat's voice.

Dakota chuckled. "You just insulted her, Laredo."

Kat's glare froze the two of them, in spite of their now shared chuckles. She stalked off, fists clenched and swinging with a man's stride, muttering curses at the both of them.

"She's a tough one to tame," Dakota said. "Many a man's tried an' they all failed."

Laredo grinned. "I don't wanna even try."

CHAPTER SIX

Dakota volunteered to stay up and keep watch on the captives. After Laredo had left he checked the tightness of the knots and squatted beside Slim.

"Can't say I understand what yer doin' with these varmints, Slim." He took paper and tobacco from his pocket and did a one-handed roll, sticking the finished cigarette in Slim's mouth and lighting it for him. "Nope, can't see it a-tall."

Slim was uncomfortable, and it wasn't just his hog-tied position. The cigarette was welcome, not just for the smoke but because it made it difficult for him to answer.

"Why'd you do it, Slim? Why'd you side with this coyote?"

"You keep yer mouth shut," Butch warned.

Slim stared at Butch, but was obviously cowered by him. He took a long drag on his smoke.

"Nope," Dakota persisted, "don't see how a nice guy like you ended up with this pack."

Slim turned to Dakota and the fear in the big man's eyes spoke volumes.

"Well, whatever the reason," Dakota said as he rose to his feet, "they're yourn and not mine." He went over to a hay bale and sat on it, where he could see all three of them. "Now don't none o' you move or this here shotgun'll be the last thing you hear."

* * *

Larson was a cautious man. He'd sent Butch, Slim and Grady to stampede the Crandall herd but he'd also sent Lefty to keep an eye on them.

Lefty had stayed back, as per orders, but had seen the three men roped by three of the Bar C hands. He rode back to Larson to report.

Larson made a comment about the parentage of the three, especially Butch, and sat down to business. "Did you recognize the three that roped 'em?"

"Nope; never laid eyes on 'em."

Larson chewed on this along with the stub of cigar in his teeth. "Heard about some new hands she was hiring. Guess that's them."

Lefty remained silent until his boss spoke again.

"If they didn't hang 'em right away, they'll probably take 'em to town to the sheriff."

"Stokes ain't gonna do much with 'em."

"No; because they'll never make it to Stokes." Larson had come up with a plan. "There's only one road from the Bar C to town. Take Bennett and wait for 'em along the trail.

"Those three ain't gonna get inta my business again. They're jobs at the Crandall ranch are gonna end right quick."

Lefty grinned.

* * *

"Waal, at least you didn't fall asleep on the job," Banty said when he came into the barn as the sun made its first shimmer of light over the hills.

Dakota laughed. Kat had brought him a pot of coffee and a mug shortly after he had started vigil.

The three owlhoots, on the other hand, had finally dozed off less than an hour before.

Dakota rose and stretched. "Seems a shame to wake 'em." He went closer and took a glance at each of them.

"They just got to sleep, you know."

"My heart's bleedin' for 'em," Banty sneered as he strode over to Butch and gave him a kick. "C'mon, get up. There's a nice comfy cell waitin' for ya."

Dakota shoved and shook the other two awake. "Yeah, we got better things to do than takin' you two to the sheriff."

Butch shook himself awake and laughed. "The sheriff! He's a joke, and you know it."

"Yeah, but Laredo believes in law and order, so we'll take you to the sheriff and *then* we'll hang ya."

Banty took a knife from his pocket and cut only the rope between their hands and their ankles, that had kept them in an unnatural backwards arch all night. Their wrists remained bound, but their ankles were now free. It took a while for each of them to straighten and relieve the cramps in their backs and legs. Grady was the first to try to stand, and his hamstring protested by twisting itself into a new knot and tugging it tight, hauling him to the floor again.

"Get up you," Banty ordered, dragging him up.

Grady kept the cramped leg bent, which didn't help the pain. He gritted his teeth and leaned against an upright for balance.

"Quit fakin'," Dakota ordered.

"I'm not. I can't stand, and I can't ride."

"We'll get you on a horse if we have to haul you up with a winch," Banty said. "Now get movin'." He took Grady by the arm and gave him a shove and the captive managed to limp just out the door before collapsing.

"Can't ya see he's hurt?" Slim said.

"He's jest tryin' for sympathy," Butch said. "Thinks it might save him from a hangin'."

"There's a rope for you too, Butch," Dakota said,

shoving him out the door.

"Yeah? Seems there oughtta be a trial first."

"Sure, I guess we can wait until after the trial ta hang the three of ya."

"Look, I don't wanna die!" Slim pleaded. "Not by a rope!"

"Shoulda thought o' that before signin' on with Larson," Dakota said. "Move."

Laredo was waiting outside with six saddled horses. "'Bout time you men showed up, leavin' me with all the hard work."

"Hey, this was your idea!" Dakota said. "If I had my say, they'd be decoratin' the rafters of the barn by now. Seems a waste o' time when we're gonna hang' em anyways, I say."

Kat came from the house. "I would've hung 'em right where you found 'em, if I'd been with you."

"I don't go much for hangin'," Laredo said, "least not without a trial first."

"Yep," Banty said as he swung into the saddle, "our

Laredo's a stickler for law and order."

Grady tried to mount but couldn't. "I just can't get up," he said. "Just leave me alone, will ya?"

Dakota ran back inside the barn and came back with a stool. "Here; use this."

Grady stepped up on the stool and managed to fork his horse, though his groans woke up the roosters.

"Aw, quite yer belly-achin'," Dakota said as he swung into the saddle. "You'll get plenty o' time ta rest that leg in jail."

Bear, Hank and Rawhide came from the bunkhouse.

"Dakota, sure yer up to ridin' herd on these three?" Rawhide asked.

"Sure. You fellers go on out and tend to the herd. We'll get these three delivered."

Kat had gone back in and came out with her hat and gunbelt. "I'm comin' too. Dakota, go an' get some sleep."

"Now Kat, I don't need no sleep. I'm so full o' that coffee you gave me last night..."

"That's an order, mister," Kat said, hand on her pistol butt.

"Yes ma'am." Dakota knew better than to argue with her.

But Laredo hadn't been around long enough to learn that lesson yet. "It's all right, Kat; we can manage." He nodded his head toward Banty. "Banty an' me have handled skunks like these before."

Kat mounted Dakota's horse. "Trouble with skunks is you might end up smellin' like 'em. An' I'm makin' sure they don't spread their stink on you."

Laredo grinned. "Why, Miss Kat; I didn't know you cared."

Kat glared green fire at him, which had no effect on his grin, and kicked started her horse. "C'mon. We're burnin' daylight."

She started off and the others had to hurry their prisoners along to follow. Kat led the way with Laredo and Banty flanking the three captives.

Laredo rode aside Butch.

"Laredo, eh?" Butch said.

"That's my handle."

"But not the name you were born with," Butch said.

"I suppose you were born with the name Butch?"

Butch chuckled. "Ya got me there. No, but I come by the

name honest anyway. Used to do a lotta huntin'. My daddy taught me. An' when we'd catch somethin', why my daddy always let me cut it up for food. Got so I was real handy with a knife."

"That so?" Laredo hid his interest.

"Yeah. My daddy said I'd grow up to be a butcher, an' he used to call me Butch. That's how I got my handle. How about you? You come from Laredo?"

"Among other places."

"Seems I seen your face somewhere before, though I don't think you were called Laredo then."

"Sounds like you got some memory. Or a big imagination."

"Nope, I don't easily forget a face. Don't know where I saw it, or on what, but I seen you before."

"So maybe we ain't strangers," Laredo said. "That don't mean we're friends neither."

"No, it sure don't. If my hands were untied, an' I had a good knife in one of 'em, we wouldn't be goin' to no sheriff."

"But they are tired, and you ain't got a knife."

"Yeah. But I know where I can get one."

"You won't have to worry about it."

"Yeah I know: jail, a trial, then the rope." Butch grinned. "But ya ain't got me in jail yet, so there ain't been a trial, and there ain't gonna be no rope. So I can still get that knife."

Laredo shrugged. "Don't see that happenin', but the Good Lord sets things goin', not me."

Butch frowned. "You believe that hogwash?"

Laredo nodded. "There was a time I didn't have no use for it either, but I come to mend my ways. There's a God all right, an' he don't like critters like you."

"Or critters like you used t' be?"

Laredo didn't answer except to pull his hat brim lower to hide his expression. Both he and Butch remained silent the rest of the way.

Kat had heard the whole thing however, and spent the rest of the trip wondering just what Butch might know about her new cowhand. From Laredo's own mouth she'd heard he had a past he might not be proud of.

Who was this Laredo, and why was he helping her?

* * *

The trail narrowed about half-way into town, and was bordered by woods on the right and high rocks on the left. Laredo rode up beside Kat.

"Looks like a good place for an ambush," he said, "if somebody wanted to ambush somebody."

Kat glared at him but her brows tensed in concern. "And why might somebody want to do that?"

Laredo shrugged as he scanned the hills. "Oh, maybe somebody might wanna save these three folks we got behind us."

Kat glanced back at their prisoners and began scanning the woods. "You think Larson might try a rescue?"

Laredo gave a chuckle that was more like a snif. "I don't see Larson 'rescuin'' anybody; don't think he's got any softness in 'im for that. But he might try to break 'em free just so he don't lose 'em."

Kat stopped her scouting of the terrain and made a study of Laredo instead. "You know, I heard what you and Butch were talkin' about before."

"Guess you did." He remained vigilant.

"Was he right? Has he seen you before?"

"I don't know; I been see by a lot of folks in my life, I recon. Butch mighta been one of 'em."

"Where you from, Laredo?"

"Now, I'm not sure how you mean that. Do you mean, 'Are you from Laredo?' or just 'Where you from?' in general?"

"Don't try puttin' me off with riddles." Kat resigned with a sigh. "All right; where *are* you from?"

"Oh, here and there."

"But were you born in Laredo?"

"Don't know. My ma an' pa didn't live long enough to tell me much about it."

Kat frowned. "You're an orphan?"

Laredo chuckled. "Seems most galoots what've grown up my size are orphans by now; either their folks is dead or they just got so far removed from 'em they might as well be dead to each other."

"And which is it in your case?"

Laredo caught a gleam of reflected light on a rock above. "DOWN, KAT!" He grabbed her reins and pulled, spurring his horse into a gallop as a bullet whizzed past his ear.

Another shot brought a cry from behind them, as the second shot caught Banty in the shoulder.

Laredo had drawn his own rifle from the boot and fired one-handed at the glint he'd seen. Rock splintered and raised a grunt from one dry-gulcher.

Banty's right arm had been hit, but he reached across with his left and wrestled iron from leather to fire at the other shooter.

"C'mon!" Butch shouted, and with a yell and three hard kicks sent his horse galloping into the woods, with Grady and Slim behind.

"Boss!" Banty called, whether to Laredo or Kat neither knew, "they're getting away!" He swung his aim toward the fugitives and saw a hat go flying. Banty cursed that he hadn't taken some scalp with it.

Laredo had released Kat's reins and was firing with both hands now, cocking his Winchester and sending rapid fire to the spot where the first shot had come. Kat was adding her .45 to the fight, though it was more of a warning than doing any damage.

Some shots came from the woods and Kat shot blindly at smoke, but heard a welcome cry of pain in response.

Laredo continued to fire at the rocks. His slugs chipped rock that struck more than one, but the ambushers were too well covered to get a clear shot.

Then the shooting from above stopped and they heard horses beyond the rocks.

Similar hoof-beats sounded from the woods and the attack was over. The attackers had finished their job.

Banty came riding up to them, his left hand clamped to a bleeding shoulder. "Should we go after em?" He tried to mask the wince of pain that contorted his features.

"No," Laredo said. "By the time we get up those rocks they'll be long gone, and we can't track 'em. An' the other three might've gone anywhere in those woods, and there's a stream about a half mile in where they'll lose us."

Kat studied him closely. "There is a stream just where you said. How did you know that?"

"I been around these parts before," he said. "No, there's no point in tryin'. Best we see to our wounded before we do anything." He pointed to Banty as he slid the Winchester back in the boot.

"I'm all right," Banty wheezed, "just a scratch." But he slid to the ground rather than dismounting and passed out, his head lying loosely to one side.

Laredo and Kat swung down and knelt on either side of him. Laredo tore his shirt from his shoulder and examined the wound. "Bullet's still in there. It's gotta come out."

Kat dug into pocket of her jeans and brought out a knife, opening it with her teeth. "Hold 'im still while I dig it out."

Laredo hesitated but braced his hands on both Banty's arms. "Sounds like you done this before."

"Sure. Many times." It was a lie but Laredo didn't have to know. She pulled off her gloves and added her own pressure to holding Banty down. She untied her patient's bandana and used it to wipe the blood away long enough to better see the wound. She stuck a finger in and felt the bullet. It wasn't in deep, but she bet it hurt like hell. At least Banty had passed out. She started to work with the knife.

Banty lurched up and howled, suddenly awake. Laredo leaned all his weight on him and Kat swung over until she was straddling him. To Laredo it looked for a moment like she was wrestling him, and she was winning. She held him there as she probed with the knife, urging it nearer the surface, its dull gray showing for a moment like a plug in a bottle bef0re she got it free. She stuck it in a shirt pocket and closed the knife. Banty continued to howl, though not as bad as before. Kat, still straddling him, swung a right to his jaw that knocked him back out.

She tore a piece from the bandana and stuffed it in the wound, tying it up with the remainder and her own. Panting heavily she came to her feet. Laredo rose next to her.

"That was something," he said. "Where'd you learn to do

that?"

"You learn lotsa things out west. Or didn't you ever pick that up?" Kat had her hands at her hips as she caught her breath.

"I've been shot plenty o' times, an' dug bullets outta men before too. But you sure got a way of makin' 'em quiet down."

"What's that supposed to mean?"

"The way you was wrasslin' him, and that haymaker you throwed to shut him up at the last. I sure don't wanna hafta to tangle with you while you're fired up like that."

"I've wrassled a few guys in my time," Kat said, "an' socked a few too. An' if that makes you ascared of me, well maybe you're not the man you make yourself out to be."

"I'm not afraid of any man or woman," Laredo said. "But a female that can fight like a man; well, that's something else."

"Yeah? Well I'm as good as any man around, and just make sure you don't forget it."

"I won't, Kat," Laredo said with a grin, "I won't." He put his hat back on his head, saluted her with a touch to the brim, and went back to Banty who was starting to come to.

Kat came back over with him. "Those bandages ain't clean," she said, "so we'll have to do 'em up all over again when we get back."

Laredo nodded. "Help me get him on his horse."

As he and Kat helped him to his feet, Banty asked, "Where's Butch and the others? What the hell happened?"

"Larson's men ambushed us and they got away," Kat said. "That's all right; we gotta take care of you first, old timer."

"Who you callin' a old timer?" He felt his sore jaw. "Somebody must've thrown a rock at me too."

Laredo was about to explain but a look on Kat's face told him he might get hit by that same rock if he didn't keep his mouth shut.

CHAPTER SEVEN

Banty leaned low, weak and unconscious, tied to his saddle to prevent falling as Laredo and Kat led his horse into town. Kat rapped on Doc Murray's door as Laredo eased him down from the saddle then both of them brought him into the doctor's parlor. They laid him on the table in the back and got him comfortable while old Doc Murray rolled up his sleeves and gathered the usual tools for treating a gunshot.

Laredo tore off Banty's sleeve and Doc removed Kat's makeshift bandage. "Hmmm. Not clean, but good work," he mumbled.

Kat knew this was high praise from the old sawbones and motioned to Laredo to step aside and let him do his work.

"Doc's the best," Kat said. "He'll have Banty up and around in no time."

Laredo's concern for his friend showed on his face. "Thanks. I know. Banty's been shot before; he'll pull through just by sheer meanness."

Kat flicked her half-grin. "Sure. Besides, we got other business to take care of." She turned back to the table. "See you later, Doc."

Doc Murray's muffled grunt was his only answer as he started work. The smell of ether filled the air as he mashed a big wad of cotton soaked in the stuff over Banty's nose and mouth.

Laredo grimaced a little at the pungeunt odor.

"Some stuff Doc uses to put you out," Kat explained. "Used it on pa one time. Stinks like hell but does the job."

"Better'n another sock on the jaw I guess."

"Depends on who's on the receiving end," Kat taunted.

Laredo smiled at the glint in Kat's eyes that dared him to respond. Instead he changed the subject. "You said we've got other business; if you mean the sheriff, I'm right behind you."

"That's who I mean all right." She led the way out and down the boarded walkway to the sheriff's office and they went in.

Sheriff Stokes leaned back in his chair, booted feet on the desk, smoke from his cigar collecting in a dark cloud around him as he read from a dime western novel about how Wild Bill Hickok killed twenty men without re-loading his six-shooter once. He was so engrossed in his literary pursuits that he didn't hear Kat and Laredo enter.

"Sheriff, we're here to report a crime," Kat said.

Stokes didn't look up from his cheap paperback. "I'm busy. Write it out, if you know how to write, and I'll get to it when I can."

"Busy," Kat repeated. "Sure you are." She took the inkwell from his desk and poured its contents over the dime novel, letting a generous portion flow down onto the sheriff's lap.

"Hey!" A string of profanity found its way around the cigar clamped in his teeth. "I was doing important research! Readin' up on the exploits of one of my fellow enforcers of the law!"

Kat took a dime from a pocket and tossed it on the desk. "Here. Buy yourself another. Meanwhile, let's talk about rustling, ambushes, and attempted murder."

Stokes' thick, dark, full mustache, boasting more hair than most of his head, bristled with his heavy, labored breath. He raised his bulk from the chair with an effort. "That's a lotta charges to talk about. Who ya got in mind ta pin 'em on?"

"We're not 'pinnin' 'em' on anybody," Laredo said. "We know Larson's responsible, and we want your help trackin' him."

Stokes glared at Laredo. "An' who in hell might *you* be?"

"He's Laredo, an' he's one of my new hands," Kat said. "An' he an' his pard were the ones attacked."

"Ahuh. An' yer goin' by this gent's say so?"

"I am." Kat's hands rested on her waist, the right one dangerously close to her gun butt.

"Laredo, huh? That the handle you were born with or did yuh just pick it up?"

Laredo stared a silent but eloquent reply.

"What's the odds that I find a pitcher or description of you on one o' my wanted posters?"

Laredo replied same as before.

"If Laredo's wanted somewhere it's on the Bar C. He's made himself useful quite a few times since he's been around." Kat looked Stokes up and down. "Which is more than I can say for some sheriff's I know."

"I'm the only sheriff you know."

Kat's one-sided grin showed Stokes he had fallen into her trap.

"Now," Kat continued leaning forward into Stokes' face, the stench of his breath testing her will, "are you gonna raise a posse and help us track that gang or not?"

"First I gotta know a crime's been committed. You said a lotta things, but that don't mean you got proof." Stokes puffed cheap cigar smoke into her face and Kat reluctantly withdrew. He grinned at his victory.

"I got witnesses. Laredo here and his pard Banty, who's getting stitched up at Doc's."

"Ahuh. Well, like I said before, swear out a complaint, in writing, an' I'll take it up when I have time." He picked up his dime novel, dripping more ink on himself before tossing it in the wastecan. "An' that dime ain't gonna cover you destroying public property."

"Public property!" Kat exclaimed. "A dime novel?"

"The public pays my salary. That book was bought with my salary. So it's public property! Now the fine is five dollars or five days in jail. Pay up or get locked up; don't matter none to me."

Kat started to reply but Laredo clamped a hand on her shoulder and tossed a coin on Stokes' desk. "Here. That's ten dollars. But yerself enough to read for a year with my complements."

Stokes took the coin and bit it. The ten dollar gold piece was genuine. While the sheriff was celebrating his new wealth Laredo took Kat by the arm and led her out to the street.

"We're getting no help from him, that's sure," Laredo said.

"I didn't expect to," Kat said, "but I thought we'd try anyway. Now when we find Larson ourselves he can't say we didn't come to him."

Laredo nodded. "You got that right. Where to next, boss lady?"

"I want you to meet Clem Grange, the editor of the newspaper." She started off then suddenly whipped around to face him. "What was that crack about?"

"What, Boss Lady? Didn't think you'd mind."

"Like I said before, just make it Kat. I don't need you callin' me nothin' else."

"Whatever you say, Kat; you're the boss lady."

The desire to knock the grin from his face was in her eyes but she somehow resisted it and swung back into her firm stride.

They reached the newspaper office. Clem as usual was setting type, his sleeves rolled up and indelible printer's ink marked his fingertips.

"Kat! Good to see you." Clem carefully set down his tray and perfunctorily wiped his hands on his denim apron before shaking hands with her. "Who's this big galoot you brought with you?" He offered his hand.

"This is Laredo, one of my new hands."

"Glad to meet you. Guess you're helpin' Kat keep the Bar C goin', eh?"

"My pards an' me are tryin'. An' those three that stayed on are doin' their share too."

"Six hands still isn't enough to run a big spread like the Bar C," Clem said. "Kat, any luck hirin' any more like him?"

"Nope, 'fraid not. Clem, there's something you can help us with."

"Glad to, Kat." He cleared a space on a worktable for them to sit and took a stool.

Kat filled him in on the visit to the sheriff's office.

"You think Stokes might be workin' for Larson somehow?"

Kat shook her head. "Stokes don't need no payoff from Larson or any other owl-hoot to avoid his duty. No, he's just a lazy buzzard who somehow can't get himself un-elected."

"So you don't want me writin' a expose on him, I take it?" Clem figured.

"No. At least, not directly. But if you can print a story of how Larson's men tried to stampede or rustle our cattle, an' how when we caught 'em the rest of the gang helped them escape and wounded one of our boys doin' it, wall maybe some folks around here might not think about votin' Stokes in again."

"An' even might try to put a burr under his butt to go after Larson's gang?"

Kat nodded. "I'm hopin'."

"Sure Kat. I'll get on it soon as I finish settin' this type. In fact, I'll make it my main story. This beats any other news I got all hollow anyways."

"Thanks, Clem."

Clem walked them to the door and told Laredo it was a pleasure meeting him. "You take good care o' Kat, won't you?"

"Clem, from what I've seen Kat can do a mighty good job o' takin' care o' herself."

As the two walked along Kat asked, "You really mean that Laredo?"

"Mean what?"

"You think I can take care of myself?"

"Sure. If it came down to a fight between you and a wildcat, my money'd be on you."

Kat tipped her hat brim a little lower as she grinned. "Thanks, Laredo." She hoped the brim hid the burning she felt in her cheeks.

"C'mon," Laredo said, "let's go see how Banty's doin'." They walked back to the doctor's office and went on in.

"Doc?" Kat called. "It's me and Laredo checkin' on your patient."

Doc Murray came from the back and adjusted his frameless glasses on his nose. He also wore his usual frown. "How ya think he is, after a bullet went into his shoulder and some damn fool tried to play doctor without a license? I mended him up best I could. Rest is up to God, an' I ain't privy to his plans."

"Can we see him?"

"Ya got eyes, don't ya?" Doc waved a dismissive hand at the treatment room and started patting his pockets for a smoke. He pulled a runt of a pipe from one pocket and a bag of tobacco from another, filled the first with the second, and Laredo offered a lit match. Doc blew it out. "Son, I been lightin' my own smokes since before your pa got a gleam in his eye for your ma." He produced a match, scraped it on the mantle to ignite it, and lit his pipe. "Well, you gonna go and see yer pard or stand here gapin' at me?"

Laredo went on in. *Some folks just don't want help or thanks or nothin;*, he figured.

Banty was sitting up, his right shoulder bandaged with clean white gauze and his arm in a sling.

"Good to see you, Banty!" Laredo said.

"Good you can see me, an' that I'm still here to see you!" He rubbed his jaw. "Ever find the guy who threw that rock? Jaw still hurts like hell."

"I'll make it my job to be on the lookout for him, Banty," Kat said. "And if I find him you'll be the first to know."

Laredo swallowed his laugh and couldn't figure how Kat kept a straight face.

Kat gave Banty an update on what they had been doing while Doc was sewing him up.

"A newspaper article!" Banty exclaimed. "Beg pardon, Kat, but paper don't do as much as a six gun."

"You'll get to use your six gun before all this is over, Banty," Kat said. "I swear it."

Banty tried moving his wounded arm. "Not with this wing all bound up I ain't. This here's my fightin' arm, Kat. Can't shoot worth a damn with my left."

"When the showdown comes, we won't cut you out Old Timer," Laredo said.

"Don't you go Old Timerin' me, you gol danged infant. These years I got on you is experience, an' that's worth a whole lot more'n youth anyday."

"Simmer down, Banty." Laredo held out his hands as though fending him off. "Didn't mean nothin' by it. An' we'll prob'ly want yer wise words afore we're done anyhow."

"That's more like it. This younger generation; don't show no respect fer their elders."

Doc Murray returned. "You three still here? You can take this ol' critter outta here. Gunshot wound; ain't nothin'. Seen plenty of 'em in the late War o' Northern Aggression. Now git outta here before somebody comes in who's *really* dyin'!"

Banty shot to his feet and faced the doc. "Who you callin' 'ol' critter?'"

"You, you ol' critter. You're all sewn up; just like patchin' a pair o' pants, that's all you needed." Doc browsed through his medicine cabinet a moment and shook out some pills into a small envelope, sealing it. "Here. Take one o' these if you got any pain. Just don't take too many of 'em. An' don't wash 'em back with whiskey."

"Ain't no fun that way doc," Banty said, sticking the envelope in his shirt pocket. "Much obliged anyways." He sized him up. "An' when it comes to ol' critters, guess you know whatcher talkin' about; looks like yer a charter member of the club yerself!"

Doc Murray's retorts pursued them until they escaped to the safety of the street.

"Anything else on your list Kat?" Laredo asked.

"Yeah; home. Let's go."

* * *

The outlaws rode back to the hideout, arriving separately in three groups. The ambushers from the rocks were one, their counterparts in the woods were the second, and the three erstwhile prisoners were the third. None of them had returned unscathed. One or two carried more lead in them and less blood than they'd had when they set out, but taking care of that had to wait until they were safe from pursuit.

All of them had been shot before, and all of them had some idea of what to do about it. Their techniques might not have been as precise as Doc Murray's, or even Kat's, but it would do.

Lefty was the only one in the hideout when the others returned.

"Where's the boss?" Butch asked.

"Larson's not here. He said he had some business, in town or somewhere I guess."

No one questioned why Lefty should know that and Butch, supposedly Larson's lieutenant, didn't. They knew better than to challenge Butch.

"Did he say when he'd be back?"

"No."

And no one asked about that either.

* * *

The shack had probably had many owners, and the wood slats were gray with age and many hung loose from the rust-worn nails that once held them. But the trail leading to the shack was just as abandoned and that meant whatever went on inside was about as private as might be desired.

Larson sat at the table which was nearly as rotted as the walls around them. Across from him sat a man in city clothes. Larson had no use for the man's dandy dress but he did have use for the money he paid. And this wasn't the first time the man had paid him, either. And for Larson it wouldn't be the last either.

"I thought you were the man we needed," the man in city clothes said. In spite of what had been perhaps days on the trail his clothes were spotless and the creases sharp. His dark mustache was neatly trimmed and Larson had never seen fingernails so well kept except on a woman. Dark brows bent down over fierce dark eyes.

"I am. No one knows the Bar C like me."

"Then how come you're not ready to hand it over to me?" the man said. "I expected you to have run this female and her pitiful crew off by now."

"She hired some new hands. And since they came on we haven't been able to drive off any more cattle."

"Are her men that good, or are yours just useless?"

"I don't know. They caught three of mine when they tried stampeding the herd."

"Caught? And hanged them on the spot, I suppose; Judge Hemp I believe he's called."

"No; they took them prisoner. But I sent the rest of my men to get 'em free. Maybe some of them Bar C boys are feedin' the crows even now."

"For your sake they'd better be."

The man hadn't mentioned it and Larson didn't want to

bring up the subject after having admitted failure but it was the only way to keep his men and finish the job.

"If this is gonna work," Larson said, "I need more cash."

"Why should I give you more cash when you haven't delivered any profit on what I've given you so far?"

"'Cause if you don't I can't pay my men. An' if I can't pay my men, they're gone, an' I'm gone with 'em."

The man shrugged. "So? Then I just hire someone else. Men like you are easy to find."

Larson grinned. "An' that's still gonna cost you. Might even cost you more'n me."

The man stared hard at Larson, cursing the truth of Larson's statement. Without a further word he pulled a roll of bills from his pocket, peeled off a fair sized portion and grudgingly slid them over to Larson who rifled them through his fingers like a deck of cards and shoved them into his jeans. Larson's smile with its brown and broken teeth was that of a demon.

The man who paid him wasn't afraid of Larson, but had a healthy wariness of him. "Get the hell out of here," he said low and even, his hands still on the table and empty of weapons.

Larson's grin still bore on the man, as the outlaw leader rose leisurely, patted the pocket with the cash, touched his hat brim in mock gratitude, and took his own time going out the door and mounting his horse.

The man watched him ride away. *Sometimes business meant making deals with the Devil*, he thought. *Larson might not be the Devil, but he's a sure candidate if Satan ever abdicates.*

He waited a long time after Larson was gone to mount his own horse, only secure that Larson didn't intend to ambush him to the extent that Larson needed his money.

The man took his path back to the town where he had his hotel room, a good fifty miles from the Bar C.

* * *

Kat, Laredo and Banty rode up to the house. Hank was there and took charge of the horses, as they told him what had happened. Hank made a few comments regarding the family life of the bushwackers and the three echoed his sentiments.

"And here I am with a arm in a sling an' of no use to you," Banty grumbled as they went inside.

Bear was getting ready to ride out and heard him. "Not that you did much to begin with."

Banty's unmeant but fiery invective followed Bear as he went out the door.

"I'd worry if they *stopped* cussin' each other," Laredo said. "My belly is screamin' to be filled."

"None of us had breakfast," Kat said.

Banty glanced in the kitchen; no one was minding the stove. "Well, guess I can still sling a skillet with my left hand. I'll have some grub for us in a jiffy." The clatter of pans and plates began.

Laredo and Kat sat at the table waiting over coffee which Bear had left in the pot.

"Kat, why do you think Larson is tryin' to put you out of business?"

"I don't know; I just figured he resents workin' for a female. Least that's what he said when he quit."

"There's got to be more to it than that," Laredo said. "The way you told me, you an' your pa ran this ranch together so he answered to you an' him."

"That's right. So you have any other ideas?"

Laredo took a long drink of his coffee. "No I don't; I really don't. An' I wish I did."

CHAPTER EIGHT

Slim wasn't the only one anxious when Larson returned and called all of them in. Even Butch shifted his feet and looked like a kid about to get whupped. And they were; a lashing by Larson's tongue, if not by his belt.

When the initial thunder and lightning and cussing out was over (even Butch learned a few new ones) Larson settled himself down and concentrated his wrath on Butch.

"And you let yourselves get caught. Slim said those Bar C boys roped you three like a bunch o' maverick steers."

Butch only gave a mute nod. Arguments and alibis weren't going to cut it, and he knew it.

"You're lucky they didn't throw ropes for each of you around the nearest trees. I've got half a mind to string up the three of you myself!" He let that sink in and while pleased with the effect it had on Butch maintained the grimace on his face and kept the satisfied smile to himself. "Only reason I'm keepin' any of you on is 'cause I need you. An' nobody's leavin' until we've driven Kat Crandall an' all those hands off'n the Bar C."

"Larson, there's one thing I don't get," Slim said.

Larson grunted a derisive laugh. "Only one?"

Slim glanced at the others, unsure now whether to continue. He hitched up his belt and his nerve with it and said, "Why're you so hard on Kat anyway? We could've gotten work at any of the other ranches round here. Why you pickin' on her?"

Larson shot him a dark look. I got my reasons, an' it's none o' your business. Your business, an' this goes for all o' you, is to do as I tell you." He let that same look pass over each of them as he debated with himself whether to pay them from the wad in his pocket. He decided against it. "Now all o' you, get the hell outta here." It boosted his sense of his own power to see them rush over each other to get out the door.

BOOK TITLE

* * *

Clem cranked away at his press, turning out another copy of the broadsheet that was the *Clarion,* his pride and joy. He was more than glad to write that article for Kat; maybe Sheriff Stokes' days were numbered, and if he had a hand in it all the better. And that big fella Laredo or whatever his real name was; he had the looks of a decent lawman.

Clem grinned as he printed the last few copies. *Yeah, and Kat could do a lot worse for a man to settle her down too.* An admirer of Shakespeare, Clem had to chuckle though; Kat reminded him of another Katherine: Kate of the Bard's *Taming of the Shrew. Wonder how Laredo might do if he tried taming Kat?*

The last copy came off the press and Clem set it aside with the others to dry. He started gathering the other copies that were ready for distribution and stacking them, tying them in bundles of thirty. After a bit the last few were dry enough to join the others and he took the whole lot outside.

He set a stack on a stand just outside his door, tacked one to the wall after taking down last week's edition, and took the others to Brody's General Merchandise for sale. Brody paid him a set amount to print ads and coupons in the paper and gave him credit in the store besides to help cover his expenses.

After the usual exchange Brody took a paper off the top and saw the headline. "Wait a minute, Clem! Is this on the level?"

"Kat gave me the story herself. She believes it's the truth, and I stand by what I print."

"She says there's been rustlin' and other stuff. And she's sure Larson is behind it?"

"That's what she says."

"What's her proof?"

Clem shrugged. He told Brody about Laredo and the others capturing three of Kat's former hands and losing them before they could get them to the sheriff.

"An' you think Larson put 'em up to it?"

"Makes sense to me. They're the ones who followed him off the ranch when he quit. Why wouldn't they still be followin' him now?"

Brody had no answer for that and Clem took his other stacks and went on his way.

Clem's stops included the various bars and saloons and a patron of such an establishment, a fellow named Andrews, glanced at the paper between beers. The headline for Clem's editorial about Larson caught his eye.

Andrews had never worked for Kat; he rode for one of the other ranchers. But he and Larson had gotten drunk together more than once, and shared other pursuits as well, so he didn't like what Clem said in the paper.

While hunting some strays for his boss a while back he had stumbled across Larson's hideout. He had recognized Bennett guarding the pass, though he was pretty sure Bennett didn't see him. And the fact that Larson had it in for the Crandall gal wasn't news; it was the talk of many a campfire or bunkhouse. And if somebody's up to no good he's gonna be hid out, and have somebody guarding wherever that is. Andrews had put two and two together and knew Larson and whoever was with him were hiding out somewhere beyond that pass. He never told; wasn't any affair of his. And Andrews had a reputation for keeping a secret.

But now it was in the paper and maybe the town might start thinking more serious about it. The town liked the Crandall gal, and so did his boss. They might get the sheriff to get off his butt and do something about it.

Andrews figured he'd better let Larson know. If the sheriff was forced to raise a posse they might even find where Larson and his boys were holed up. And some of the stuff they might have done could buy 'em a rope.

Andrews downed the last of his beer in a gulp, dropped a coin on the bar-top, and went to his horse.

* * *

He remembered the way; he'd grown up in these hills. Andrews found the trail and started through the boulders that formed a natural gate to the pass. A cool wind blew through it.

A shot spattered rock next to him and a splinter of it struck his horse. Andrews gripped the reins and cooed easily to his mount to calm him.

"Halt!" a voice cried out from above. "Turn yourself around and get the hell outta here."

Andrews knew the voice. "Hiya, Butch."

Butch skylined himself on the rocks above, but kept his rifle ready. "That you Andrews?"

"Yeah. Got a message for Larson. He around?"

"What makes you think he's around here?" Butch asked, his fingers playing about the rifle.

Andrews shrugged. "You're here, ain't ya? Folks say you're his right hand man."

His ego fed, Butch stood a bit straighter. "Yeah? What if I am?"

"Then you'd want Larson to see what's in this paper." He held up the broadsheet.

Butch hesitated. Orders were not to let anyone through the pass. He should've shot Andrews on sight, but he'd also shared a few of those beers and women with Andrews and Larson.

"Leave the paper."

"What? Leave it where?"

"Right where you are. Put a rock on it so it don't blow away."

Andrews got down slowly and did as told then forked his horse again.

"Now ride, back the way you came. An' you tell anyone about this..."

"I won't. I swear it."

"You'd better not." Butch patted his rifle.

Andrews turned and rode back up the trail.

Butch watched until he was gone then climbed down from his spot. He picked up the paper and swore when he saw the article. He went a few yards into the pass. Lefty was on guard there.

"Hey, I heard you jawin' with somebody," Lefty said. "Who was it?"

"A friend." He handed Lefty the paper. "Take this to the boss; he'd like to see it."

"Sure." Lefty went to where his horse was tethered and once he started on his way Butch returned to his post.

He had a few words to say regarding the editor of the newspaper, and for that matter the whole institution of the press. The reader can use his or her imagination to fill in the details. Butch hoped the boss would send him to teach Grange a lesson.

* * *

Butch might have learned a lesson in the fine art of cussing if he had been present when Larson read the article. His efforts were but a baby's prattle to the wide spectrum of fluency that the boss exhibited.

His instructions were terse. "Grady, you take over Butch's watch. Lefty, you and Butch go into town and make sure Grange don't print no more. Savvy?"

Lefty grinned. "I savvy."

Lefty was about to turn when Larson grabbed him by the shirt front. "And don't mess up."

"We won't."

* * *

Laredo and Bear had the night off so they decided to spend some of their pay in town. They took their beers to a table and Bear took a couple of sniffs. As usual the bar was filled with the smells of whiskey, tobacco, and sweat. The cheap perfumes worn by the girls employed by the establishment did little to remove the odor.

"What's the sniffing about?" Laredo asked. "The place smells just as foul as any other liquor joint."

"Yeah," Bear agreed, "but at least it don't smell like any o' Larson's crowd."

Laredo laughed and lifted his glass. "Yeah; I'll drink to that."

Both men rolled their own and smoked them, talking little and minding their own business. A card game was going on at a nearby table and Laredo felt the weight of the wages in his pocket and wondered if he might make it heavier. He turned to his pard and said, "Feel lucky?"

Bear eyed the game doubtfully and shook his head. "Not me. If you wanna blow your wad on some cards it's your funeral."

Laredo downed the rest of his beer and like some conjuror's trick one of the half-clad bar girls appeared at his side. "Like another?" she asked, her smile and eyes suggesting she offered something in addition to the beer.

Laredo grinned up at her. "Sure, doll; and bring it over to that other table. I'm gonna try my luck." He rose and hitched up his gun-belt, drawing the gun briefly to verify a full cylinder before slipping it in place loose and ready. He went over to the table where a chair had just been vacated by a cow puncher who'd just lost his last nickel and said, "Mind if I join in?"

"Sure," one of the men said. "You got money to lose just like that young amateur that left?"

"I got money," Laredo said, pulling back the chair, "but I think I got luck too."

The girl came with his beer and said, "And if you do good maybe your luck'll hold out later." She added a gentle sliding pat of her hand on his cheek as she glided off.

Laredo watched her go.

One of the card players noticed. "Kat better not see the way you're ogling that little number."

Laredo's voice was calm. "Meaning what?"

The card player shrugged. "Nothin'; 'ceptin' she'd probably rip the hide off both of ya."

"I'm here to play cards," Laredo said. "I'm willin' to ignore your poor manners as long as you understand my patience is only so long."

"Sure," the player said as he dealt. "I don't mean nothin' by it. It's just a friendly warnin' is all."

Laredo looked at his cards. "OK; I'll take it that way." He put his hand under the table. "Now, I can bring this hand up holdin' silver or iron; and the iron's full o' lead. So which'll it be?" His eyes remained on his cards, their expression hidden.

A little sweat broke out on the player's brow. "If you're gonna play," he said trying to cover a tremor in his voice, "we need to see some silver."

"Fine with me." Laredo set a couple of coins on the table. "I'm in."

Bear pulled up his chair so he could see the game, sitting just behind Laredo. Both were facing the entrance and saw the wing doors open and two familiar hombres enter. A sort of telepathy passed between the two without removing their eyes from the newcomers.

Butch and Grady had just stepped into the saloon and saw Laredo and Bear. The four were still for maybe a second or two and Butch jerked his head to the door. He and Grady retreated to the street.

"Something wrong, gents?" a player said.

"No; not now," Laredo said.

"Guess they decided to get lickered up somewheres else," Bear said between closed teeth.

Laredo nodded and played his hand.

Bear waited a moment and straightened. "But I guess I'll go make sure they got enough to pay their way. Even varmints is allowed a good drunk now an' then." His tone was casual but he was checking the loads in his sidearm at the same time.

"You see that them boys behave gentle-like," Laredo said without removing his eyes from his hand. He tossed some more silver on the table. "I see that an' raise you another five."

Bear stepped out in the street and looked up and down. There was no sign of them. The Fancy Free was across the street and he crossed to it and entered. They weren't there either. He checked another bar on the way, again with no luck.

Laredo joined him. "I got enough," he said. "I thought I might lend you a hand."

"No sign of 'em," Bear said. He jerked a thumb over his shoulder. "But that's their horses, I think."

"Yep; them's theirs." He glanced up and down main street. "Wonder where they've gone?"

A crash down the street sent them on the run. The lights were on in the newspaper office and they saw two familiar shadows moving about inside. Another crash and Laredo and Bear burst in.

Laredo caught a glimpse of Clem lying on the floor, out cold (he hoped) with a nasty gash in the side of his head. Trays of what were probably type lay spilled along the floor. Butch had a sledgehammer raised in his hands, ready to smash the press but stood like a stone when he saw Laredo.

Butch came at him, swinging the hammer. Laredo dove under it and tackled Butch to the ground. Bear strode toward Grady and the smaller man backed away. The blaze in Bear's eyes burned red.

"Please! Don't hurt me!" Grady kept backing up.

"I don't like hurtin' smaller guys," Bear said, "but sometimes I make an exception." He continued to advance.

Grady, retreating, tripped over the fallen figure of Clem. Bear bent down and picked him up with one hand and held him about a foot off the ground. "Is he dead?" When Grady didn't answer Bear cocked his ham-sized fist and asked again. "Is he?"

"No; least, I hope not. We're just supposed to scare 'im, and mess the place up a lot."

A certain stench formed in the bundle Bear held. "You made a mess all right." He turned to Laredo. "How you doin', pard?"

Laredo sent a left to Butch's stomach and a right to his jaw. "Doin' fine."

Butch came back swinging, but Laredo dodged them and sent two more to Butch's jaw. The big man fell against the press and when Laredo came at him again used it to lean against as he kicked Laredo in the crotch. Laredo bent clutching his privates.

"Excuse me," Bear said. "Gotta help my buddy." He tossed Grady down like so much dirty laundry and came after Butch. A low, hard punch delivered at least as much damage as Butch had done to Laredo, and when Butch caved to nurse himself Bear delivered a hammer blow of his fist that toppled him to the floor. Both Larson men were down for the count.

Laredo gulped deep breaths; the pain was severe and he knew riding home was going to be agony tonight, but he'd live. He shoved the unconscious Grady away from Clem and knelt beside him. "Clem, you OK? Wake up, pardner." He shook him a little and heard a groan. "Bear, get some whiskey." Bear ran to fetch a flask he kept in his saddlebag.

Laredo made Clem comfortable and used his bandana to

splash some water on Clem's face. Bear came back with the whiskey and Laredo poured some on the bandana and used it to clean the wound.

Clem grimaced and let out a howl. "What the devil is that stuff?"

"He's all right," Laredo said. "It's us, Clem, Laredo and Bear." He turned to Bear again. "Get the sheriff and Doc Murray."

"That's me," Bear grumbled, "the errand boy. Make the big boy run."

As he started on his way Laredo grinned at Clem's confusion. "He's always like that." Clem tried to get up. "Just sit tight; you got a nasty bump. I cleaned it a little with some whiskey but the doc's comin'."

"What happened?"

"You got hit on the head. Butch and Grady were tryin' to wreck your press, but we stopped 'em. The sheriff'll take care of 'em."

"I don't know... I don't remember."

Bear, puffing and panting, returned with the sheriff and the doctor behind him. Bear looked about, found a bench that looked solid enough for his weight, and dropped himself on it.

Stokes placed a hand on Laredo's shoulder. "Take your hand away from your gun or I'll take it from you."

Laredo turned on him. "You just wanna try that, Sheriff?" His voice and even his smile purred with menace.

"Just cool off; all o' yuh." He looked about the shop again. "Ain't no damage I can see, 'cept what mighta happened in a fight. Butch, you say Laredo an' Bear jumped you?"

"That's right, Sheriff. We got no quarrel with them."

"Well, I've got plenty o' quarrel with you," Laredo snarled.

"Just simmer down," Stokes warned again. "I'm not sayin' it a third time or I'll haul in the lot of ya for disturbin' the peace."

Clem was sitting on a stool, his head bandaged. Laredo found the editor's glasses and handed them to him. Remarkably they weren't broken.

"Grange, what've you got to say about it? It's your place."

Clem started to his feet, wobbled a bit until Doc steadied him and he found a table to lean on. He looked around. "It's a mess, but nothin' I can't clean up." He used the table for support as he went round it to the press. He took off his glasses, rubbed his eyes, and put them back on to inspect it. "Nope, nothin' broken here. Sheriff, whatever happened won't set me back none."

"That's 'cause Bear an' me stopped 'em before they could finish," Laredo said.

"Is that right, Grange?" Stokes asked.

Clem scratched his head. "Don't know, Sheriff. Somebody hit me on the head; at least, that's what Laredo tells me. Other than that, I don't remember nothin'."

Bear joined in now, towering over the Sheriff. There were words you don't use to describe a lawman to his face, and Bear was about to use some choice ones when Stokes shouted him down.

"I've had about enough! There's some stuff layin' around here, and I have to admit that sledgehammer looks suspicious. But all I got is your word, Laredo, against Butch; an' I've known Butch a lot longer than I know you. Fact is, there might even be a poster with your face on it in my office, for all I know. Is there?" He studied Laredo close up.

"Can't say, Sheriff; ain't never been in your office an' me and Bear would like to keep it that way."

Stokes gave an exaggerated nod. "A wise choice; stay outta trouble an' you'll stay outta my jail." He gathered them all in his gaze. "An' that goes for the lot of ya. Now git, before I run ya all in just for the hell of it."

Laredo and Bear helped Clem close up and put out the lights as Butch and Grady left. Clem's rooms were above the newspaper office and Laredo helped him up the steps, carrying a lamp. Clem claimed to be all right and Laredo came back downstairs. He and Bear stepped out into the street. Butch and Grady were waiting for them by the hitching rail.

"This ain't over yet, Laredo."

"I know it ain't," Laredo answered.

Each watching the others warily, the four mounted their horses and rode off, one pair heading for the Bar C, the other to report to Larson.

It occurred to both Laredo and Bear that if they followed the others it might lead them to their boss, but it had been enough for the night.

But all four knew Butch was right; it wasn't over.

CHAPTER NINE

Dawn had risen nice and pretty, as though to put the lie to the fracas the night before. Bear was out riding heard with Hank and the others. Banty was still on the mend, but even one-handed he wrangled a mean skillet. Breakfast had filled their bellies before they rode out. Laredo leaned against the post supporting the roof over the porch, smoking a cigarette and enjoying the cool of the shade. It didn't cool his temper any though, and the fight the night before and the Sheriff's refusal to do anything about it still rankled in him.

Damn that Stokes anyhow, Laredo thought. *Any fool could see Clem was hurt bad; did he think we did it? Did he think Clem tried to take on two big lugs like Butch and Grady by himself?* Laredo ran through a list of names he had for Stokes; probably a few of them were the ones he had stopped Bear from using the night before. They had Butch and Grady red handed; not good enough for Stokes though. Was he on Larson's payroll too?

Yeah, there was a question. Larson had to be paying his men from somewhere; what was the source of his payroll? Butch and Grady always seemed to have some ready cash; where was Larson getting it? There hadn't been any robberies in the area he knew of. Someone had to be paying Larson, but who?

A dark haze was on the horizon against the rising sun. It was just a spot, and Laredo squinted trying to make it out. The spot was moving and getting closer. Then he heard the sound of hoof beats and saw it was a rider approaching. He didn't recognize the man and loosened his gun in the holster.

The rider spurred his horse a bit as he drew nearer, as one does when approaching a familiar destination. When he was within sight Laredo took his measure. He was tall, about Laredo's height, slender but wide shouldered with limbs of corded muscle. His features were sharp, clear, too pretty for Laredo's taste; but he figured the rider had certainly had his share of female conquests.

He pulled up to the hitching rail and dismounted. As he tied his horse Laredo threw away his smoke and strode out to meet him. Their eyes met as they took stock of each other.

"Stranger, aren't you?" the rider said.

"No; you're the stranger, mister. I work here. What's *your* handle?"

"Billy Holcomb!" The voice was not the rider's and it came from behind Laredo. Kat came from the ranch house, all in her usual flannel and jeans, her hat hanging down her back on its cord. Laredo wasn't sure whether it was just surprise or some discomfort too in his boss' reaction. "What the hell are you doin' here?"

"Kat!" Billy ran toward her, arms out to embrace her, and Kat met him with a stiff-armed shove that held him off and a cocked right fist.

"You try anything like that an' I'll sock ya again like I did when we were kids." Her eyes said she might do it just because.

"OK, I'll hold off." Billy Holcomb stepped back a pace or two. "Man it's good to see you again, Kat."

Kat held her punch ready a moment or two more before dropping her hand. "Yeah? What kept you away, anyhow?"

"Aw Kat, you know how it was. Sometimes a man's gotta go out an' make his own way in this world. I wanted to prove to pa I could do that."

"An' your pa died less'n a year after you left an' you didn't even have the guts to come back for his funeral."

"I know, Kat, I know." Billy took off his hat and hung his head low.

Laredo tried to figure whether his manner was real or he missed his calling for the dramatic stage.

"But by the time I heard he was gone I was too far away to get back in time. You know I sent some money to buy him a good headstone."

"I guess. Well, you still didn't answer my question. What brings you back?"

"I heard you need hands and well, I'd like a job. That's all it is: I wanna sign on."

"How'd you hear about it? Where were you all these years?" Kat strode forward to look up into his eyes, probing them for the truth.

"I came across one o' Clem's newspapers. Somebody was passing through here I guess about the time your daddy passed an' musta picked up a paper. He left it in a bar I was in an' I saw the announcement in it. Figured you might need some help running the place, with your dad gone an all."

"Ahuh." Kat's hands were on her hips. "An' just what kinda help are you offerin', Billy Holcomb?"

"Why, I'd like to be your foreman. I done some cattle punching around Wyoming, and was trail boss a coupla times. Kat, you need a man to run this place an' I'm applyin' for the job."

It was an open-handed slap that stung his cheek, but it hurt just the same. "Hey, what's that for?" Billy complained, nursing his jaw.

"That's a warnin'," Kat said. "An' I got a foreman already."

"Yeah? Well where is he? You can tell him he can step down, 'cause Billy Holcomb's here to take his place."

"You can tell him that yourself," Laredo said, stepping forward. "I'm him; an' I'm not about to step down for a kid like you."

Billy went for his gun and Laredo wrenched his arm up behind him in less than a blink.

"I wouldn't try that," Laredo said. He applied a little extra pressure on the arm.

"Hey! You're gonna break it!" Billy sounded like he was about to cry.

"That's not a bad idea, unless you agree to learn some manners."

"Let me go! Kat, call off your ape."

Laredo gave the arm one last tug before releasing him.

"Still all talk an' no grit, eh Billy?" Kat sneered.

"I'll take on anybody in a fair fight," Billy protested. "He took me off guard, that's all."

"Ahuh." Kat wasn't buying it. "All right; we're short one hand right now anyway while one of our guys is recovering from a gunshot wound. You say you can punch cattle?"

"Yeah, been doin' it all over it seems," Billy boasted.

"Laredo, let's see what he can do."

"You're the boss." Laredo touched his hat as Kat started back inside. He turned to Billy. "C'mon, I'll show you where to stack your gear."

"You don't have to show me. I had the run of this ranch when Kat an' me were kids." He unhitched his horse and led him toward the corral.

Laredo followed from a distance. He watched while Billy untied his blanket and saddle bag, uncinched his saddle, and opened the corral gate for his horse to go in. He closed the gate, secured the saddle where the rest were stored, and with his saddle bag over one shoulder and his bedroll in his hand he turned and saw Laredo. He just stood and stared a moment and Laredo returned the favor. Then he made his way to the bunkhouse, found an unclaimed bunk, and set his gear down. He turned to face Laredo.

"I get the feeling you don't like me much," Billy said.

"No, I don't. But if Kat vouches for you, that's enough for me."

"She'll vouch for me, you can bet on that." Billy got a cigar from a pocket, hesitated, and got a second to offer to Laredo.

"Thanks." Laredo took the cigar and struck a match to it. He lit Billy's for him and shook the match out. "So you an' Kat grew up together."

"Yeah. We were pretty close too, if you know what I mean."

"Sure. Sounds like you got close enough for her to deck you, at least once."

Billy grinned in spite of the color coming to his cheeks. "Yeah, she's packs quite a punch."

"Don't I know it."

"She socked you too?"

"Nope; but I once saw her knock out a pal o' mine. She was diggin' a bullet outta him at the time."

"An' she put him to sleep so's to make it easier on the both of 'em, right?" Billy chuckled and Laredo laughed with him.

"Yeah, that's about it. I'd say Kat can handle herself right well."

"For a woman."

Laredo removed the cigar from his mouth slowly, his mouth twisted as though it was suddenly bitter to him. "I'd say Kat can handle herself right well; I've known men not half as tough."

Billy was smart enough to see that last remark was aimed at him. "Yeah, guess you're right at that."

Laredo waited; when Billy didn't add any further observation he seemed to discover the cigar in his fingers, regarded it a moment, and drew another draft from it. "Pretty good smoke."

"Yeah. Got a pal back East in the Carolinas that ships 'em to me."

Laredo nodded. "Interestin'. Guess when you're a-driftin' you let him know where you a-driftin' to, eh?"

Billy fidgeted a little. "Yeah, somethin' like that. Now that I'm here I'll have him send some to town. There's a telegraph office, right?"

"Ahuh. All you gotta do is send him a wire?" Laredo showed no more than casual curiosity.

"Yeah. You'd be surprised how quick they get out here."

"I can imagine."

"Say, would you like me ask him to throw in another box of 'em for you?"

"Much obliged," Laredo said. "I do enjoy a good smoke. Just so no one's blowin' it in my face."

Billy's chuckle was nervous. "Yeah; nobody likes that much."

The clang of the triangle announced lunch.

"C'mon Billy," Laredo said. "My pard Banty's actin' as one-armed cook these days until his busted wing gets un-busted."

"Banty? Is he the one Kat dug the bullet out of?"

"Yeah. If you put in a good word about his cookin' maybe he'll tell you about it himself."

"Sounds like a bargain, if his food's good." He crushed out his finished cigar.

"He ain't poisoned no one yet that I know of." When Billy laughed Laredo added, "'Course, they say there's a first time for everything." He took one long last drag on his cigar, crushed it under his foot, and strode toward the house.

Billy watched him go a moment before he set his shoulders and followed.

* * *

"Yep, Kat saved my life all right." It was just after lunch and Banty sat at the table with Laredo, Billy, and Kat. "She dug that bullet outta me and plugged it up real pretty until Doc Murray fixed it up proper. I remember puttin' up a fuss while she was a-huntin' for it though; thought she'd hit me with a rock to shut me up."

"Just used this," Kat said, displaying her right fist.

"Put me out o' commission, just the same," Banty finished.

"So you way this Larson is tryin' to put you outta business?" Billy asked.

"Yeah, an he's doin' a heluva job of it," Kat said. "Lost a good part of my stock, kept some supplies from comin' in, even tried to stampede the herd I got left one night."

"Laredo, Bear an' me stopped 'em," Banty said. "It was when we were tryin' to take 'em to the Sheriff that some o' Larson's men ambushed us an' they got away, an' I got shot."

Billy smiled. "Well, old timer, maybe it's for the best."

Banty peered at him through slitted eyes. "How you mean that?"

"Just that yer too old t' be ridin' herd, but you fry up a mean steak an' potatoes."

Banty didn't seem re-assured. "I'm not sure which part o' that to take: the insult or the complement."

Billy shrugged, his face all innocence. "Why, the whole thing was meant as a complement. I didn't mean nothin' by it." He reached in his pocket. "Here, have a cigar."

When Banty looked at it doubtfully Laredo said, "Go ahead; it's good tobacco. I had one myself before lunch."

"Have another." Billy offered one to each of them and lit a third for himself. "Call it a peace offerin'."

"OK," Banty said, accepting the cigar. "Don't mind if I do." He stuck the stogie in his mouth, stacked the plates, and started toward the kitchen. "Thanks."

"I guess I'd better ride out an' check on the other boys,"

Laredo said. He stood and hitched up his belt. "Billy, wanna come along an' meet 'em?"

"Oh, I'll ride out an' join you a bit later. I think I can find my way." He noticed the glance exchanged between Laredo and Kat.

"Suit yourself," Laredo said. "I might stay out overnight with 'em, Kat."

"You keep an eye on the herd and don't let any Larson men cut any out," Kat ordered. "If you do, it'll be your hide."

"Yes ma'am," Laredo said with a tug at his hat.

The glare Kat gave him at his "ma'am" brought a grin to his face and she looked about for something to throw. There wasn't anything worth tossing so she just glared some more, which widened Laredo's grin.

But she didn't see the frown of suspicion toward Billy just before he went off to his horse.

"So he's top hand now, huh?" Billy said, pouring himself another cup of java even though it had cooled.

"Yeah. He and his two pards came outta nowhere and signed on. I wasn't so sure about 'em at first, but they've proven they're loyal."

"Yeah? What do you know about 'em?"

"Nothin', 'cept they can ride and shoot and handle a herd. That's enough, in my book."

"Then your book don't have many pages," Billy said. "Seems I've heard o' that Laredo from somewhere."

Kat leaned forward. "You think he might be an outlaw?"

Billy shrugged. "I dunno. Not sayin' he is, an' not sayin' he ain't. Just think on it this way, Kat: you know me, an' you don't know him."

"Yeah, Billy; I know you." Kat sounded like she wasn't too happy about what she knew.

"There ain't nothin' — romantic goin' on between you, is it?"

"That's none o' your business." Kat's cheeks burned nearly as red as her hair and her hands clenched on the table.

"I'm makin' it my business 'cause I care about you. I always did."

Kat relaxed a little. "I know. But you don't have no claim on me, Billy Holcomb; let's keep that straight."

"I know. Just wanna look out for ya."

"I don't need lookin' out for." Kat nearly knocked over her seat getting up and storming out of the house.

Billy sat for a minute finishing his coffee and started out. Kat was already mounted and riding and he grinned as he watched her go before saddling his own horse and riding after her.

His horse was fast and he caught up with her.

"Say, if you're not sweet on this Laredo hombre what about me?"

"What about you?" She started to pull ahead but curiosity slowed her.

"Well, you remember I was always sweet on you."

"I remember." Her hands tightened on the reins.

"What'd happen if I tried kissin' you again like I did?"

Kat's half grin curled itself. "Depends. Which eye did I blacken for you that time?"

Billy grinned too. "The left one, I think."

"OK. Go ahead and kiss me, if you wanna go for another shiner on the right."

Billy chuckled. "I'll take a pass for now." They rode a little further, still side by side, and he said, "Bet you wouldn't slug that Laredo if he tried to kiss you." He spurred his horse and went off the trail to escape, leaving his laughter behind.

Kat was tempted to follow but figured it wasn't worth it. She urged her horse ahead and soon saw Laredo. She caught up to him and rode beside him a bit.

Laredo kept pace with her and noticed her mood. "What's wrong?"

"Nothin'." Kat spurred her horse and was nearly out of sight in a moment.

Laredo saw Billy riding to cross the trail behind him and chuckled.

Gunshots sounded ahead and both men cried to their mounts for speed. Dust clouds rose behind them as they raced toward the firing. They saw Kat turn her horse toward where they now saw whiffs of gun smoke and raced to join her.

Kat saw it first: Bear, Hank, and the others were trading shots with what seemed an army of men. Kat let out a scream as a bullet struck Hank from his saddle. She drew her own gun and fired toward the man who had shot him. It missed and she tried again. A startled cry told that she'd hit somebody; whether it was the one she aimed at didn't matter, as long as it was a Larson man.

Laredo and Billy caught up to her and the three spread out, adding their aid to the others. Laredo pulled a Winchester from the boot beside him, cocked it one-handed without stopping, and let off a shot. Another raider fell from his saddle. Billy fired his six-gun and emptied it in a quick barrage, turning and spurring out of range to reload.

Bear, Rawhide and Dakota were preparing a charge, and Kat and Laredo joined them. Lead singing past them they sent slugs of their own, some of which hit home and some missed.

Kat saw Bear flinch once, and again, but he kept firing and shouting to his horse. He was like some fierce warrior god riding into battle.

Billy returned to the fray, firing into the now retreating band.

The Larson men fled and Laredo and Rawhide started after them.

Bear had pulled up, and sagged in the saddle. Then like a heavy sack of grain he slid to the ground, a spur catching in his stirrup. Kat was nearby and grabbed the reins or Bear would have been dragged by his own horse.

"Laredo!" she called. "Bear's hurt!"

Laredo stopped, hauling rein, and turned back. Rawhide followed him.

They pulled up where Bear lay and swung from their saddles. Laredo knelt next to his friend. "Bear! Bear, it's me: Laredo. Take it easy, pard; you'll be OK."

Bear's eyes were closed and even when he opened them they seemed shut. "That you, Pete?"

"It's me, Laredo," he said again.

The others had heard the name Pete and Rawhide exchanged a questioning glance with Billy who shook his head but listened for another slip of Bear's tongue.

If Kat had taken notice she didn't let on. "It's all right, Bear. You been shot and fell off your horse. We'll take care of you."

Bear's smile was a grimace. "Much obliged, ma'am."

Laredo noted that Kat didn't take exception to the term as she took out her pocketknife and cut and ripped open his shirt. Bear was wounded in three places.

Laredo had to chuckle in spite of his fear for his friend. "That tough hide o' his can stop a cannonball."

"Maybe," Kat said, "but it didn't stop these slugs."

Laredo got the flask of whiskey from Bear's saddlebag. "Seems we did this once before," he said.

"Yeah." Kat examined the wounds. "But these look pretty deep; he needs Doc Murray, not me."

Dakota came running up. "So the big guy got it too."

"He'll be all right. How's Hank?"

Dakota shook his head. "Pretty bad. I did what I could for him but I don't think it's enough."

"Where?" Kat demanded. "Where is he?"

Dakota led the way and Kat obviously thought he went too slow. Hank lay face down, his limbs stretched and angled unnaturally. His blood soaked into the soil around him, a brown stain spreading from both sides.

Kat knelt beside him. Her eyes burned with the tears she dared not show, and the fury that seethed in her. She'd known him all her life. Hank wasn't just a hand, an employee; he had been like an uncle to her as she grew up. She realized she was still clutching the knife; so hard her fingers hurt.

Kat's lips were a firm line as she stood up and put away her knife. "Well we can't do nothin' for either of 'em standin' here flappin' our jaws. We'll rig up a couple of blankets to pull 'em along Indian-style. We gotta go slow, so I hope we can get 'em in town in time."

After the wounded men had been placed in the makeshift travoits each started back to his horse.

"Hey, Pete!" Billy called.

Laredo paused only a second and kept on, climbing on his horse.

Billy mounted and pulled next to him. "How come Bear called you Pete?"

"He's wounded an' a little outta his head. Musta mistook me for somebody else, I reckon."

BOOK TITLE

"Yeah," Billy said, "guess he did."

CHAPTER TEN

Doc Murray had shooed all of them outside while he worked on the two injured men. Kat had insisted on helping and Laredo nearly had to haul her out bodily to get her out of the way. Laredo and the others were surprised when all the fight seemed to have gone from Kat once in the open. She just stood, only her hands reflexively closing and opening revealing her tension.

"He's gotta pull through," she whispered. Kat wasn't one for prayer, but those four words were sure close to being one.

Laredo heard them and said, "Bear's pulled through worse than this." He was assuring himself and Banty, who had joined them, as much as Kat.

"Yeah, sure," Kat said. "Bear can take it."

Billy nodded as he realized what Kat meant.

Without a word Kat strode off. Laredo started after her but Billy put a hand on his chest to stop him.

"Let her be," Billy said. "She's got to be alone. I seen this before. An' she ain't just worried about Bear."

Laredo frowned a question to him.

"It's Hank. She's worried about Hank too."

Laredo's shoulders sank. "Sure. I shoulda known. Hank didn't look so good."

Hours passed. Billy had offered to buy the first round if they went to the saloon but there were no takers so he just waited with the rest of them.

Doc finally came out, wiping his hands. "It's done. I got the last slug out of that big one — what do you call him?"

"Bear," Laredo said.

Doc gave one soft chuckle. "Suits him. He'll live."

Kat had come it seemed out of nowhere when Doc had appeared. "What about Hank? How about him?"

Doc put a hand on her shoulder. "I'm sorry, Kat. He — he

was already dead when you brought him here."

Kat shrugged loose. "No. It ain't so. Say it ain't." Her hand gripped her gun butt, knuckles whitened by how tightly she held.

"There was nothin' I could do for him, Kat. I'm awfully sorry."

Kat was frozen a moment, the hand looking like it was ready to draw on Doc any moment. A sudden turn and she mounted her horse and was gone.

They watched her go in silence until she was out of sight.

"Hank was the first hand her father hired years ago. He was almost like an uncle or something to her," Billy explained.

Laredo started for his horse.

"Don't go after her," Billy said. "She won't wanna talk or see you or nobody for a while." He waited before adding, "I saw her like this when we was kids an' a mare she loved died after droppin' her first colt."

Laredo continued to look down the road where Kat had disappeared for a long time. Rawhide and Dakota were talking to the Doc about arranging for Hank's burial.

* * *

The tears didn't come, but Kat didn't need them. Loss and mourning were tempered in here with an anger, a hate hotter than any smithy's fire.

She sat on her bed, her door locked, brooding over the situation.

The cattle were gone; *all* of them. What hadn't been rustled before were stampeded and vanished during the gunfight. Larson's men had probably rounded up most if not all of them by now. There might be some strays, but nobody will want to round 'em up until after Hank's funeral, which won't be for a couple of days, and by that time who knows where they'll be?

Market time is coming up, Kat thought, *an' I won't have nothin' to sell unless we find where the rustlers have been hidin' the cattle.* They could start on that task once Hank was planted anyway. *Maybe we can even find where the Larson bunch have their hide-out.* Meanwhile there were supplies to be bought an payroll to fill.

She went to the strongbox that had been in her father's room and she now had hidden in her own closet. The key was on a chain around her neck. She opened the heavy padlock and looked inside. Just about enough, she reckoned. After that it was up to Fate or God or Whatever or Whoever took care of such things.

* * *

Hank was buried in the same plot where Tom and Molly Crandall were, and the parson read the same verses over him. The only ones who came this time though were Kat, Laredo, and the rest of the hands including Billy. Kat noticed Rawhide and Dakota were fighting tears and she kept her own back. Hate and grim vengeance were her substitutes for grief. She'd get whoever fired the shot that killed Hank; she'd get him personally.

The service over they rode back to the ranch house. As soon as they were all there Kat called a meeting in the door yard.

"Hank is gone, an' we'll all miss him, but this ranch has got to keep goin'." She paused as they knew she was speaking business. "Most of the cattle are gone, we know that. But there's always a chance of strays, still somewhere on the Bar C range or maybe roaming back. Laredo, you and Rawhide make one pair lookin' for 'em and Billy, you an' Banty are the other. Sure could use Bear and Hank right now, but — Dakota, we need some supplies. Come on in an' I'll give you a list and the money. The rest of you, get goin'. The sooner we have some cattle back the sooner we can take 'em to market. We might not have many this time, but we can sell what we got until that Larson mob is found.

"An' it goes without sayin'," Kat added, "that if any o' you four find any o' Larson's men, fill 'em with lead before they can draw on you." She fingered her own gun butt as she said it, itching to take down an outlaw or two herself."

The four men forked their horses, rode off in pairs, and Dakota joined Kat inside. She had already put the money in a small sack and was just about finished her list.

BOOK TITLE

* * *

The four riders returned to the scene of the gun fight to see if there were any tracks. There were; but much of it was a confusion of hoofprints between horses and cattle. And circling the area much of what might have been a trail either of cattle or escaping horsemen had been obliterated by the wind.

But even so there was some impression and Laredo called them to gather.

"There's what might be cattle tracks goin' that way," he gestured to his left, "an' horse tracks goin' that way," to his right. He tugged a coin from his jeans. "I'll flip; Rawhide an' me'll take heads. Heads goes left, tails goes right." He flipped the coin. "Heads." He showed it to them so there was no mistake. "Ready, Rawhide?"

"Ready." The two rode off.

"Guess that means you an' me go thataway," Billy said.

"Well c'mon," Banty said. "My arm ain't sore no more but I'm achin' ta get me some rustlers!"

Banty kicked heel to his mount and sped away. Billy had to spur his own horse to catch up. When they were a good bit along, with no sign of any tracks, Billy had a suggestion.

"Why don't we split up here? I'll go up that draw —" he indicated the way, " — and you go up the other."

"Suits me. An' we meet back here in one hour; an' if one of us isn't back the other goes after him."

Billy nodded. "Right." He started up the draw and Banty rode the other way.

Banty was good at spotting trail, and he kept an eye to the ground. There were other markers possible as well: broken branches, or signs of a former camp. Banty kept watch for them all, at the same time alert in case of a trap. The way he went was open but there were high rocks around which might conceal a bushwacker. He'd been caught that way before and swore it wouldn't happen again.

He stopped after a time and checked his watch. He'd been out nearly half an hour. He gazed around him and decided to take one more look in an area he'd missed then head back to the rendezvous point.

There was no sign of anyone having passed so Banty returned to where they had split. Billy wasn't there so Banty got out some tobacco and rolled a cigarette.

* * *

Dakota had no trouble getting to town. And Mike, Brody's big hired man, helped him load the wagon. He was on his way back now and even had a little of the money Kat had given him left. At one time he might have blown it on a couple rounds of drinks for whoever was in the saloon at the time, but Dakota knew enough about the sad state of the ranch right now not to even think of it.

It was only another ten miles and he'd be home.

Horse hooves rolled behind him. He hazarded a look over his shoulder.

Three men, masked, their guns drawn.

One of them fired.

A bullet nicked Dakota's hat, knocking it from his head. Another shot zinged by his ear.

"Hi-YAH!" He snapped the reins, cracked his whip, and shouted to his team to speed up. They picked up and started to run, but the load was heavy and soon tired them. One of the horsemen came up beside him, gun leveled.

"Halt, or you get what your pal Hank got."

It didn't take any further warning for Dakota to haul back the reins and call the team to halt. They pulled to a stop and he raised his hands.

"Toss your iron," the gunmen said as the other two pulled up to the wagon.

Dakota tossed his gun away and raised his hands again.

"Just sit tight an' we won't hurt ya none," the gunman said.

The others started to rummage through the supplies in back.

"Whatcha got?" the gunman asked, his eyes still on Dakota.

"Flour, an' coffee, an' feed for hosses." He dug a little further. "An' some ammo; hey, we can use this stuff!"

"That's the idea," the gunman said. He getured with his gun. "Get down off there."

Dakota climbed off the wagon.

"Cover him, boys." One of the others covered Dakota while the gunman who had watched him got off his horse. "We're takin' your stuff; an' the wagon too. But to show we're hospitable, I'll let you have my horse."

"Much obliged," Dakota said.

He held his horse while Dakota mounted and climbed into the driver's seat. Without looking at them he called to his men, "Go on, mount up."

Dakota took a good look at their masked faces. Their bandanas covered the lower half and their hat brims shaded their eyes. He thought he recognized at least one of them, but wasn't sure.

"All right," the gunman said, "start walkin'."

Dakota started on the road to the ranch. He glanced behind him and saw the gunman turn the team and drive them in the opposite direction.

He turned back to his road. He had several miles to go.

Kat wasn't going to like this.

* * *

Banty had just about finished his third cigarette when Billy came down the path.

"Ain't nothin' or nobody up there," Billy said. "Guess we'd better go back."

They started toward where they had split with Laredo and Rawhide and heard a sound that's music to a cowhand's ears.

"They found some o' the herd!" Banty shouted. He waved his hat and yelled "YIPPEE!" three or four times.

"Shut up, you fool," Billy said, "you'll scare 'em into stampeding again!"

Banty was in too good a mood to argue. He yelled again and Billy had to grin at his enthusiasm.

"C'mon," Billy said, "let's give 'em a hand."

It was only about a couple dozen head, but they all had the Bar C brand. Banty joined in getting them going toward the Crandall range and Billy hung back riding rear guard.

"Found some of 'em only a little ways off the main range," Laredo told Banty. "An' Rawhide found some more. Then we ran into two or three more and here they are. Not much when you consider a couple thousand head, but it'll do, I reckon."

"Yep," Banty agreed, "it'll do for now."

They had gone a couple of miles and were on the road back to the ranch when Rawhide spotted a figure on horseback, distant and to the rear of their direction. "Hey, hold up," he said.

The others stopped and looked. The cattle continued moving, sounding their complaints, but at least they still went toward home. Rawhide stood up in the saddle a moment. "That looks like Dakota!"

The figure, recognizing them, waved, hallooed, and broke his horse into a run. The sight of his friends urged him on and he joined the group.

"What happened to you?" Laredo asked.

"That sure don't look like no cart to me." Banty said with a laugh.

"Somebody robbed me," Dakota said. "They stole the supplies and the team and wagon with them." He looked around. "But I see you found some cattle."

"Just a few," Laredo said. "But at least it's somethin'."

"So you're headed back to the ranch?"

"Yup," Laredo said. "We're headin' these cattle right up to Kat's front door."

Dakota scratched his head a moment. "Think you an' Billy an' Banty can take 'em in yourselves?"

"If you weren't a friend," Banty said, "I'd take exception to them words."

Dakota chuckled. "It's just that I'm thinkin' Rawhide and me can track what happened to the wagon, while you're ridin' herd."

"Suits me," Rawhide said.

"OK by me too," Laredo said. "I'll tell Kat what happened."

Rawhide grinned. "Better that your ears get scorched than ours."

Laredo called to Banty and Billy to follow and they turned the herd toward the ranch. Rawhide and Dakota watched them go a moment.

"Got your six gun?" Dakota asked.

"Yeah. What about you?"

"Had to leave mine behind. We can pick it up on the way. C'mon, maybe we can catch 'em before they get too far."

"Or maybe even track 'em back to the hideout."

Dakota swung a friendly poke at Rawhide. "Brother, you read my mind."

* * *

First there was the sound of heavy hooves, far more sound than that made by four horsemen. Kat rose from the ledger she'd been calculating in and went to the door. Next the strong smell of cattle came toward her. Then the dark mass of beef on the hoof, driven by four men whose grins shone through the grit on their faces.

Kat stepped out onto the porch and stood speechless. She just stood and watched the spectacle. True, it only seemed like a couple dozen but maybe it was enough for now. And maybe where they found the cattle they might find signs of where the rest were hidden.

Banty and the other steered the cattle back to the range as Laredo rode up and dismounted.

"We found some of 'em anyways, Kat," he said.

"I see you did. Any sign of the rest?"

Laredo shook his head. "No. But it's worth another look. Maybe if we all go next time one of us might find somethin'."

"Might work at that," Kat agreed. "C'mon in. I just put on some fresh coffee." She led him inside.

"Much obliged." He followed her in. He wasn't too anxious to tell her the bad news; not just yet.

* * *

Dakota led Rawhide to the spot where the cart had been stopped. He dismounted and picked up his revolver where it lay and looked around. There were plenty of tracks and the wagon itself left a good trail. The bandits had turned the wagon around and looked like they headed back toward town. But there was a sign where they went off the road and the two friends followed it as far as they could. The ground was rocky and the trail was soon lost. They searched around for a while before giving up. Then they decided to back trail them and they found something quite interesting.

Up behind the rocks alongside the road there were tracks of several horses having stood for a time. Rawhide and Dakota dismounted to get closer looks.

"Here's where they waited for you, Dakota," Rawhide said.

"Yep; three horses, three men. Wonder how they knew I was a-comin'?"

Rawhide shrugged. "They were probably waitin' for whoever come along. You mighta just been the lucky one."

"Huh. Yeah, lucky they let me go. Guess they figured nobody'd recognize 'em with those masks."

Rawhide noticed another set of tracks and followed them a bit. "Hey, here's another set." He knelt and studied them a moment. "Looks like somebody came up here to meet 'em an' then went back down." He pointed the direction of the departing tracks as he stood then turned to Dakota. "Wanna follow 'em?"

Dakota shrugged. "Suits me. C'mon."

They mounted their horses again and Dakota followed Rawhide who eyed the tracks as they went. There was a patch of rocky ground where the tracks disappeared but instead of giving up they scoured around to see if they picked up anywhere. Past the rocks there was gravel again, right before a road. The tracks led to that road and down.

"Funny," Dakota said, "Looks like somebody came up this road, turned off, met up with the bandits, an' came back again."

"Maybe it was their boss."

"Larson?"

"Wish we could prove it," Rawhide said. "All we got is tracks, an' nothin' special about 'em. Shucks. In the dime novels the bandits always got a lame horse or a missing or broken horseshoe or somethin' the hero uses to track the bad guys."

"Yeah, but this ain't no dime novel. Told you before not to waste yer money on them things."

Rawhide gave Dakota a look. "Yeah; well, I'd take more

stock in yer advice if you didn't insist on readin' 'em when I'm done."

Dakota started a string of insults that just brought a laugh out of Rawhide.

"C'mon. It ain't much, but at least we got somethin' to tell Kat." Rawhide swore. "At least when Laredo and I went out we found some of the cattle."

Dakota nodded. "An' at least I can say they was Larson's men all right who robbed me. One of 'em was Grady, I'm sure of it."

"Even with masks?"

"Those eyes o' his; there's none mistakin' 'em."

"Yer right about that," Rawhide said. He turned his mount. "Let's go back."

* * *

Kat was surprisingly calm when Rawhide and Dakota returned with their report. Laredo had told them that he'd already told Kat about the robbery so she had vented her rage on him.

"You boys did the best you could," she said. "But Dakota, I'm sure you're right: Larson's behind this. An' if we can find out where he's hidin', we'll find the cattle an' the supplies."

"You want Rawhide an' me to ride back out an' try again to pick up a trail?"

"No; it'll be dark soon. You can't read trail in the dark. Banty's rustlin' up some grub; go put your feedbags an' we'll try to figure things in the mornin'.

That sounded fine to the two cowboys and they went to claim their dinners.

Kat returned to her room. She sat on her bed, brooding. The supplies were a loss; no doubt Larson and his men will make short work of them. There was a payment due on the ranch, and the cattle were nowhere near ready for market. Especially if the boys could find more strays in the next week or two.

She'd just have to swallow her pride and go into town tomorrow and ask Hopkins the banker for an extension. Her daddy had never asked such a thing from anybody, but she couldn't let that stop her.

Kat turned in but sleep refused to come. She lay on her back, her hands clasped behind her head, and by morning she had memorized all the knotholes in her ceiling. Not that that helped matters any.

* * *

Next morning Kat, Billy, and Laredo rode into town. Laredo was to try his charm on the Brody's for another shipment of supplies, this time on credit, and if he was successful hire a buckboard and team from the livery stable to cart them back. She and Billy were going to see Hopkins about that mortgage.

Morgan Hopkins was the typical, prosperous looking banker: tall, a bit stout and well-fed, always wearing the latest style and always cleanly groomed. It made you wonder how much of the citizen's funds were actually in the safe and how much of it went toward Hopkins' upkeep. He had a wife and two sons; one was fresh from college back east and Hopkins planned for him to be his successor. The younger son was ten and attended the town school. Morgan Jr., the college graduate, was working inside the cage as teller today. Kat went to him first.

"Morning, junior; is your daddy in?" Morgan Jr. hated when someone called him "junior," which was why most people called him that. Growing up he'd liked "Morg" or Morgan; now he preferred Mr. Hopkins, same as his dad, regardless of any confusion that might cause.

Morgan Hopkins Jr. burned crimson with anger behind the vertical bars that separated him from his customers. But he kept his voice cool and polite as he answered. "Yes, Miss Crandall; he is." He knew Kat hated being called "Miss Crandall" as much as he hated "Junior." "Just a moment and let me see if he's available." He locked the cash drawer, though it was inaccessible from the front, pocketed the key, and went through a connecting door on his side of the counter.

"He sure ain't changed," Billy said. "He was the most stuck up little kid back in school..."

"Yeah," Kat said. "I got so mad at him once I beat him up.

He had to go runnin' home an' tell his daddy he got beat up by a girl."

"We all took our turns usin' him for punching practice," Billy said. "An' he wasn't the only boy you beat up back then, Kat."

Kat laughed. "Guess not."

"You settled down a mite?" Billy knew he risked a punch just by asking.

Kat thought a moment. "I dunno; maybe I have."

Junior emerged from a door on the customer side that was marked MORGAN HOPKINS – PRESIDENT on a brass plaque. "Father will see you now."

Kat mouthed the word "Father!" with a sideways grin and a wink to Billy. Junior was still a brat with airs. College had just made Junior into an *educated* brat with airs.

Morgan Hopkins sat behind a desk the size of a freight car, yet it didn't dwarf him one bit. The chair behind him was rich dark wood, like the desk, and luxuriously upholstered in wine red leather. Hopkins didn't rise; he only did that for customers he considered worthy, and Kat Crandall certainly was not worthy.

To Kat however he was just another bully, and Kat had stood up to bullies all her life. Hopkins didn't frighten her one bit.

"Mr. Hopkins," she began, "we got a payment due on the Bar C."

Hopkins drew himself up even more stiffly than he had been, which was quite a feat. "Yes, and I intended to draft a letter to you regarding that later today. Since you're here, I imagine you plan to make that payment now. It saves me the trouble of writing to you about it."

"Nope; I'm not here to make the payment," Kat said.

Billy watched Hopkins' reaction and calculated his chances at winning at poker against the banker as being slim but possible.

"Oh? And just why *did* you come?"

"We need an extension; maybe a month."

"An extension," Hopkins parroted, "maybe a month. Miss Crandall, do you realize what it takes to run a financial institution such as this?"

"Sure," Kat said, "it takes money."

"Money; yes, it takes money."

"None o' yours, though," Kat said.

"What do you mean?" he asked, eyes narrowing.

"Oh, the money in your safe ain't yours; you're just holding it for people who give it to you, right?"

"Well, a bank like any business has employees; and employees need to be paid, and a part of that money goes towards those salaries."

"Sure, an' I don't grudge against any salary you and Junior make; as long as it's legit."

"Are you implying I'm doing anything illegal, Miss Crandall?"

"'Course not. But you've got all that money in your safe, an' some of it's my dad's, an' some it's other folks', an' you dole out some of it to yourselves. So if you got enough in that safe to do all that, you got enough to hold you until I can pay again."

"Miss Crandall, as I said this is a business; and a business must abide by certain rules and regulations. One of those regulations is requiring those who owe money to the bank to make their payments on time."

"What if I can't pay?"

Was that a smile on Hopkins' lips? "If you cannot pay on time I'm afraid the bank will have to foreclose."

"You mean you'll take the ranch away from me?" Kat's voice smouldered with heat and her hands flexed in a steady rhythm.

Hopkins shrugged. A little perspiration dampened his brow. "That is the fate of those who cannot meet their obligations. I'm sure you understand."

"Yeah, I understand." Her hand started to close on the gun.

Billy gripped her arm; she wrestled free but the look in his eyes warned her.

"Guess you're right," Kat said. "All right; just so we're talkin' the same language, an' since you were aimin' to write a reminder letter anyways, write a memorandum with the date due, I'll sign it, and you'll sign it."

Hopkins hesitated. "Fair enough. All right, I will." He took a piece of paper and wrote upon it, handing it to Kat. She read it and signed it.

"All right then," Kat said. "I'll see you in two weeks with the payment." She glanced at Billy. "C'mon, Billy; let's get to work." She strode out of the office with Billy following.

Once they were gone a back door of Hopkins' office opened. "Good work, Hopkins," a grumble of a voice said. "Good job."

* * *

As Kat and Billy stepped out into the street they heard two horsemen ride away from somewhere behind the bank. She saw them pass the alley between the bank and the livery stable. *Looked like Butch and Grady,* Kat thought.

"Billy, I think I just saw Butch and Grady leave Hopkins' office."

"What?" Billy exclaimed. "Kat, yer seein' things. You got Butch and Grady on the brain. What would they be doin' in the bank?"

"I don't know, but it can't be good."

"Nothin' them two do is good. Just forgit about 'em. Besides, why would they show themselves around town?"

"Guess you're right." Curious she went into the alley in time to see the two ride toward the end of town. Mulling it over she came back to where Billy was waiting. Laredo rode out of the livery stable with a buckboard.

"Good news, Kat. The Brodys came through; at least a part."

"What do you mean?"

Laredo stepped down from the buckboard. "They wouldn't give us the full list but I got 'em to give us credit on some staples. There's some flour, coffee, an' sugar waiting for us."

"At least we can live on biscuits and coffee for a while," Billy said.

Kat had barely noted Laredo's announcement. "What is it, Kat?"

"I think I just saw Butch and Grady ride away from the back of the bank and head for Hopkins' place."

"Hopkins, the banker? Ain't he the guy you went to see?" Laredo asked.

"Yeah; an' he wouldn't give us the loan. But if that was Grady an' Butch, they might've been persuadin' him."

Laredo nodded. "I got ya. This Hopkins, he got a family?"

"A wife and young son. The son's in school, but the wife's probably home."

"You think they might be in danger?"

"Some of Lawson's other men might be holdin' the missus," Kat said.

"One way to find out," Laredo said, drawing his gun and checking the loads.

"Sure. Let's head out there an' make a friendly visit. Coming, Billy?"

Billy seemed to emerge from somewhere else. "Huh? Yeah. Lead the way."

* * *

Hopkins house was just out of town, where there was some privacy. The other side of the road and behind the house were rocks and woods. It was a nice house, a banker's house for certain, larger and better built than most other houses in town.

There were four horses hitched to Hopkins' fence when the three arrived. And as they dismounted the horses' owners came from the house. Butch saw them first and fired his gun. A bullet zinged past Laredo's shoulder, and he fired back, missing Butch only because he ducked back inside.

Kat drew and shot one of the others, the bullet shoving his shoulder around with its impact and spinning him as he fell. He lay still as red stained his blue flannel shirt.

Brady and the other also ducked inside as the three Bar C riders sought cover. Glass shattered as someone broke a window, firing at their running figures. None of them were hit but there was little shelter available; just a few rocks across the way.

A bullet from the house splattered rock splinters into their faces.

"Didn't reckon on a siege," Laredo said. He thought he saw a face and fired. A cry came from within.

"Me neither." Kat shot and a window frame cracked.

"Maybe we better just cut and run," Billy said. "They were about to leave when we showed up anyway."

"You yellow or somethin'?" Kat asked. Green fire burned in her eyes.

"No; but we might hit Mrs. Hopkins if we're not careful, an' isn't she the one we came to rescue?"

Neither of the others answered but sent more fire into the house. "Shut up and aim for the ones shootin' at us," Laredo said. "You ain't fired none since we started, an' I gotta reload anyway."

Billy drew his gun with hesitation but started firing. Laredo and Kat both reloaded. They each fired a couple more rounds.

"I got an idea," Kat said. "Cover me."

Before either could say anything she had cut to the right where there was a little cover and was soon out of the line of fire, circling the house.

"Damn fool," Laredo said. "She's gonna try to get in the back way and take 'em all by surprise."

"Is she tryin' to be a hero or a corpse?" Billy fired again.

"We better make sure it works." He fired again at a face in the window and scouted the area. "You stay here; I can make it to the side and the front door."

"What? You insane too?"

"Just do like I tell ya. An' watch where you're shootin'." Laredo followed the same route as Kat and when he was out of eyesight of the house got to the side. Ducking low he sidled around to the front. As he neared the door a bullet nearly got him. *Damn that Billy! Is he just a bad shot or was that on purpose?*

Before he could decide he heard Kat's voice inside.

"Drop your guns and put up your hands!"

He kicked the front door open and stepped inside to cover her.

Grady decided to be brave for once and shot at Laredo; Laredo ducked and rolled, knocking Grady to the ground. Grady lost his grip on his gun and Laredo clubbed him once with his.

"You can come in now, Billy!" Laredo called.

Billy slowly came through the door, unsure if it was safe. His gun hand shook a little as he tried to keep them covered.

Kat had things under control even if Billy didn't, Laredo figured, so he turned his attention to a middle-aged frail woman tied to a wooden chair in the corner. "Mrs. Hopkins?" He started setting her free.

"Yes. Who are these horrible men, and what was this about?" Her voice had only a slight tremor of fear; defiance was in it too.

"Don't worry about them, Mrs. Hopkins. Did they hurt you any?"

"No. Did a lot o' talk, though. Talk ain't nothin' if you don't back it up."

Laredo grinned. "I admire your spirit, Mrs. Hopkins."

Kat moved a little closer. "What did they say, Mrs. Hopkins?"

"I don't know; something about my husband and a loan. A loan to you, Kat."

Kat nodded. "That's what I figured."

Suddenly Butch had grabbed Billy's gunhand and twisted it back, sending a fist hard against Billy's jaw.

Kat fired but Butch was out the door before she was ready. She ran after him but he had already forked his horse and was nearly out of range.

Grady used the confusion to run out back and disappear into the woods. Laredo ran and sent a shot after him and he heard a cry but when he pursued, hoping to have slowed him down, he realized he'd lost him.

Laredo went back inside. As he came indoors he heard a slight ruckus in the front room. The fourth man, a fresh scar along the side of his head probably from one of Laredo's early bullets, was on the floor. Kat was digging her boot heel into him. "He came to and tried to lam like the others," she said. She made a clubbing motion with her gun. I stopped him."

Laredo grinned. "Looks like you did."

Kat let up her boot on the man and Laredo hauled him to his feet. "C'mon, you." He dragged him outside where Billy was crouching over the man Kat had shot.

"He's dead; you got him, Kat."

"Well, at least we got one to take to Stokes," Kat said. "If only he believes us this time."

Mrs. Hopkins came out behind her. "Oh, he'll believe me all right. The town funds that pay his salary are in my husband's safe."

* * *

So it was one for the jail and one for the coroner. Kat didn't recognize either of them; they weren't former Bar C hands. Larson must have been recruiting from outside. Did that mean he was getting desperate?

Mrs. Hopkins accompanied Kat and company to the bank. Hopkins Sr. and Jr. were both surprised to see her.

"You've got these three to thank, Morgan," she said. "They told me about comin' to you before. I'd say Kat needs not just an extension but a loan to tide her over for a while, don't you? Ain't that the least you can do for her and her hands savin' my life?"

Laredo and Kat swapped grins and chuckles. Hopkins was a big man in more ways than one: big in the town and big in size. But this little lady scared him.

"Of course," Hopkins stammered. "And Ethel, you're exactly right. Morg, let's give Miss Crandall..."

"Kat."

"Yes, of course. Kat about oh, say a thousand?"

"Much obliged, Mr. Hopkins," Kat said. She tried to hide her amazement and saw that Laredo couldn't hide it at all. Billy, for some reason had a different reaction; but she let that go.

"Interest free, of course," Mrs. Hopkins added.

"Interest free, of course," Hopkins repeated. "I'll draw up the papers while Morg counts out your money."

"Pleasure doing business with you, Mr. Hopkins," Kat said.

"The pleasure is all mine, Kat," Hopkins said.

Though Laredo doubted his sincerity in that last statement.

CHAPTER ELEVEN

They counted them: just under thirty head. That was all they had; a pitiful number to take to market. First thing next morning everyone mounted up and started hunting for more strays. Bear had recovered enough to ride and joined in.

He rode with Laredo and they searched beyond the fertile Kat had shown them. It was still part of the Bar C property, but not suitable for grazing land. But it was possible some of the cattle might have wandered there.

And at least one had.

They came upon its carcass, or what was left after the carrion birds and coyotes had fed off it. Laredo swung down from the saddle; Bear took a little longer. It always took him longer due to his size, but the wounds still pained him a bit if he stretched certain ways. Banty had suggested to him, "Just don't stretch them ways," and Bear had offered to stretch him a couple different ways in reply. But Bear had survived enough wounds of one kind or another to know Banty simply meant not to take chances, and he didn't.

Bear waddled over to where Laredo knelt beside the remains and squatted down

carefully next to him. "What d'you think got it?"

Laredo shook his head. "Don't know." He surveyed the country. "Coulda just died o' thirst, out here."

Bear nudged his hat back and scratched his chin. "Yeah, maybe." He joined Laredo's survey of the land. "Sure is dry here. Funny how it's not that far from all that green over thataway." He shaded his eyes with his hand. "There's somethin' over there." He hauled himself up and made his way toward it. Laredo rose and followed. There was a marshy pool, and a dark substance oozed from it. They knelt beside it as they had by the cattle carcass.

"What the hell is it?" Bear asked.

Rawhide put a finger to it, licked and spat.

"Hey, I didn't ask ya ta drink it!" Bear scolded. "Serves ya right."

"I don't know what it is, Bear. Sure tastes nasty. It might be what killed our late friend over there."

"Maybe; maybe there's more of it around."

They straightened. "Yeah, there might. And there might be more beef out here; live ones. An' that's what we're out here to look for, not black ooze. C'mon."

But as they rode Laredo thought about it. The spot looked like it had been dug a while back and covered over again, and the black tarry stuff was trying to find a way out again. Maybe they weren't the first to find it.

* * *

When everyone got back they took another count; they had nearly tripled the original count. That still wasn't much, but with the loan from Hopkins they might have enough to hold them until market. And maybe they might even find the others that had been rustled in the meantime.

Evening spread its vast darkness over the ranch. Laredo and Kat stood on the porch leaning against the rail. Laredo was having one last smoke before turning in. They stood silent, just enjoying the stillness and cooling air.

"Bear an' me saw something today," he said. "Not sure what to make of it."

"What's that?"

"We saw a dead cow; or what was left of him." He went on to tell of the black liquid oozing from the ground.

"You know what it might be?" Kat asked.

"I got a hunch," Laredo said, "though I don't know much about it."

They both had the same hunch, he figured. But no sense saying anything until you know for sure.

"Kat, how did your pa die?"

Kat stayed silent.

"Sorry; if you don't wanna talk about it, that's fine."

"No, you should know. He had gone to town on business,

alone. When he didn't come back I sent the hands out to look for him. I looked for him too. Slim was the one who found him."

"Slim? He's workin' for Larson now."

"Ahuh. He fired three shots..."

"The distress call."

"Yeah. I must've been closest. It looked like he'd fallen from his horse. His neck... his neck was broken."

"Any sign of his horse stumblin'? I mean, from the tracks or anything?"

Kat shook her head. She sniffed, squinting her eyes in a forced blink to turn off the tears. "No. But it had been a day or more before we found him, and there'd been a storm the night before."

"Will you show me the spot?"

"What good will it do?"

"I dunno; but maybe seein' it will give me some ideas."

"All right. We'll ride out there in the morning."

* * *

While the rest of the hands continued the search for strays or signs of the rustled cattle Kat and Laredo rode out toward town. Laredo glanced over at her as they rode. *She's had to ride this road everyday since her father was killed. That took guts.* Not that he ever doubted she had them; he knew that from their first encounter, in the barn.

She led him off the road now to a poor excuse for a trail through a rocky gorge. It widened after a bit into an older road that didn't look like it had been used much in recent years. Laredo glanced on either side of them: high piles of rock, almost like a wall on either side. It got him to thinking.

Kat halted at a certain spot between those stone walls and dismounted. Laredo got down beside her.

"This is where Slim found him," Kat said. With her finger she drew a long figure in the air above the ground. "He was layin' right here."

Of course there were no signs left; it had happened months before and time and weather had obliterated any clues there might have been. Not that he expected Stokes had made much of an investigation. Laredo again studied the rocky border of the old road. They were about twenty to thirty feet high on the average, he reckoned. Plenty far to kill a man if he fell.

"You're sure he fell from his horse?"

"That's what Stokes an' Doc said. Not that I believe it. Dad was an expert, an' never fell off a horse in his life."

"Did you find the horse?"

"Yeah. He was standin' right over him." Kat sniffed. "That's what made 'em figure he was thrown or fell."

"But you've always doubted it."

Her reply was adamant burnished with fire. "My pa never fell from a horse in his life. An' especially not Rex."

"Rex? That was your father's favorite horse?"

"Best damn horse that ever was," she said. "He'd never stumble an' he'd never throw my dad."

Laredo put a hand on her shoulder and was surprised when she didn't shake it off. "I'm sure Rex is a fine horse, and I don't think you're father was thrown."

"You don't?"

Laredo shook his head and looked up at the rocks again. "Did you or anybody go up and take a look at those rocks?"

"No; why?"

"Are you up for a climb?"

"Sure. What you got in mind?"

"I don't wanna say until we look around. C'mon."

They searched about first for a good place to start and began the ascent. Laredo offered his hand to Kat once only to have it slapped away. He let her make her own way from there on, and she proved to be a steady and fearless climber. The way up the rocks wasn't too hard, though there were a couple of places where footholds required quite a stretch of the legs, and one or two where footholds were almost non-existent. But they made it to the top and stood looking down on the spot where they had stood.

Laredo indicated the place below. "That's where your father was found?"

"Yeah."

He looked around. "It's been a while, but we might find

somethin'." He knelt and looked on the edge. "There's what looks like the mark of a bootheel here."

Kat knelt next to him to see it closer. "Yeah. An' whoever it was stood with his back to the road below."

"And probably not for long," Laredo added. He ran his eyes over the area a little more and saw something glint through some scrub. He picked it up. It was a rowel from a spur. "This look familiar?" He handed it to Kat.

She examined it and shrugged. "It's just a spur. Could be anybody's." Her fist struck her knee. "Or it might be dad's. I'd forgot; one of his rowels was missing. We didn't notice 'till we got back to town an' didn't figure it was worth looking for."

"Then that might be your father's?"

"Might; but what was he doin' up here?"

"Is there a road or path that leads up here?"

"Sure." Kat pointed the curve of the trail. "You can ride a horse up it too." She peered into his face. "Just what are you drivin' at?"

"It's hard to say now," Laredo replied slowly, "but if he was up here, an' that rowel suggests he was, he may have fallen... or mighta been shoved from here."

"Shoved?" Kat exclaimed. "You think my pa was murdered?"

"I don't know," Laredo said, "but it's possible."

"But why?"

"Why is Larson or somebody trying to drive you out of business? Seems to me if we solve one question we'll answer the other." They stood and Laredo looked at the trail Kat had pointed out, leading from the road up to this point. There was another trail that branched off from it into some trees, where it seemed to continue. "Where does that lead?"

"That? Oh, there's a clearing an' an old shack a little ways into the wood. It's been there since Methuselah's time, I reckon."

"I doubt that, but I get the idea. Let's have a look."

They climbed down from the rocks, which was a bit harder than climbing up, and took to the trail. The scent of pine blessed their nostrils from both sides and soon they found the clearing. It looked like there had once been more land cleared but at some time decades before it had been abandoned and started to grow back up again, encroaching on whatever space had once surrounded the little shack that bravely stood in its center. They were boards, planed and measured, but now gray and twisting with dry rot and decay, peeling away from the frame beneath. Whoever had put this together knew what he was doing; too bad nobody else could enjoy it now. It needed some work for sure; but it might be worth it.

Laredo went up to the door, which hung on by one rusty hinge. He rapped once.

Kat laughed. "You don't think anybody really lives here?"

Laredo shrugged. "You never know. An' it's always good to be polite an' don't barge in on folks." He gingerly opened the door and somehow it maintained its tenuous hold on its one hinge. They stepped in.

The inside was almost as dilapidated as the outside, though the furniture hadn't rotted as badly as the outer walls. It was a one room affair, with a cot in the corner, a table, a chair, and a potbelly stove. Mold emitted its effluvium to the closed atmosphere. There was a coffeepot on the stove that didn't look as rusty as it should and a few plates with nothing worse than a chip or three.

Laredo grunted when he saw the shelves, stocked with canned goods. He took a couple off the shelf; none had collected much dust.

"Somebody's been livin' here," Kat said.

"Yeah. Or at least stayin' once in a while. Wonder who?"

"Might just be some trapper or drifter. Prob'ly out in the woods huntin' right now."

"Maybe," Laredo said. He looked the place over again. "Well, whoever he is we don't want him findin' us here."

"You think it might be Larson?" Kat rested her hand on her gun.

Laredo shook his head. "No. He'd be somewhere with the rest of his gang. Only room for one in this hole."

They left the place as they found it and followed the trail out of the woods, to the rocks, and down where their horses waited.

"No use tellin' Stokes what we seen," Laredo said.

"No," Kat agreed. "He wouldn't do nothin' about it anyhow."

As they untied their horses Laredo said, "Thanks for takin' me out here, Kat. I know it was prob'ly hard."

"Kinda. But you showed me things I didn't see; an' it makes me think on my pa's death a little different now."

"Don't know if that's good or bad."

Kat grinned a little as she mounted up. "It's good; an' thanks." She frowned. "Things are startin' to come together a little."

"Yeah," Laredo agreed as he eased up in the saddle. "I was thinkin' the same thing." He mused a moment. "Though that shack brings up some questions of its own, don't it?" He clucked to his horse and the two rode back the way they came.

CHAPTER TWELVE

Billy tied his horse to the rail and strode down the boardwalk until he reached Sheriff Stokes' office. The afternoon sun flashed on the glass of the windows on this side of the street, a last flare before dipping below the rooftops and finally the forested hills beyond the town. He entered the office; Stokes was leaning back in his chair, his feet up on the desk, a thick stinking cigar burning between his lips. Stokes regarded Billy through the smoke.

"Billy. What brings you to town?" He didn't move from his position.

"Somethin' I heard the other night, Sheriff, that I been wonderin' about."

"What's that?"

"Remember when there was that fracas at the newspaper office?"

"Yeah; what about it?"

Billy pulled up a chair and straddled it backwards, crossing his arms over the back of it. "That big guy, Bear they call him."

"Yeah, I know him."

"Well, we had another fracas with the herd, an' Bear got shot up bad."

"I know that too; Doc had to patch him up. Shame about that fellow Hank, though." He blew some more smoke, clouding his expression.

"Bear mumbled somethin'; like he was kinda out of it, but not all the way."

"Delusional is what the docs call it," Stokes said, smiling proudly at his own intellectualism.

"Yeah. Well, he called out the name Pete."

"Pete?"

"Yeah, Pete. I got the feeling he was calling to Laredo when he said it."

Stokes shrugged. "So? A lotta men out here hide their names. An' there's as many reasons for it as there is men who do it."

"Yeah, but I think I seen this Laredo somewheres before."

Stokes frowned. "Now that you mention it, I had the same idea. But I don't remember where."

"My guess is on a wanted poster. I think he's hidin' from somethin'; or somebody."

"Could be. We get a lot of handbills, but I don't remember seein' his face on one. But like I said, I saw it somewheres."

"Maybe he run into some trouble in Laredo, or somewheres else. Maybe he was from Laredo, got into trouble, an' just took the town's name as his own hopin' no one could find him."

"Maybe." Stokes eased his feet off the desk an' sat up. "It has got me curious," he admitted.

"Then you'll look an' see who he is?"

Stokes thought about it over a few more puffs of his cigar. "I don't think I'll bother. It's too much like work."

Billy thrust himself to his feet, knocking the chair over with a crash that startled Stokes. "Work? Why, I can find out with a simple telegram."

Stokes leaned back and started to raise his feet again. "Then go right ahead. It's a free country. I'm not stoppin' ya."

Billy came round the desk and swept Stokes' feet from the desk with a swing of his arm. Stokes almost bit half of his cigar and nearly choked.

"Hey! That's strikin' an officer of the law!"

"Officer of the law. Afraid to even check up on somebody that might be an outlaw. Afraid he might have to do somethin' other than sit behind his desk, smoke cigars, and look important."

Stokes came to his feet. "All right, sonny. I'll send a telegram. Bet there's plenty o' Petes in Laredo born every year." He looked hard into Billy's face. "Probably a lotta Billys, too."

"Just send the telegram."

Stokes sat down and took paper and pen. "Sure, Billy. I'll write it up right now." He started writing and then handed Billy the finished message. "Here; will that suit you?"

Billy looked it over. "Looks fine. I'll even take it to the

telegraph office for you. Pay for it too."

"Much obliged." Stokes put his feet up again and re-lit his cigar.

Billy shook his head. "I'm not doin' this outta the kindness of my heart. It's to be sure the message gets sent." He gave the Sheriff one last look of contempt and stepped out.

He went down to the telegraph office and entered. Clem was there paying for a message he had just sent.

"Hello Billy," Clem said.

"Hello, Clem." Billy went up to the counter. Hayes, the telegrapher, set Clem's message down and turned to him. "How much to send this?" Billy asked, handing over the message from Stokes.

Hayes was a grizzled old coot who looked ninety; but then he had looked ninety for about twenty years. Suspenders held up pants that he'd never lose because no one ever saw him rise from his seat, and he seemed to wear the same shirt everyday, sleeves rolled up and held by elastic. A green eyeshade sheltered his eyes; from what nobody knew, because the telegraph office was never what you'd call brightly lit. The telegrapher counted the words and gave him a price. Billy dug in his pocket and paid. "By the way, any messages for me?"

Hayes checked the pick-up tray. "Nope; nothin' for you."

"OK; thanks." As Billy turned to the door Clem was waiting.

"How are things at the Bar C?" he asked.

"All right," Billy said.

Clem blocked his way. "All right? Not the way I heard it. Is it true Larson and some of Crandall's old hands are causin' the trouble Kat is having?"

"I ain't seen Larson, so I can't tell ya."

"Bet Kat was glad to see you come back to help her," Clem went on, refusing to budge. "And I guess those three, Laredo and the others, are doing good. Sad about Hank; always did like him."

"Yeah; Hank was a good guy. Excuse me, Clem; I gotta go."

"Sure. Just one other thing: like you I been around this town a while. I remember you were always sweet on Kat. An' it seems now she's taken a shine to that Laredo. Hope there isn't any jealousy goin' on between you two."

"Jealous? Me? No. But that Laredo might not be what he seems. An' I still like Kat an' wanna look out for her. Anything wrong about that?" He towered over Clem, though the smaller man didn't back down.

"No Billy, nothing at all." He took out his watch. "I've gotta get back to the office anyway. Pleasure talkin' to you." He touched his hat and went out the door.

Billy followed. "Same here," he called. Then a thought came. "Hey Clem, that little powwow wasn't for the paper, was it?"

Clem turned. "The paper? No Billy; I was just makin' conversation; passin' the time of day. Why? Is there something you said you don't want made public?"

"No. Why do you say that?"

"Just making sure," Clem said. "Say Hi to Kat the boys for me when you get back to the Bar C."

"Sure." Billy still mulled over it as he swung into the saddle and rode out of town.

* * *

He got in after dark. Banty, on cook duty again, was just cleaning up when Billy came in the door.

"Where in tarnation you been all day?" Banty asked.

"Had t' go in town," Billy answered.

"Well, supper's over an' I'm not heatin' nothin' up. There's some cold beef, some bread, an' when I finish with the dishes I was gonna make a fresh pot o' coffee. If y' can live offa sandwiches for tonight, an' gimme a few minutes to finish cleanin' up, I'll brew you somethin' to wash it down with."

"Tell you what," Billy said, "you go ahead clean up an' I'll make the some sandwiches an' the coffee too."

"That's a deal," Banty said. "Just so's you save some coffee for me." He carried some dirty dishes out back where the pump and basin were.

Billy made four sandwiches while he was waiting for the coffee to brew. He set two on one plate and two on the other, poured coffee into two mugs, and sat down to eat. Banty came back a minute or two later.

"Hey, I already et," Banty said.

"I know what it is to cook for a passle o' hungry cowboys," Billy said. "Bet you didn't get t' eat anywhere near as much as you wanted." He slid the plate toward Banty. "An' drink your coffee while it's hot."

Banty sat opposite him. "Much obliged." He bit into a sandwich. "You're right liberal with the mustard."

"Yeah. Hope it's not too much?"

"Nope. I like it that way." He took another bite and washed it back with the coffee. "Good sandwich, good coffee. Say, maybe *you* oughta be chief cook an' bottle washer around here."

Billy laughed. "I've done it before, an' I'll do it when it's my turn again. But full time? Uh unh; not me."

Banty laughed with him.

"How long you known Laredo?" Billy asked.

"Quite a spell," Banty said. "We been ridin' together for years."

"Same with Bear?"

"Yeah. We three been saddle pals for some time. Why?"

"Oh, just askin'. You know, me an' Kat go bak a long ways too."

"Ahuh. She told us about when she turned twelve."

Billy chuckled. "Yeah. Guess the whole town remembers that too."

"For some females that age, that's how they tell a boy they like him." Banty started on his second sandwich.

"Yeah, guess so. Well, mainly I'm askin about you an' your pals 'cause I still like Kat an' wanna look out for her."

"Sure; I figured that. That's why you come back when you heard she was havin' troubles, right?"

"Yeah. I just wanna be sure you're here to help her an' she's got nothin' to worry about from you."

"Don't worry about that." Banty grinned. "An' if you're worryin' about Laredo tryin' to take her away from you, well you've got no worries there."

"That's good. I don't know if I got a chance with Kat; it's been so long since I was around, you know."

"A female makes up her mind, an' then she changes it. An' she expects us menfolk to keep up."

Billy chuckled. "Wise words."

"All I know about women," Banty said, "is that you can't know 'em."

"Even wiser." He'd finished his sandwiches and poured more coffee for the both of them. "I bet you been around some, even before you hooked up with Laredo."

Banty nodded. "Yeah, some."

"Ever ride with anybody called Pete?"

Billy saw a slight flicker in Banty's eye before he covered. "Not sure. So many go by handles instead o' the names they were born with, you know?"

"Yeah, that's true enough. O' course, I kept my name; an so did Larson."

Banty slowly set his mug down. "Why'd ya have to bring him up?"

"Sorry. It's just that I remember Larson from back when. You're right though, I shoulda thought o' someone else."

"Hey, it's all right. Let's just leave him outta the confab though. We were havin' a nice chat 'til you said his name."

"Yeah. Never rode with any Pete?"

If he hoped to surprise Banty by bringing the name up again he failed.

"No. I been thinkin' on it; never rode with no Pete."

Billy rose from the table and started gathering up the plates and mugs. "Banty, it's been good talkin' to ya. An' I'll clean this up."

"Much oblighed," Banty said. He dusted crumbs from his shirt, took one last swig of coffee, got his hat from the peg and went outside.

He made right for the bunkhouse and signaled to Laredo and Bear to step out with him. "It's a nice clear night," he said. "I just want a little more fresh air before I turn in."

The other two agreed and they walked a distance from the bunkhouse.

"Billy was askin' after Pete," Banty said.

"You told me I called you Pete when I got shot a while back," Bear said.

"Yeah," Laredo said. "We told Billy you were just mumblin' an' confused."

"Think he bought it?" Bear said.

"I dunno," Banty answered. "He asked me a coupla times. Guess he thought waitin' a while might catch one of us off our guard."

"Where was he all day, anyways?" Laredo asked.

"He says he was in town."

"Did he say what he was doin' there?"

"No."

Laredo rubbed his chin. "Maybe one o' us oughtta go into town tomorrow an' find out where he went."

* * *

Banty had volunteered and decided his first stop would be the newspaper office. If the editor of the town paper doesn't know what's happening, nobody does.

"Hi Clem."

"Hi Banty! What brings you to town?"

"Oh, just checking something. Say, did you see Billy around town yesterday?"

"As a matter of fact I did. He was at the telegraph office same time I was. We had a little chat."

"What about? Don't mean to pry."

"Not at all." Clem chuckled. "I did most of the talking. Seemed like he wished I hadn't seen him; he couldn't wait to get on to whatever he was doin'."

"Why was he at the telegraph office? Was he sendin' or receivin'?"

"Both, I guess. He had a message to send out an' he asked if there was any message for him. Don't know who he'd be getting a telegram from, but that's none of my business."

"Any idea where else he went?"

"No; except I saw him ride out of town, an he wasn't goin' in the direction of the Bar C."

"So it looked like he had other business when he finished here."

"Guess so. I supposed Kat sent him out to do some errands for him."

"Maybe; she don't always tell us everything. Thanks, Clem."

Banty made the telegraph office his next stop.

"Hi Hayes. Remember me: Banty from the Bar C."

"Sure, Banty. What can I do for you?"

"Did that telegram Billy had for Kat go out all right yesterday?"

Hayes blinked a moment beneath his green eye-shade. "The telegram went out, but it wasn't for the Bar C."

"Huh?"

"The telegram was signed by Sheriff Stokes. I figured Billy was doin' it as a favor for him."

"I see. Oh, by the way: Billy asked me to check and see if any telegrams came in for him. I know he was just here yesterday, but he's kinda anxious about it."

"No; nothing today."

"Billy get a lot o' telegrams?"

"Some. Now Banty, you know I can't talk much about other folks' business, even if you do work with him."

"You're right; sorry, Hayes. Guess I'll be headin' back now. Thanks."

* * *

Banty reported what he had learned to Laredo and Bear.

"Interestin'," Laredo said. "Did you check with the Sheriff to see what the telegram was about?"

"Nope; didn't wanna take no chances playin' into their hands."

Laredo nodded. "Prob'ly right. I'd like to know what that telegram was about." His mind started turning things around.

"You think it might have something to do with his questions about Pete?" Bear asked.

"That's what I'm thinkin'. Suppose he went to the Sheriff an' told him about your sayin' 'Pete' when you were out of it. Maybe Stokes thought he'd check up on the name an' find out the connection."

"I wouldn't worry, Laredo," Banty said, slapping him on the back. "There's plenty o' Petes in the world. That don't mean it'll lead back to you."

"I hope not. We got a job to do here, pals, an' we can't let anything stop us from getting it done."

CHAPTER THIRTEEN

A horse was already tied in front of the shack when Larson got there, so his financial supporter had arrived ahead of him. Smoke rose from the iron pipe chimney and the aroma of coffee beckoned from the open window. He also noticed something else: tracks on the ground. Larson opened the door.

"Don't you think it's takin' a chance usin' the stove?" Larson said.

"No." The man was calm and his self-assurance irritated Larson. "If someone sees the smoke it'll only be from a distance. Besides, you said no one comes up here anymore."

"I may be wrong. There were tracks outside; somebody's been nosin' around here just recently." Larson poured himself some coffee and sat down.

"Oh? I hadn't noticed."

No, Larson thought as he sipped. *City folks like you don't know nothin'.* "I know you have to wait for me here a day or two sometimes, an' that's whey you got the supplies. But you gotta keep watch too. Anybody might ride up an' catch you with yer britches down."

The man drew himself up. "That is something that I shall never permit to happen."

"Oh?" He made a crude remark regarding the man's bathroom habits, or rather the lack of them.

The man stared at Larson and rose with cold menace. "You know, there are easier ways of achieving what my backers want. There is always the direct approach. And in fact, that will cost me less time and money."

"I'll get the ranch for ya," Larson said, rising and laying his hand on the man's shoulder in an attempt to shove him back to his seat. The man resisted and regarded Larson's hand like some vermin that had somehow landed on his expensive coat. Larson removed the hand and the man returned to his seat on his own.

"I'm giving you a time limit," the man said. You have another week." He leaned forward. "You first came to me as the appointed representative of the late Mr. Crandall, just prior to his demise. And there was the matter of his untimely death, which I'm sure was not quite the accident it has been reported to be."

"If you say anything to the law about it," Larson said with a vile grin, "I'll say it was your idea."

"You can't prove it."

"You can't prove it *ain't.*"

"Isn't, is the correct word, Mr. Larson."

Larson used a word to characterize his opinion of the man's grammar. "Just remember, threats ain't gonna do you do good."

"There are a few more errors in grammar in that sentence, Mr. Larson, but I see that attempts at rehabilitating your education are in vain, so I will not point them out. Two weeks, Mr. Larson; I want news from your town that Miss Crandall has lost her ranch and that it is up for public auction in two weeks."

"You're pretty sure of yourself that you'd win that auction."

The man smiled. "Mr. Larson, though our funds are not limitless they are certainly sufficient to outbid anyone else who vies for it."

"The bank will foreclose on the ranch," Larson said. "I'll see to it."

"I understand you thought you had accomplished that just a few days ago but had failed again."

"I won't fail this time. I got a plan."

* * *

Larson rode through the opening that Nature had disguised as being closed and down into the valley. It was rich and fertile grassland; perfect for grazing livestock. The lowing of cattle welcomed him and he sat his horse a long moment looking down at it. All Bar C cattle; none stolen from any other ranch. Over five thousand head, if their count was right. He knew there were some the men had missed, and a few strays had probably found their way back home. Those hands of Kat's were good, judging from what his men had said, and they were stubborn too; stubborn as their boss. They wouldn't give up looking; especially now that more was riding on their finding the missing herd.

Only Larson's men knew of this secret entrance; and only Larson knew why the Bar C was so important to certain interests. And as long as his men were paid he knew they'd stay loyal; but loyalty didn't always buy silence.

He rode down to the cabin. Not many of the men were there; he wasn't surprised about that. He'd seen several of them among the herd, guarding it just in case. Tiny was filling his cavernous belly in the cabin and Bennett was with him. Didn't matter if they were the only two around; it only took one of them to carry out the job he had for them.

He looked between the two; Tiny needed the exercise more than Bennett, but then Tiny always needed the exercise. "Tiny, I got a job for you."

"Yeah, boss?" Tiny was eating a plateful large enough for three men.

"I want you to ride into Silver Gulch and send a telegram." Larson found a pencil and paper and sat down to write.

"Sure. Where you want it sent to?"

"You'll understand when you see it." He started writing and had it done inside of a minute. Handing it to Tiny he waited for the big man to read it and said, "Well?"

"Sure, boss. I get it." He didn't like it, just as he didn't like a lot of what was going on here lately. But it was too late to pull out now. "Just let me finish my snack here an' I'll get going."

Larson eyed up the "snack." "All right. But make it quick."

"Sure, boss."

* * *

The men had done their jobs well: the strays they rounded up doubled the number they had. That still wasn't much but maybe they'd get a good enough price.

Kat knew this was wishful thinking, and she'd been raised

to be a realist; that's what her dad was, God rest his soul, and she tried her best to be just like him. But another lesson he'd taught her was that when the chips were down you had to look up; and that's what she was trying to do.

It had been a week since they had gone to the bank; only another week before the mortgage was due. And this time there was no getting around it.

Kat sat her horse and eyed the pitiful excuse for a herd that they had. The railroad was only a day or two away, so the trail drive wouldn't be far. That was one good thing anyway. The railroad had moved in here several years ago. Some of the ranchers had fought it at first because it meant losing some of their grazing land, but the advantage of shortening the distance to market turned them around.

Dakota rode up beside her. "Not much to look at, but they is prime."

Kat nodded. "They are that, Dakota. And I hear some buyers are gonna be at the train station in three days. That'll give us plenty of time to move 'em."

"It will. Hope we get somethin' out of it."

Billy rode up to join them. "Laredo and his pals just came back. They still haven't found any more."

"Then we'll have to go to market with what we got," Kat said.

"Yep," Billy agreed. "Guess that'll have to do."

* * *

The next day was payday and Kat hadn't decided what to do. The men had proven their loyalty, and had gone without pay the last two months. The necessities were met: they had food, home, and clothes on their backs; even though the latter were mostly what they owned when they first came on. But none of them had been to town except for errands. If they had any pleasure money they'd somehow saved it up. Kat figured with market day coming, and the good job they'd done in rounding up about fifty head altogether, they deserved a payday and a lark before driving the cattle to market.

She walked over to the stable where Laredo was currying

his horse. "Laredo, I'm gonna let you boys have a fling before the drive."

Laredo stopped brushing. "You sure you wanna do that, Kat? All you have is what's left of the loan Hopkins lent you, an' that can't be much by now."

"I know. But you boys have done a good job an' I wanna do somethin' for you now. An' there'll be some left after meetin' payroll. Besides, we'll make it back; even with only fifty head, we should clear the thousand Hopkins lent us, the mortgage, and maybe have some to spare."

Laredo nodded slowly. "Maybe. All right."

"Where are the boys?"

"Bear, Rawhide an' Dakota are ridin' the east end where we found some o' those strays, hopin' to find some more. Banty and Billy are scoutin' north to try to pick up sign of the stolen cattle."

"Good. Come with me an' we'll count out the pay. Then you ride out after them and pay it out."

"You trust me to do that, Kat?" His grin was teasing.

Kat didn't find it amusing. "*You* can trust if you up an' run off with it I'll find you, fill you full of lead, an' drag your carcass an' the money back."

"I think you would." His grin was wider.

Kat's angry frown dissolved into a grin of her own. "C'mon. Let's open the safe." She led him into her room. "Don't get any ideas."

"I've never been in a lady's boo-dwoir before."

Kat glanced over her shoulder at him as she knelt at the safe. "Never?"

"Nope; not in a *lady's,* anyway."

Kat got the joke. "I'm not a lady, but I'm not a saloon baud either."

"I know. That makes you even more interestin'."

Kat wasn't sure how to react to that so she concentrated on turning the dial, keeping herself between Laredo and the safe as a precaution. She yanked the handle and opened the heavy door. Her dad's pocket watch was there; so was her mom's jewelry. So were a couple of other keepsakes more valuable by attached sentiment than by monetary value.

But the cash was gone.

"What's the matter?" Laredo asked, unable to see inside but sensing Kat's shock. "What is it, Kat?" He bent down beside her.

"It's gone. The money's gone!"

"Gone?" He looked inside, felt all around.

Both indulged in some language.

"How?" he asked. "Does anyone else know the combination?"

"No. Dad and I were the only ones who ever knew."

"And the lock hasn't been tampered with?" he said, examining it as best as his untrained eyes could.

"No. I don't know much about it but if it were I prob'ly couldn't open it."

Laredo nodded. "Prob'ly right." He stood up and Kat closed the safe and rose beside him. "Fact is, somebody broke in or figured out the combination. An' they musta done it in broad daylight, too."

"How do you figure?"

"If somebody crept in here at night to rob your safe while you were sleeping right there in that bed, there wouldn't be no money missin' but there'd be a dead robber on the floor."

Kat's expression burned with manslaughter. "You're right about that."

"An' another thing: whoever it was just took the money. Your other valuables are still there, so far as you can see, right?"

"Yes, it's all there. Only the money is gone..."

"So that's the only thing they were after."

"They?"

"Whoever did this was sent by somebody else."

"You're right. And 'somebody else' is Larson."

"Sure." He shook his head. "Hate to think it's one of the men."

"Why does it have to be one of the men? Larson could send somebody else here just as easy."

"Yeah, but there's more risk that way."

They walked the floor uneasily, neither knowing what to do or say next.

"One thing for sure," Kat said. "No matter what we make at market, it won't be enough to pay Hopkins next week."

"Not unless we find the thief and the money before then."

Kat searched his face. "You think we will?"

Laredo didn't want to answer that.

CHAPTER FOURTEEN

Laredo and Kat agreed to keep it quiet both about the payroll and the robbery. If it was one of the hands maybe he'd make a mistake and they'd catch him. Kat knew she must control her temper; never an easy task for her. The thought that one of her men was a traitor seethed inside her, and she was ready to shoot whoever it was if she caught him.

Meanwhile, there was a cattle drive to manage.

It took less than half a day to guide the cattle into line; a record, if it hadn't been for the small number of animals to herd. Laredo and Kat rode up to lead and at Laredo's call they started off.

The noon sun burned down on them, the wide brims of their hats the only things shading their eyes. The heat seared through their clothing, no matter how lightly dressed, and patches of sweat soon decorated everyone's backs. Even though the distance wasn't great, a slow moving herd was a safe moving herd. Try to get too much speed out of the dumb, lumbering critters and you have a stampede on your hands. There was nothing worse or more dangerous on a cattle drive than a stampede.

Bear and Rawhide rode left flank and Banty and Dakota rode right; Billy brought up the rear. Keeping a slow, steady pace with the herd, guiding strays from leaving the ranks, and maintaining a watchful eye on the country around them kept them occupied.

Lunch was a real feast that one consumed in the saddle: some jerky, chewed until it was moistened by your own spit, some even drier biscuit, and a brief pull from your canteen. Even on short rides water in this country was valuable and you didn't waste it.

Other ranchers were taking their cattle to market as well, and the sounds of lowing and the rumble of hooves that you felt rather than heard announced their presence.

Kat looked off in the direction of the vibrations and a long dark shadow crept slowly along, approaching yet keeping a wary distance. Beeves were unpredictable, that was the only thing predictable about them. If they sensed others of their species they might seek to join them, they might stampede, or they might just ignore them entirely. The third, of course, was the most desired course.

She didn't recognize the trail boss, though her distance sight was keen. Maybe it was somebody hired new for this drive, though that wasn't the usual way. You always wanted someone you knew and trusted running the drive. Oh well, it wasn't her herd they were driving.

But then Kat studied Laredo. Just how much did she know about him and his pals? She had resisted hiring him when he first showed up and had only hired him and Banty because they came along with Bear, who she'd already hired. And there was that mysterious time Bear called him Pete, when he was half unconscious from gunshot wounds. Who was Pete?

Everyone had a past; and whatever Laredo's past was he wasn't the only one to hide it under an assumed name. Rawhide and Dakota obviously had names they were born with that they no longer wanted known, and they were two of hardest working most loyal men she could want.

But Laredo and his pals had come out of nowhere and won her over. Now they were on a cattle drive which meant everything, even if the pay for fifty head might not be all they needed. If they were going to make a move against her it was going to happen in the next couple of days.

Kat was going to watch them, and watch closely.

* * *

Sheriff Stokes's feet had gone to sleep during his morning nap so he eased them off the desk, stamped them on the floor, and figured it was time for a stroll. He wandered down the boarded walk pretending to make rounds, frowning and glancing about to look official. Some of the townfolk spoke to him, wishing him good morning, and he responded with a curt nod for the men and his version of a charming smile and a touch of his hat to the ladies. The men generally knew even the nod was phony, and the women pulled their shawls and capes a little tighter to better conceal what the Sheriff seemed to see underneath.

He was just about to pass the telegraph office when he stopped. *Might as well see if an answer has come,* he thought. Who this Laredo or Pete or whoever really was meant nothing to him, but a chat with old Hayes gave him something to do for a while, if nothing else. He went in; Hayes was tending to a young woman who was sending a message. Stokes leaned against a table in a corner and bit off the end of a cigar, spitting the end into the corner. He struck a match on his holster and lit up. The smoke was choking for anyone but him; he happened to like the "aroma" himself. He puffed away until the young woman was done and gave his wolf smile to her as she passed him on the way out. She gave a polite cough and made a speedy exit. Stokes congratulated himself on another feminine conquest and strode over to the main desk.

"Mornin', Windy." He knew Hayes hated the nickname, a sarcastic remark on Hayes' laconic nature. That's why he used it. "Any reply to that telegram I sent?"

Hayes glared at him under the eyeshade and turned in his chair to check the pigeon-holed case behind him. He pulled out a folded paper. "Yeah; here."

Stokes took the paper and said, "Much obliged." He tucked it into his belt and left the office.

The young woman he had seen at the telegrapher's was just coming out of a shop and he decided to follow her for a bit just to enjoy the movement of her hips. But she entered another shop and his entertainment was over so he sighed and went back to his office.

Time for lunch, and he took a sandwich out of one drawer of his desk and a flask from another. The sandwich was big, and before he was done he loosened his belt. He didn't notice the piece of paper that fell to the floor at the time but went back to his lunch.

It was late afternoon before he thought of the telegram again and felt for it in his belt, which was still loose. He was genuinely surprised not to find it there and looked about his desk for it at first. Then he felt something scrape under his boot and looked down. There it was on the floor. He bent down as best he could, which wasn't very well, to get it.

What he read was interesting; *very* interesting.

His pants threatened to fall as he stood up so he fastened and belted them again and stuck the telegram in his belt. For the second time today he left the office, this time mounting his horse and riding out of town. No one paid any attention to him, which was the way he liked it anyway, so his destination was of no interest to anyone.

* * *

"Fifty head, eh?" the man said. "That isn't much, Miss Crandall."

"It's all I've got," Kat replied, swallowing his way of addressing her. "We've had a hard time these last few months."

"I remember your pa saying he had a couple thousand that would be ready for market about this time."

"I'm sure he did. Most of our herd was rustled." Her patience was wearing thin. Laredo stood behind her and she shook off the calming hand he had placed on her back. "They're good beef, even if they are few. What will you offer for them, Mr. Marley?"

Marley looked them over again, grazing and moaning in their pen. "They are prime, I'll give you that. What's the exact count?"

"Fifty-three," Laredo said.

"Ahuh." Marley scratched his head. He wore eastern clothes but a good western Stetson. White sideburns bordered his jaws and a thick white mustache formed a horseshoe around his mouth, masking his expression. "I can offer you ten dollars a head." He peered closely at Kat for her reaction. "I'd offer more, if you had more to sell. As for rustlers, that's too bad; but none of my affair."

Laredo saw Kat's hands curl at her side. "Kat, lemme talk to you a moment." He took her arm. "Excuse us, Mr. Marley."

"I don't need to talk to you, Laredo or Pete or whatever your name is." She pulled herself from his grasp.

If Laredo was bothered by her calling him Pete he only showed it a second. But Marley frowned as he watched them. "Just for a minute, Kat." He took her arm again and this time she couldn't wrestle loose.

"All right." She stepped away with him.

Laredo put his back to Marley at first as he winked at Kat and hoped she took the signal to play along. "I know your pa dealt with this Marley for years," he said, in a supposed whisper loud enough for Marley to hear. "But Spencer over there offered us twenty a head, when he spoke to me."

Kat's eyes widened and at Laredo's second wink she got the idea. "He did, huh? Why didn't you tell me?"

"Well, you said you wanted to give Marley first choice 'cause he always did good by your pa. So I figured I'd wait and see. Now Spencer..."

Marley came over. "Excuse me, I know you're having a private conversation, but I couldn't help but hear. If Spenser offered twenty then I can certainly offer fifteen." Kat and Laredo shared a wary glance. Marley waited, a friendly smile covering his own doubt.

"I don't know, Mr. Marley," Kat said. "If Spencer said he'd offer us twenty, I don't think I can turn him down."

"No," Laredo said, "I don't think you can." Turning to Marley he added, "Thanks anyway, Mr. Marley. I'm glad to know you." He shook hands and started to guide Kat away.

"Wait!" Marley called.

Laredo and Kat halted.

Marley chewed over his words before saying them. "In honored memory of your father, who was a good friend as well as a business associate, I'll offer eighteen dollars a head. Cash on the barrel."

Kat drew a formless sketch in the dirt with her boot. "I don't know, Mr. Marley. If Mr. Spencer offers us twenty why that's —"

"Twenty-five!" Marley said. "I won't let you go for any less."

Kat and Laredo regarded each other, mulling it over while Kat fought to hide her excitement. "Twenty-five? You're sure?"

Kat asked. "I mean, I'm glad an' all that but I don't want you to think we're pulling a trick on you."

"No trick. I *want* to pay." He stuck out his hand. "Have we got a deal?"

Kat glanced at Laredo again who nodded. "It's a deal, Mr. Marley; it's a deal." She stuck her strong hand into Marley's fattened one.

Marley was surprised at the girl's grip and winced slightly. "Good. Come on over over here and we'll sign the papers." He put an arm around Kat's shoulders which she remarkably did not try to shrug off and Laredo waited until they were done. "Thank you, Miss Crandall. Your father would be proud."

"I sure hope he is, Mr. Marley. And call me Kat."

"Kat. Yes, I will. Thanks you again, Kat."

Kat and Laredo celebrated in the saloon. After the second round Banty and Bear came in and Kat bought a round for the both of them. She told them of what had happened with Marley and they congratulated her on the sale.

"There's another guy got a good deal over yonder," Banty said, pointing vaguely toward the cattle pens. "Huge herd; the Box O, I think they were."

Kat frowned. "Box O? Never heard of them."

"That's what Dakota said. He's never seen any of their hands, neither."

Kat drank down more of her beer. "Well, we got enough to pay Hopkins anyhow. As for after that, we'll have to see."

Laredo had pulled a notebook and pencil stub from a pocket and was doodling.

"What's that you're doin'?" Kat asked, ""figurin' your share? There won't be any pay for a while..."

"No. Just somethin' that occurred to me. The Box O, you say?"

"Yeah," Banty answered, peering over Laredo's shoulder. "Well, I'll be a sheepherder's cousin. Will you look at that!"

$\overline{\text{O}}$

Kat started to turn red as her hair and Laredo saw one fist curl and the other tighten around her gun.

"Unh uh," he said, laying a hand on her gun wrist. "This might look bad but it's not proof."

She glared at him. "You got the proof right there. All it takes is a running iron to turn the Bar O into a Box O. Whoever they are, they got my cattle."

"Maybe." He turned to Banty. "See anybody we know from Larson's bunch?"

"Nope."

Bear shook his head No.

"And we're sure Larson rustled your cattle." Laredo asked.

"As sure as hell," Kat said. "What's your angle?"

Laredo finished his beer and straightened up. "I'd say this Box O outfit is worth a look, if nothing else."

Kat patted her gun butt. "I'm for that."

"But no shootin'. Just let me talk."

Kat was about to do some talking of her own but decided for once in her life to shut up and listen. She followed Laredo out and they used Banty's directions to find the Box O outfit.

The cattle, a couple of thousand head, were in a pen and Kat strode right up to the fence. A few of the animals were close enough for her to read the brand. The others examined it with her. The brands were interesting in their own right, to say the least.

"You lookin' or buyin'?" a voice asked behind them.

Kat turned to see a tall broad-shouldered man, skin weathered to leather toughness. He still wore some of the dust of the trail. Kat wasn't sure but she figured he was the rider she had seen leading the other trail drive as they were nearing town.

"Just lookin'," she said. "That your brand?"

"It's the brand I was hired to bring to market." It was a response rather than an answer.

"That your *boss's* brand, then?" Laredo and his friends were standing just behind her, as implacable as she.

"What business is it of yours?" he asked, though he took a half-step back, wary of the three pairs of male eyes studying him.

"It might be none of my business," Kat said, "Or it might be all my business." She took a glove from her belt. "See the brand on that?" It bore the Bar C brand, stitched into the leather.

"Yeah. Bar C. What of it?"

"It just strikes me the brands are a mite similar," Kat said, her voice flat.

Laredo knew what that tone meant.

The man looked at the glove, glanced at the herd, and said, "Yeah, guess it is. Must be one o' them coincidences you hear about."

"Maybe." Kat tucked the glove back into her belt. "You been punchin' cows long?" Her question was casual.

"Most o' my life."

"Then I guess you've heard o' what they call a running brand. Maybe you've even seen one or two."

"Sure. Anyone that's been around cattle ranches've seen running brands."

Kat found a stick and knelt down, drawing in the dirt. "Now, like I showed you, this is my brand." She drew a Bar C. "And here's yours." With a few quick strokes she turned the Bar C into a Box O. She looked up at him and said, "See what I mean?"

"Yeah. Right fancy drawin'. Still don't mean nothin'."

Laredo stepped in. "I think it does."

The man stepped back. "Now let's just stay nice an' friendly, OK?"

"Sure," Laredo said. "If you answer a couple of friendly questions."

"Like what?"

Kat joined in. "Like, who hired you to drive these cattle?"

"The man who owned them. A guy named Dawson."

"Oh?" Kat glanced at Laredo. "What did Dawson look like?"

The man gave a good description but it didn't sound familiar.

"I see. And he said they were his cattle?" Kat continued.

"Yeah."

"Didn't seem odd that a man named Dawson would have a brand with an O instead of a D?"

The man was even more uncomfortable. "No; well, yeah, I guess."

"So you didn't question the brand?"

"No; they was branded that way when he hired me."

"Funny thing about some o' these brands," Banty said, leaning against the fence rail to look in at the herd. "Some o' these just don't look right."

"How do you mean?" the man, eager to avoid Kat and Laredo's eyes, came beside him and looked into the pen.

"Well, some o' those brands look a little lop-sided. Look at that one, for instance." He pointed to one of the steers closest to them. The two vertical lines and the bottom line of the box were at a different angle than the top line. "Looks to me like some o' that was added later." He turned and glared at the man as Kat and Laredo were still doing. "Kinda like my boss lady's little drawing over there."

The man straightened and backed away a bit. "Look, this guy who called himself Dawson hired me to drive some cattle for him. He said I could hire whatever men I needed, an' I did."

"You sell 'em yet?" Kat asked.

"No. But I got a buyer who's comin' soon to look at 'em."

"What's his name? I know most of the meat buyers around here."

"Says his name is Spencer."

Laredo and Kat again exchanged glances.

"You mean that's a phony name too?" the man asked.

He was relieved when all four of them laughed.

"No; he's real all right," Kat said. "My pa used to deal with him and with Marley. Depended on which one offered a better price."

"Well, Spencer's due any time," the man said.

"Ahuh." Kat twitched her head at Laredo and they stepped aside while Banty and Bear continued to watch the man. "I think this guy's on the level."

"I think so too. Larson might have hired him to bring the cattle to market, not thinkin' we'd run into him."

"Why don't we wait here for Spencer?" Kat said. "We might be able to work something out."

"Sounds good to me." Laredo looked about. "Say, I just realized Billy ain't around. Wonder where he got to?"

"i don't know. Maybe he's just drinkin' his pay. You and Banty see if you can round him up while Bear an' me wait for Spencer."

"All right." He signaled to Banty who followed him off.

Kat chatted with the man, and learned his name was Bill. That's the only name he gave. Bill was a pretty common name; common as a real name and an assumed one, so she let it go. She assured him they figured him to be innocent of rustling, but would want him to lead them to the man who sold them the herd.

"Sure thing. Like I said, I been in this business since I could ride, an' one thing I hate is a rustler."

A tall man with expressive blue eyes, a ready grin, and sparse hair that he covered with his hat came toward them. His smile grew broader when he saw Kat.

"Why it's ol' Crandall's daughter! How are you, Allie Kat?" He offered his big hand for her to shake.

Her grip almost matched his as she vented her anger at her girlhood nickname. "Fine, Mr. Spencer. How are your son and daughter?"

"They're doin' fine. I was so sorry to hear about your pa."

"Thanks. I've taken over the ranch and this is our first drive."

"That's terrific." He looked in the pen. "But these are those Box O cattle that Bill here wanted me to look at."

"I might have been doin' you a bad turn, Mr. Spencer," Bill said.

"Oh? How do you mean?"

Bill showed him the sketch Kat had made in the dirt and how she had done it.

Spencer frowned; Kat rarely remembered him looking grim or angry. "If that's right, this Box O brand was made with a running iron."

"That's what I think," Kat said.

"Then, you're sayin' this is your cattle?" Spencer said,

aiming a thumb at the herd in the pen.

"That's what I suspect." Kat told him about Larson leaving and the trouble she'd been having, and that Larson was probably behind it. "Bill here described the man who hired him an' he sure sounds a lot like Larson."

A second figure had been attracted by the scene.

Spencer grinned and held out his hand again. "Howdy, Marley. You been buyin' today?"

Marley shook with him. "Yeah, from this little lady here. You buyin' from her too?"

"My client is this man, Bill here." Spencer indicated Bill who was beginning to feel either mighty important or totally useless; he couldn't make up his mind which it was.

Marley looked over the fence at the herd. "Box O? Never heard of 'em. Where you from, son?" he asked Bill.

"Look mister, I was just hired to drive the cattle to market, get a good price for 'em, an' bring the money back. That's all."

"I think he's tellin' the truth, Mr. Marley," Kat said. "An' I think Larson hired him. Guess he didn't think we'd cross paths or notice how alike the two brands are."

"If I remember Larson," Marley said, "he was never much on brains."

"A man come to me a little while ago," Bill said, "an' said he was one o' Dawson's men sent to collect the money when I get paid."

"Oh? What was his name?"

"I don't recollect; I'm not even sure he gave it. But I know where I'm supposed to find him."

Spencer put one hand on his shoulder and waved a stern finger at him with the other. "Listen, son, you go find that man now an' bring him to us."

"I'll do that." He hurried off.

Kat and Bear showed the two cattlemen some of the irregular brands that suggested a running iron had been used. Both men agreed that seemed to be the case.

"There's a U.S. Marshal in town," Marley said. "When Bill comes back with this man from Dawson or Larson or whoever we'll see that they get acquainted."

"Thanks, Mr. Marley."

A shot sounded from about a hundred yards to their right. Cattle started getting agitated, and cowboys tried to sooth them.

Kat started into a run and the four others trotted behind, unable to keep up, though Bear proved surprisingly nimble for a man his size.

A crowd was already gathering but of her group Kat reached the scene first and pulled to a halt.

A man lay in the dirt behind one of the tents, part of his head blown off by a .44 slug. But there was enough of him left that she recognized him.

He was the trail boss Dawson or Larson had hired; the man who called himself Bill.

CHAPTER FIFTEEN

Billy Holcomb came at a run and skidded to a stop near them. "I heard the shooting. What happened?" He looked down at the body. "Any idea who he was?"

"No," Kat said. "He was here to sell some cattle; the Box O brand."

"Box O? Whose brand is that?"

Kat sniffed a laugh. "Mine."

"Now, we're not sure of that, Kat," Marley said. "There's a herd of cattle here with a brand that looks like it might have been run from your Bar C, but you still have no proof."

A man of medium height and massive weight, his features fused into a perpetual scowl in the center of his heavy face, and his mustache bristling over pursed lips came riding up. With unexpected ease he lowered himself from his horse and strode over. A marshal's badge shined from his vest.

"All right, spread out here." His voice was a low bass growl to match his expression. He gazed down at the body and looked around at the crowd. "Anybody see what happened?"

A mute chorus of shaken heads answered in the negative.

"Anybody know who he was?"

Kat stepped forward. "All I know is he called himself Bill and was selling cattle with the Box O brand."

The marshal turned to her. "And how do you know that?"

The Bar C men had again gathered around her. "Because I think they were my cattle."

"You? Do you own the Box O?"

"Nope. I own the Bar C. These are some of my men."

The scowl somehow tightened even more. "Miss, I don't understand. How can they be your cattle?" The obvious struck him. "Did you accuse this man of rustling?"

"No; but I think he was paid by the man who has rustled my cattle to sell them here. He didn't reckon I'd be here too."

The Marshal looked around him again; he could spot the men who must be working for this woman. "Anybody here workin' for the Box O?"

There was a shuffling of feet and a couple of men came forward. It was clear from their breath and their uneasy attempts at standing straight where they had spent their pay.

"We were hired along with him," the shorter of the men said. He was a dusty, unshaven runt who would surely lose an argument with a stiff wind. His pal was equally dusty and unshaven, but tall and lanky. "Me and Burke here. I'm called Peewee."

The Marshal nodded. "We're all goin' to my office and get this straightened out." He glanced up and beckoned to a newcomer, a gnome in formal funereal black, complete with an aged top hat that refused to sit upright. "Doc Stone is our town doctor, coroner, and undertaker. Doc, I leave the corpse to you. The rest of you follow me."

* * *

Marshal Conrad took Kat's story first then Marley and Spencer. Last he turned to Burke and Peewee.

"We worked with Bill before," Peewee said. "He came to us and put us on the payroll with a bunch of other fellas. I don't know why they didn't show."

"Prob'ly too dead drunk," Burke said, belching loudly and filling the air with the stink of cheap booze. "Pardon, Miss," he added to Kat.

"How long have you known him?" the Marshal asked.

"Near all our lives," Peewee said. "An' we've worked with some o' them other boys too, one time or other. Bill is on the up and up, let me tell you." His jaw drooped. "He was."

"Did either of you see the man who hired him?"

"Nope; all we saw was his money. We got a week's pay up front."

"Any idea who might have had it in for Bill?"

Peewee turned to Burke and they both shook their heads. "Nope; everybody liked Bill. Poor ol' Bill."

Both men started sniffling. The others in the room made

various sounds or gestures of discomfort.

Marshal Conrad broke the moment by standing up, forcing his hips free of the curved arms of the desk chair. "Next thing I'm taking a look at those beeves."

* * *

They led him to the pen where the Box O stock waited. He examined the brands and agreed they appeared to be done by a running iron. He turned to Peewee and Burke.

"I'm ready to arrest you two and any others I can find your bunch as rustlers, unless you can prove different."

"Honest, marshal, we're not rustlers!" Peewee insisted. "I told you, Bill hired us."

"What's Bill's last name?" Conrad asked.

"Simmons. I'm tellin' the truth, marshal!"

"All right. I'm gonna hold these cattle until I can locate the owner, this Dawson character. That brand's gotta be registered if its legal, an' I'm gonna trace it down."

Kat came forward. "What am I gonna do in the meantime, marshal? I'm sure they're my cattle."

"But we can't prove it for sure until we find who changed the brands. Miss Crandall..."

She'd had enough of that. "Just call me Kat; everybody does."

"All right: Kat. I don't doubt the brands were changed, but I haven't seen anything that proves they were originally Bar C; you understand, don't ya?"

Kat fumed. "I guess so."

"I'm sorry for the trouble this causes," Conrad added, his voice suddenly mild and his hand on Kat's shoulder in a man-to-man sort of way. "But I'm wearin' this badge to uphold the law, an' whatever I might think is only opinion in court. If I find proof that this brand is unregistered, an' we can locate this Dawson fella, the cattle are yours."

"All right." Her men nodded agreement. "Should we hang around until you find out?"

"No, that might take some time. Go on back to your ranch an' when I know somethin' I'll get word to you."

Kat put out her hand. "Thanks, Marshal. I know you'll do what's right."

Marshal Conrad was surprised at Kat's grip. "Thanks. I'll do what I can."

* * *

Kat was silent as they rode back. The others kept their own silence as well. Each had something to ponder.

Kat's primary concern was the cattle: they were Bar C cattle, re-branded with a running iron; no doubt. The fact that the cattle remained in Peewee and they had to return to the ranch without payment rankled in her. She wasn't angry at Marshal Conrad; he seemed honest enough, and as a U.S. Marshal had the authority to investigate not only within the state but across state lines if necessary. And Spencer and Marley were old friends of her father's, and she knew to rely upon their loyalty.

The body of the young fellow called Bill who was killed mysteriously preyed upon Laredo's mind. Who killed him, and why? The most likely reason was because he knew something and someone feared he might reveal it. Or perhaps he had bungled the job he was hired to do. Either way the penalty he paid was death. Whoever was behind this, Larson or someone else, was deadly serious.

Another thing bothered Laredo: where had Billy Holcomb been? Then again, he did smell of bad whiskey when he rejoined them. He had probably just gone celebrating a bit while waiting for him and Kat to make the sale. They hadn't seen him in the bar where *they* had done their celebrating; but like any self-respecting town out west, this one had more than its quota of bars and brothels. Billy was most likely in some other establishment, that was all.

Banty had been around longer than any of them here, and had seen just about everything the west had to offer, good and bad. He knew running iron work when he saw it; and that so-called Box O was done with one, that was for damn sure. That Marshal seemed to know his business, and he figured the man knew the brands were fake just as he did.

BOOK TITLE

* * *

"What's the verdict, Doc?" Marshal Conrad asked.

"What you think it was? Single gun-shot to the head, close range." Doc Stone pulled a sheet over the body and rolled the bed to the side.

"Close range? You think he knew who killed him?"

"Maybe. I'm a doctor, not a detective. I'll keep on doctorin' if you keep on marshalin'. That a deal?"

Conrad's grin was hidden by his mustache. "Sure doc; that's a deal." He took one last look at the shrouded form. "Let me know if you need any help with the funeral."

"Sure. Just like I always do."

He never did; but that was a running joke between them. Doc Stone followed Conrad outside and entered his undertaker shop next door. Young Thad Barker did the carpentry work for the town, including coffins, and since the death rate in a cattle town was usually high he used the undertaker's shop as his headquarters for both. Conrad hauled himself up into the saddle and rode back to the area where the cattle pens stood.

Marley and Spencer were staying in town until this was settled, and had agreed to put up Peewee and Burke as well. The two itinerant cowpokes were probably living high for now, but at least they'd be nearby in case Conrad needed to question them again.

Conrad reached the pen. A deputy had kept watch for him. "I'll take over, Lester." The deputy headed back to the office while Conrad cautiously opened the gate of the pen and stepped inside, fastening it securely behind him. It was risky but the only way to get a close look.

Reaching in a vest pocket he pulled out a notebook and turned to a page with two sketches: one of the Bar C and the other of the Box O. Anyone could see the similarities between the two, but that wasn't what he was here for. An old cowhand himself, he made the kind of soothing, cooing noises he had done back in his cattle ranching days as he moved among them, looking at the brands closely.

Some of the brands were perfect, like they had been Box O brands all along. But others were slightly off, crooked or askew. That is, part was askew; and that part was all that was needed to turn a Bar C into a Box O. The brands that had obviously been tampered with had Bar C's that looked all right, but the rest of the curve that turned the C into an O left gaps, and the lines that formed the sides and bottom of the box were at an angle to the top bar.

Conrad had seen enough. He made his way through the cattle again and out of the gate, shutting it securely. Spencer saw him and ambled over.

"I see you're lookin' at those beeves, Marshal," he said.

"Yeah."

"See anything interestin'?"

"Maybe."

Spencer grinned. "I get it; you're not tellin' just yet."

"That's right. I got my suspicions, but that's all I'm sayin' for now." Conrad started over to his horse.

"Marshal, if those cows are Kat Crandall's who do you think she'll sell 'em to, me or Marley?"

Conrad took a grip on his saddle pommel. "Mr. Spencer, that's not up to me; that's up to Kat. Those two cowboys still in the hotel?"

"I don't know; I don't think they left town though. Marley said somethin' about showin' them a good time."

Conrad nodded. "That's a temptation few cowboys can resist." Stepping into a stirrup he hauled himself to the saddle. "Hope they resisted enough to stay sober until I question 'em some more. Excuse me, Mr. Spencer."

"Sure, Marshal; sure."

The Marshal rode into town and started making the rounds of the saloons. One the third try he spotted Marley and the two cowhands. They were seated at one of the tables, a half empty whiskey bottle making the rounds. Conrad walked over to the table and intercepted the bottle between hands.

"Hey!" Burke protested, "Mr. Marley bought that for us and just for us. He ain't had any himself, for a fact!"

"I'm not havin' any," Conrad said, placing the bottle on a nearby empty table, "an' neither are you until you and your pardner answer some more questions."

Peewee eyed the bottle and licked his lips. "OK; but I don't know what else we can tell you."

Marley eyed Conrad. "Do you need me, Marshal?"

Conrad shook his head. "No; but I left Spencer over by the cattle pens. You might wanna join him, just to keep him honest." He was going to say "to keep each other honest," but thought this might be a better incentive.

Marley rose. "Sure, Marshal. I'll do just that." He went straight for the door and out.

"Now. You say you never saw this Dawson that your pal Bill Simmons dealt with, right?"

"That's right. Say Marshal, you know we're hangin' around for Bill's funeral. You don't have to get Marley an' Spencer to nursemaid us."

"I know; but it's in their interests too that you hang around, an' I'd think you'd be glad they're bankrollin' your stay."

Burke gave a wide grin. "That's for sure." And he shot a thirsty glance at the lonely bottle.

"OK, so you can't help me there," Conrad said. "What about the herd? Were you with him from the time he picked up the cattle?"

"Well, sure," Peewee said. "We were the first he called. An' when he told us the kinda money we'd make, well it was a sure deal. Like I said, he paid us a week in advance an' promised us more after the sale."

"We was countin' on that extra too," Burke said. "A week's wages don't go too far no more."

Conrad dismissed the hint. "Do you think you could show me where you picked up the herd?"

"Sure," Peewee said. "Why, we're two o' the best trackers you can hire. Drunk or sober," he added with a nod toward the bottle.

"I'm gonna give you a chance to prove it," Conrad said, pushing up from the chair. "It's getting late now." He picked up the bottle. "I want you at my office at sunup tomorrow and ready to ride."

Peewee took the bottle. "We'll be there, Marshal." He took a long swig and passed it to Burke. "Say, is there any reward for leadin' you to these rustlers?"

Conrad was thankful for the many times, like now, his

mustache hid his grin. "You can take that up with Kat."

"Cat? What cat?"

"Kat Crandall, the lady rancher."

"Hey, she's a good looker too," Burke said.

"Yeah; an' she was lookin' at me," Peewee said, drinking from the bottle.

"You're crazy; she was lookin' at me the whole time. She even smiled at me." He made a grab for the bottle and Peewee let it go just so it didn't break.

Conrad doubted Kat had smiled at either one of them; or at him or any other man, for that matter. With the sound of their good-natured (he hoped) argument behind him he started out the door. Nothing to be done until tomorrow; and maybe this will be over then.

* * *

Peewee and Burke were there just after dawn; they'd stop to buy some sandwiches to pack for on the way and a couple more bottles of whiskey. Conrad accepted a sandwich from Peewee and they mounted. Munching this makeshift breakfast as they rode, Peewee and Burke led the way.

It was the main road out of town to what passed for a highway and the three took their time. The cowmen said it had been several days' ride driving the herd so it might take that long going back.

Night came and they finished the last of the sandwiches around their fire.

"We'll need something to eat for tomorrow," Burke said, "an' maybe the day after that too."

"I packed bacon an' flour in my saddlebags," Conrad said, "an' a couple o' cans an' some coffee in that extra sack." He pointed to the burlap sack beside his saddle. "I always keep it on hand for cases like this."

"You're prepared all right," Peewee said. "Bacon an' beans an' biscuits: the three B's. Tell the truth, I'm kinda tired o' sandwiches anyhow."

Conrad allowed himself a short chuckle. He liked these two; maybe when this was over Kat Crandall might even hire them.

She could use a couple more hands.

They rolled themselves up in their blankets and went to sleep. The ground was hard, and their saddles weren't the most restful pillows. And the owl and the cricket and the coyote seemed to be competing for loudest noisemaker. But these were men of the open, and hard ground and saddles were more familiar to them than the softest mattress or downiest pillow. And the song of owl and cricket and coyote were only lullabies that settled them into sleep.

* * *

They awoke at dawn and Conrad proved his cooking skills as he heated up beans, fried bacon, and mixed up some biscuits which didn't resemble rocks at all. His coffee was just the way they all liked it: scalding hot, black as tar, and almost as thick. Once filled they put out the fire, broke camp, and Peewee again took the lead.

About mid-afternoon Peewee led them off the highway and across country, finally picking up another poor excuse for a trail that wound like some bewildering maze. Conrad remembered a story from childhood about a maze; a labyrinth it was called, and guarding it was a creature half man and half bull. He was pretty certain no such creature haunted this winding path but he wished he had a ball of twine like the hero of that old story had, to find his way back out again.

"Not much further," Peewee said. "But Marshal, I don't know about you but I'm getting hungry."

"Me too," said Burke. "I could use some more o' those biscuits an' beans."

Conrad halted and considered. There was no sign of an opening ahead, so the valley Peewee had told him about had to still be a ways. Chances were whoever was on guard wouldn't see a campfire, or if they did might not be suspicious. He heaved his bulk down from the horse and said, "All right; I can eat too. Help me get it started." He opened up the saddlebag and tossed the burlap sack to Burke.

The meal was soon cooked and sooner eaten. They put out the fire with the last of the coffee and mounted up again.

The path was narrow, just wide enough for two or three cows to walk abreast, and bordered by trees that reached across at each other above them. Twilight was settling in, and shadows turned the path into a tunnel. Conrad had good night vision, and Peewee and Burke shared that skill. The way continued to twist and turn and he imagined what this might have been like driving a herd through.

At last it widened a bit and they reached a ridge that sloped gently down into a valley. The valley was good grassland, with a cool clear stream running along one edge. It seemed a nice place for a ranch; or for rustlers to hide stolen cattle.

Full night had come, a sickle of moon slicing through the stars, but Conrad could see enough to guide him. He led now, as the three left their mounts and eased down the slope. They reached bottom and saw a small lean-to not far to their right. He crossed to it as they followed, his gun loose in his holster and the other two holding theirs ready.

He entered the lean-to and lit a match. There was an oil lamp on a small table but he didn't dare light it. The brief glance afforded by the match was enough. There were ropes and heavy work gloves, a pile of firewood, and two or three interesting pieces of iron. He picked up one of them: it was exactly the shape he expected to see, a curve that completed the C into an O surrounded by three bars forming the bottom sides of a box. This was the running iron the rustlers used.

There had to be another entrance that led to the hide-out, where they might even find this Dawson or whoever he was.

A shot splintered a wall of the lean-to and Conrad dropped the iron to grab for his gun. Peewee and Burke were already firing back, hoping to find targets revealed only by the flash of gunfire.

Another bullet zinged close, and Conrad fell to the ground to avoid being a target. He thought he saw a flash and fired at it; only the crack of a ricochet answered. Peewee and Burke were firing back blindly, and he called them to be careful. They might run out of bullets without hitting anything.

A cry answered the blast of a gunshot; one of his friends was hit. He fired at where he thought the shot had originated and crawled toward them. Burke lay on his face, twitching and moaning with pain. Peewee had found shelter behind a rock and tried covering fire, but without a clear target his shots were useless.

Conrad edged his way toward Burke. The shooting from their hidden attackers was heavier now; maybe reinforcements had joined in. just as he was a few inches away from him another bullet struck Burke and his body jumped once and lay still. The moaning had stopped. As though to be sure another shot sounded and Burke's head exploded.

Wiping blood and what was probably brains from his face Conrad crept back, hoping the rock where Peewee was hiding was large enough for the two of them. It was probably big enough for Peewee and an ordinary sized man like Burke; but Burke didn't need any cover anymore and Conrad was not your average sized man.

A bullet thudded against his shoulder-blade, and Conrad's left arm went limp. Pulling himself with his right he crept closer. A second bullet narrowly missed him as he was within a yard of shelter.

He reached a rock near Peewee who had stopped firing. He was frantically re-loading when Conrad reached him, but was unhurt. Conrad pulled himself to a sitting position with his good arm.

"How many shots you got left?" Conrad called.

"Enough for two more loads."

That meant ten or twelve, depending on whether Peewee normally loaded five or six rounds at a time.

"We've got to get out of here," Peewee said.

"We haven't got a chance," Conrad said. "They can pick us off as they please."

"Then what do you suggest? Give up?"

He had exposed himself to ask the question; just enough for a sniper to get in a lucky shot that sent Peewee's skull in every direction.

Conrad swore; at least he had gone the way of his pard.

There was nothing to do but try to escape; it was his only chance. Peewee had fallen within his reach and he grabbed hold of the dead man's shirt, trying not to look at what was left above the collar. He got a grip on the cartridge belt and unbuckled it. There were about a dozen cartridges left. Conrad filled his gun and Peewee's fortunately they were both Colt .44's.

It was desperate, but maybe the twelve shots would cover him until he reached his horse. His horse wasn't smart or trained like a horse in a dime novel; he didn't come at command or a whistle. Conrad wished he did, but that wouldn't help now. His only chance was a covering fire while he climbed up that slope to the horses. Yeah; his only chance.

No time like the present.

He shoved to his feet, fired a couple rounds, and sprinted as best he could to the slope. His left shoulder hollered its pain at him from the recoil, but he fired again. He doubted he hit anything or anyone.

But they did.

A bullet struck his shoulder, spinning him around and knocking him off his feet. He propped himself on his right elbow, trying to rise. Another shot struck his leg and he felt the warm blood soaking his Levis. Another struck him in the head. He had just enough time to remember his ma saying what a hard head he had before all went black.

The guards and bushwackers didn't bother to check their work; there was no way those men were alive. The explosion of a skull when a bullet strikes it was quite distinctive; and satisfying, when you're in the killing business. The guards went back to their posts and their compatriots returned to theirs, to swap stories of how great they were and how each one claimed to have fired the killing shot for each of the three intruders.

* * *

Clouds had come in, and obscured the vague light there was. The guards, their job done as they thought, went to sleep at their posts.

One figure stirred in the valley below. He had fallen near the stream and dragged himself to it. It was slow; minutes were hours if not years. With the only good hand he had he untied his bandana and dipped it in the stream. He squeezed its contents between parched lips and into an arid throat. He did it again and again until he had enough to go on.

One arm and one leg; that's all that worked now. But it was enough to reach the slope where he hoped the horses waited. He wasn't a praying man, but he prayed God for the strength to get up that hill and to his horse.

CHAPTER SIXTEEN

Dobie and Red watched the sunrise over the ridge and each looked for signs of the other on either side of the valley. The morning shift was on its way and both needed the rest. Night duty came by lot: whoever picked the black pebbles "won." Red spotted Dobie and swung his rifle in a wide overhead arc. Dobie answered the signal. Red stood up and stretched his aching limbs. The cold nights with nothing for light but stars and nothing for warmth but a ragged blanket weren't new for either of them. Like about a half dozen others they had joined Larson's gang for the promise of money and what that money bought them. And men like Dobie and Red wanted only the simple pleasures: enough liquor to get drunk and enough women to satisfy another type of appetite. And one could never have enough of either.

The night had been eventful: whoever those three intruders were who had stumbled onto the valley they were dead now. Marksmanship was one of the skills men like Larson most prized in their guards, and Red and Dobie had proven those skills in the late War of Northern Aggression. Larson had hired several men like them; in fact Red and Dobie had put Larson in touch with some of their old buddies who had lost home and land in the War and needed some way to scratch out a living.

Hoof-beats approached as their replacements came on. Harris, here to spell Red, dismounted and tied his horse next to Red's and hiked the rocky slope to the spot where Red stood waiting.

"Had some excitement last night," Red told him.

Harris, one of Red's War buddies, glanced about and asked, "What kind?"

"Three men found the valley. Dobie an' me took care of 'em." He pointed down below. "They're still layin' there, what's left anyway."

Harris followed Red's finger and saw two bodies lying below. The crows were having breakfast on them. "I see only two. Where's the other one?"

"He can't be far; we poured lead into the both of 'em. He prob'ly tried to get back to his horse but he couldn't've made it."

"Well, we can bury 'em or let the crows take care of 'em."

Red shook his head. "The Boss don't like loose ends. He'll prob'ly want you an' Gunner to bury 'em. An' hunt up the third one and toss him in the hole too."

Harris scratched his head. "Guess you're right." His chuckle wasn't really for humor. "Guess we left so many on the field I got kinda used to it."

"We did that 'cause we didn't have time for any other way. You don't gotta be fancy; just dig a hole and shove them in. Dobie's prob'ly tellin' Gunner the same."

"Awright. There's some shovels in the lean-to, ain't they?"

"Yeah. You might as well go ahead an' get started." He saw Dobie signaling across the way. "Looks like Dobie's got Gunner all set. See you, Harris."

"S'long." Harris didn't look forward to manual labor first thing in the morning but Red was right: it had to be done.

Red mounted and rode back the way Harris had come. The trail skirted the edge of the valley and curved, meeting with the trail from the other side. Red waited until Dobie joined him; the latter had a little further to go to reach the rendezvous spot. Dobie pulled up beside him.

"Got Gunner straightened out?" Red asked.

"Yeah. He an' Harris oughta be diggin' that hole by now."

"Guess they'll have to drag that third guy back from wherever he fell," Red mused with a single chuckle. "Guess it'll take both of 'em to handle him. He was a big one."

"Yeah, but not so big a buncha bullets can't stop him."

Red clucked to his horse. "C'mon. We gotta report to Larson an' get some sleep." He gave a little nudge with his spurs and started toward the hide-out. Harris followed.

Red had been no more than a private; no higher than Dobie, Harris, or Gunner. But if liked giving orders, Dobie wasn't going to argue; neither did the other two. After all, one of the things they learned in combat is with the giving of orders comes the taking of blame; and if anything went wrong, Dobie would rather that blame fall on Red than on him. Especially if Larson was doing the punishment.

They reached the hide-out and tied their horses. Red went in first. "We had some action last night, boss," he said.

Larson was finishing his breakfast and wiped some grease off his chin with a sleeve that showed it had performed that office for some time. He glared up at him narrowly, still chewing as he asked: "What kind of action?"

Red told Larson about the three intruders.

"You're sure they're dead?" Larson asked.

"Dead as that damned Lincoln," Red replied. "We told Gunner and Harris to bury the bodies."

Larson nodded. "Good job. Draw your rations from Slim then get some sleep."

"Thanks, boss." Red turned to Dobie and with a jerk of the head led the way outside. "Told you he'd say we done good."

"Yeah. Wonder who them three were?"

"Don't know an' don't care. Let's get some grub an' a empty cot."

* * *

There was the usual midday traffic in Clear Springs when Kat, Laredo and Billy rode into town. Women went into the shops, some men gathered in clumps and others spent money in the saloons. The three from the Bar C tied their horses in front of the bank and Kat and Laredo started inside.

"I'll meet up with you later," Billy said. He patted his six shooter. "There's something off about my gun that seems off; maybe the gunsmith oughta look at it."

"OK," Kat said. "Last one there buys the first round."

Billy laughed. "That won't be me." He started down the street to the gun shop and turned in.

Kat and Laredo entered the bank. Junior Hopkins grimaced when he saw her.

"Miss Crandall." His voice was as stiff as his spine.

"Hey, Junior," Kat answered. "Your daddy in?"

Morgan Hopkins, Jr., somehow straightened even more. "I will see if he is in for you, Miss Crandall." He went through the same business of locking the cash drawer and knocking on the inner connecting door to his father's office as he always did. A moment later he came out. "Is this about the loan the bank proffered to you, or some other matter?"

Kat untied the small sack from her belt. "It's about the mortgage payment, Junior. Tell your daddy we're here early. That might perk him up."

Junior's eyes brightened just an instant at the word "payment." "I will give him your message." He disappeared into the *sanctum sanctorum* again.

Kat bounced the money sack in her hand and turned to Laredo. He was amused by the whole thing and she had to smile as well. "Hopkins is the biggest wheel in town," Kat explained, "and he's never let anybody forget."

Laredo shrugged. "A banker has a lotta power anyway. He's got everybody's money. An' somebody said anybody with power always wants more."

Kat frowned. "You don't think..."

"Father will see you now," Junior said, appearing in the outer door.

Kat passed by him without a word and Laredo tried a grin which received only a glare as a reply. Junior closed the door behind them.

Morgan Hopkins, Sr., might as well have never moved from the leather throne behind his desk-fortress. "Good morning, Miss Crandall. I understand you want to see me about your mortgage?"

"Yeah." She spilled the contents of the sack on his desk. Hopkins jumped slightly at both the sound and the possible scarring to the perfect polish of the rich wood.

He carefully gathered the gold pieces into piles on the leather desk pad, counting it as he did. Then he counted it again, not trusting his own first count. "Yes, it is all here. And somewhat ahead of your due date, if I recall."

"Yup; you bet." Kat leaned forward, resting her hands on the desk. Alarm again shone from Hopkins face; he'd definitely have to have the entire desk refinished once she was gone. "An' we're hopin' to make another payment soon."

Laredo placed a cautioning hand on Kat's arm but she shrugged it off.

"We might have found the rustled cattle. An' now there's a U.S. Marshal named Conrad who's backin' our play. Soon as we hear from him we'll know for sure."

Hopkins nodded; an empty gesture. "I see. Quite interesting. But we are not done; as you know there is another year of payments before the land is yours, free and clear."

"Yeah, I know. An' we'll make those payments too, you can bank on it."

Laredo laughed out loud; it was first real joke she'd ever heard from Kat.

Kat grinned at her own wit. "Yeah, Mr. Banker; you can bank on it, all right." She turned to Laredo and nudged him. "C'mon, let's see if we can beat Billy to the saloon."

They crossed the lobby and onto the boarded street again.

"We saved his wife an' son a while back, an' he didn't say a word about it."

Kat threw a skeptical glance at him. "An' you're surprised about it?"

Laredo shrugged. "No; guess not."

* * *

One of Larson's many jobs before becoming a cowhand for the Crandall outfit had been stringing wire for the telegraph. The main trunk of the telegraph company ran a couple of miles from their hideout, and it had been nothing for him to tap it and run a private wire for himself. All he needed do was teach a couple of his men to read and decipher Morse and he had his own message service.

Slim was on duty at the key today and about noon he brought in a message. It was short, but it spoke volumes.

CATTLE STILL AT DOUBLE ROCK UNSOLD

Larson read the six words and crumpled the paper in his fist. Even Slim's ample form shuddered at the wrath he knew was coming. But Larson's ire was low and cold. "Wire Dawson at Double Rock. One word: COME."

"Sure, boss." Slim waddled out to send the message.

Something had gone wrong, Larson figured, and he was going to find out what.

* * *

Billy was standing at the bar when Kat and Laredo arrived. His first beer was half done, and he gulped the rest as soon as he saw them. He raised the empty glass at them. "Told you I wasn't gonna be last."

Laredo and Kat glanced at each other and Kat dug into her jeans. "I'll pay."

"A gentleman doesn't let a lady pay for her own drinks," Laredo said.

"Right." She looked around between the three of them. "I might see a gentleman or two here, but I sure don't see a lady. I'm buyin'." She tossed a dollar on the bar. "Three beers."

The bartender drew the three, re-filling Billy's, and Laredo raised his in a toast. "To the Bar C; an' Marshal Conrad. Let's hope he stays on our side an' we get a good price on them steers."

The other two clinked glasses with him.

"Say Billy," Laredo said after he had downed most of his beer, "what was wrong with your gun?"

"Huh? Oh, just needed a little cleanin' that's all. Oughta take better care of it myself, I reckon."

"You can use my grease anytime you want," Laredo said. "Just ask."

"Much obliged." Billy lifted his glass to him in thanks.

Kat glanced at Laredo and decided they were thinking the same thing. It takes longer than that to fully clean a gun.

* * *

Harris and Gunner rode I after their shift and Larson strode over to the corral as they unsaddled their horses.

"Hear you were on graveyard duty this mornin'," he said.

"Hope you said a nice proper prayer over the dearly departed."

All three got a great laugh out of that one.

"Yeah, sure. We sent 'em off to hell quite proper," Gunner said. "Only thing: Dobie told me there was three of 'em."

"Red told me the same thing," Harris added.

"Yeah; three is what they told me. So?" Larson peered keenly at them.

Harris was getting nervous. "Well boss, there was only two. We buried both of 'em an' nobody'll find 'em."

"Didn't you look for the other one?" Larson stepped closer.

Harris retreated a step but Larson got up inches from him.

"Sure boss," Harris said, the sweat running down his brow and back. "We saw where he tried to pull himself up to where they prob'ly came in, but there was no body. An' no trail, once you reach them rocks."

Larson nodded. "No sign of him, eh?" Harris shook his head. "What about horses? See any horses?"

"No. Horses prob'ly run off durin' the shootin'."

"Boss," Gunner said, "you want we should go back an' look again?"

Larson seemed to consider it a moment. "No; he prob'ly crawled into some hole and died. The birds or the coyotes have taken care of him by now."

But Larson wasn't so sure. He'd have the next shift look for the body before they took over. That was another eight hours away, but how far can a man get with a bunch of slugs in him and on foot?

* * *

A couple hundred yards from the edge of the rustler's valley a prone figure lay. Blood soaked his clothing and stained the sparse grass under him. Weak, sick, and dazed he stretched one hand forward, sought something to hold, and pulled himself along. There was a long time before he mustered the effort to do it again. The hand crept forward, grasped at some weeds, and the arm pulled the body a few more inches. He had been doing this all his life, it seemed. He was born on the

BOOK TITLE

ground, in pain and bloody, his life leaking from almost a half dozen holes in body and limbs. Thirst was but a word; his mouth and throat were as devoid of moisture as the sands of Death Valley.

But he had to keep moving. He snaked his arm out, grasped, and pulled again, and lay until strength returned. And he did it once more. And once more. Somewhere ahead was the road, the highway. If his prayers were answered someone was bound to come along on that highway sooner or later and find him. It had better be sooner; even if he reached the road he might not last long enough if they took their time coming or missed seeing him.

He reached and pulled one last time before darkness cloaked his senses.

* * *

Blue Warton was a tall, pleasant skeleton of a man, bald since his twenties and a loose collection of long bones beneath weathered skin. He had been driving the stage for five years now, and was always on time. He was due at Clear Springs in four hours and he planned to make it early on this run.

He shaded his eyes with a knotty hand and looked ahead. A large, dark shape lay alongside the road. And as he concentrated on it to be sure it was real he saw a slight movement. Calling "Whoa!" to his team and gently pulling back the reins he brought the stage to a stop just before the figure.

"Why are we stopping?" A passenger, a large, city-clad, self-important man asked, sticking his head out of the stage.

"Looks like somebody needs help," Blue explained in his high, self-effacing voice. He clambered down from the box, his long legs making the task easy and awkward at the same time. He went over to the man who lay beside the road. He was a big man, heavy, and when Blue turned him over he saw the U.S. Marshal badge. "He's a Marshal! He's been hurt bad."

The man of importance got out of the coach, and helped the other passenger, a young woman, descend with him. He went over to Blue and the Marshal.

"What can we do for him?"

"I hope we kin halp him," Blue said, going back to the coach. He grabbed a couple of blankets from inside and the canteen from the box and came back.

The young woman knelt beside the wounded man. She was in a fine dress, but showed no sign of being overly prim. "What can I do?"

Blue directed her in propping him up with one blanket and covering him with the other. "Maybe we can do something about them wounds," he said. "I got some bandages an stuff; maybe not enough, but we can try."

"I'll get them," said the businessman, rummaging around the box until he found them. He knelt on the other side. "I learned some first aid in the war," he said. "You know how to make a tourniquet?"

"To stop the bleeding?" Blue scratched his bald head. "Yeah, I think so." He hunted around for some good thick wood and found two or three sticks. They used lengths of the bandages and the sticks for tourniquets on the arm and leg wounds as the young woman made gauze pads for the body wounds. It took time but they managed to get the bleeding under some control.

"R-rustlers," the Marshal murmured. "Val-valley."

The businessman pulled out a pocket flask and poured a couple of sips down the Marshal's throat. He coughed and sputtered, but swallowed enough to doze off again. He lay still and quiet, but breathing.

"Thanks," Blue said. "That's probably just what he needed."

The businessman nodded as he replaced the flask in his pocket. "Kills the pain." When the young woman cast a questioning glance he added, "Pardon."

"That's quite all right. I don't use spirits myself, but I'm not a temperance crusader, either."

Blue and the businessman carefully lifted the Marshal into the carriage. Both of his passengers agreed to stay inside and Blue started to climb the box. "It's gonna be a bumpy ride anyways you do it, but I'm gonna try to make it easy for him." His long arms and legs easily pulled him into the driver's seat.

"We'll try to keep him still as best we can," the young

woman said.

* * *

Kat, Laredo and Billy came out of the saloon and saw Clem standing at the stagecoach office. He glanced nervously at his watch two of three times in the short minute it took to walk over to him.

"Expectin' somebody on the stage Clem?" Kat asked.

"Yes; the new schoolmarm. I'm gonna feature her in the next paper. Stage was due about a half hour ago. Hope bandits didn't hold 'em up." He checked the watch again.

"You know," Laredo said, "it always seems to me time goes slower the more you look at your watch."

Clem chuckled. "I guess so." A rumble and dust cloud was heard and seen at the end of town. "Here it comes now."

"Bet the new schoolmarm is an old maid an' ugly as sin," Billy said to Laredo.

"Bet she is," Laredo agreed. "My ol' schoolmarm sure was."

"I hear she's young and pretty," Clem said, winking to Kat.

"Oh?" Billy straightened his bandana and brushed futilely at his clothes. "Maybe we oughta stick around an' find out. Whattayou say, Laredo?"

"Sounds like a good idea to me." He ran a hand through his hair.

"We've got a ranch to run," Kat said, placing a hand at the back of each. "For now anyways, the only female you two are gonna see is the one payin' you. Now git to your horses!" She gave each a shove and they pretended to lose balance stumbling to their horses.

"She ain't no fun," Laredo said as he lifted a foot to his stirrup.

"Nope. Never was," Billy said.

Kat gave Billy a swat on the behind as he swung up. "Git." But she was trying to hold back a grin at their teasing as she mounted her own horse.

They were at the other end of town by the time the coach pulled up.

"Hey! We need halp here!" Blue cried as he clambered

down. "Somebody get the doc! I gotta wounded man here!" He was already opening the coach and helping the new schoolmarm down as the businessman exited from the other side and came around. A bystander, after rubbernecking a moment to see the exhibition, ran to get the doctor. Clem helped Blue and the businessman ease the Marshal out of the coach and carried him to the doctor's as Doc Murray met them about half-way.

"Where did you find him?" Doc asked first off.

Blue filled him in as they carried him into Doc's office. The schoolmarm followed at a little distance at first before coming in and standing in the parlor waiting room. She paced a bit while she heard them tending to the man inside.

It was nearly an hour later when Doc and the other two men came out.

"Will he be all right, doctor?" the schoolmarm asked.

Doc shook his head doubtfully. "He's lost a lot of blood. He's still unconscious right now, an' I don't think he'll be wakin' up anytime soon." He frowned at her curiously. "Are you any relation, miss?"

"No. I just hope he'll be all right. It's terrible, the way he was shot."

"Yeah, an' I've seen more'n my share of 'em since movin' out west."

"Pardon me, miss," Clem said, "but are you the new schoolmarm?"

The title took her a little by surprise but she recovered with a smile. "Yes, I'm the new schoolteacher."

"I'm Clem Grange, editor of the local paper. I'd like to do a story on you for the next edition."

She smiled again. "Thank you, Mr. Grange. I'm Amy Sawyer."

"A pleasure." Clem took her hand and led her toward the door. He wanted to steer her away from the operating room where Doc still had some work to do. "If you'll wait here a moment?"

"Of course, Mr. Grange."

Clem took a step or two back to Doc. "Let me know if there's anything I can do. And let me know if he wakes up or says anything."

"Sure will, Clem," Doc said.

CHAPTER SEVENTEEN

As they rode back to the ranch Billy trailed behind Laredo and kept his eyes on him. When they were in town Sheriff Stokes had gestured to him to come into his office. He had shown Billy a telegram received by him while Billy was away on the cattle drive. The contents of the telegram was very interesting.

"I was gonna take it to... a certain party," Stokes had said, "but since you took the trouble of sendin' it for me in the first place I thought I'd let you look at it first. You can deliver it to whoever you please."

The telegram was still hidden in Billy's pocket. He hadn't decided just what he was going to do with it.

The possibilities multiplied themselves like jack-rabbits in his mind.

* * *

Clem saw Miss Sawyer to her hotel room and she agreed to an interview once she was settled. On his way out he passed by the businessman who had arrived with her on the stage. There was something familiar about him, but Clem couldn't place it. He shrugged and started down the walk. He had some time to kill so he stopped in the telegraph office.

"Hi Gabe," he said. "Anything new over the wire?"

"Clem. No, nothing today."

"Billy Holcomb pick up anything when he was in town a few minutes ago?"

"Clem, I've told you before I can't discuss customers' business. An' I haven't seen him, neither."

Clem smiled a little. Gabe Hayes had said plenty without saying much.

The key started to click. Hayes started to grab pencil and

paper but put them back.

"That's a message coming in, isn't it?" Clem asked.

"Yeah, but not for here."

"What do you mean?"

"There's a code at the beginning of each message saying what station the message is intended for. That code's for another station."

"So you don't have to take down the message."

Hayes nodded. "It's a kinda honor system we got in the telegraph business so we don't intercept messages we shouldn't."

"That's interesting." Clem sat on the corner of Hayes' desk. "A little bit of information I might slip into the paper sometime when I need to fill space."

Hayes shrugged. "No skin off my nose."

"Then you know what those codes are, in addition to the Morse?"

"Have to. I might need to send a message to one o' them stations sometime."

Clem rubbed his chin with his forefinger. "Where's *that* station, for example?"

"The one for that message? It's some private station up the line."

"Individuals can have their own telegraph stations?"

"Sure. There ain't many of 'em, though."

"Get many messages from it?"

"Been a couple for Billy once in a while."

"Really?" Clem concealed his rising interest. "Any idea where that station is?"

"Not exactly." Hayes eyes narrowed and his brows overshadowed them. "Now listen here, this is getting awfully close to private information."

Clem stepped back a bit. "Sorry Gabe; didn't mean any offense. Any problem though with my usin' that bit about private stations in the paper?"

Hayes' glare remained on him a moment longer before easing up and saying, "No; guess not. Just don't mention about anybody getting messages like that."

"I won't. But thanks, Gabe." Clem stepped back outside and

headed for his office. *Suppose those telegrams have something to do with whoever rustled Kat's herd? Does that mean Billy's working against her too?*

He entered his office and sat at his desk, pondering what he'd learned. Maybe Kat ought to know about it; or maybe not. Billy might be getting those messages for her. But if so, where was this private telegraph station, and who ran it?

The little bell over his street door jingled as it opened.

"Mr. Grange, I'd like to do that interview with you now."

Clem looked up and a charming smile warmed his face. He rose from his chair and pulled another one close to the desk. "Of course, Miss Sawyer. Please, have a seat. Would you like me to put on some coffee or tea?"

* * *

The telegraph key started clicking again and Hayes took down the message. It was from that private station and addressed to someone named Hammond. Hayes was puzzled as he decoded it; there was no one named Hammond in town or at any of the ranches or farms outside of it. But obviously it was somebody and it was his duty to take any messages to the Clear Springs station.

He had no sooner signaled receipt of the message when a large man in city clothes entered. "My name is Hammond. I expect to receive a telegram some time today. I'm staying at the hotel; can you send word when it comes?"

Hayes' jaw dropped open.

"What, do fools run the telegraph around here? Pick your jaw up, man, and answer my question."

Hayes gulped. "Sorry, mister. It's just that a message just came for you. I just finished decoding it." He handed the paper to Hammond.

Hammond snatched it from him and read it. Hayes could see Hammond didn't like what he read. Hammond crumpled the message, tossed it, and went out the door.

Hayes watched him go and did something the townspeople swore he never did: he rose from his chair. Then he circled round his desk, and picked up the fallen message. He already knew what it said, having deciphered it, but it might be of interest later.

* * *

The man who called himself Dawson knew he was on the last leg of the trip.

The road, if you wanted to call it that, was narrow and surrounded on both sides by high rocks. He didn't know just where Larson had his place but he expected to be led the rest of the way.

He was tall, clean-shaven, and about forty. He wore business clothes, but not so fancy or expensive as businessmen back east did. The suit was dark and the vest gray; not much different from a man of business in the west. Dawson was more comfortable in typical range wear, flannel and denim, but he had worn all kinds of clothing in his time, and the suit fit the role he was playing now.

A warning shot spat gravel and stones at his horse's flank. He struggled to steady him.

"You Dawson?" an unseen voice called from the rocks above.

"If I say 'yeah,' are you going to kill me for it?" Dawson answered.

"No. Just makin' sure. The boss don't want nobody comin' in unless they're expected, y' see?"

"Sure." He saw the upper body of a man rise from the rocks just far enough to wave to someone below him before vanishing behind his little fortress again. A second man appeared from behind the lower rocks and descended the rest of the way to the trail.

"Follow me," the man said, taking a firm grip of the reins which prevented any argument.

The way was circuitous and there were several offshoots. If he had tried to find his way back on his own he'd surely get lost. The trail opened into what resembled a typical front yard and a small house stood beyond a hitch rail. A few similar outbuildings were scattered about.

"Just tie up an' I'll tell Larson you're here," his guide said as he vanished inside the cabin.

Dawson hitched his horse and waited. As he had assumed the role of a businessman he continued to play the part.

His guide re-appeared. "What the hell you doin' standin' out here for? Get the hell inside!"

Dawson shrugged it off; Larson had probably told the man off for not bringing him in right away and the man was taking it out on him. He thanked the man and stepped inside. Larson was smoking a big cheap cigar; that matched Larson, a big cheap bully.

Larson leaned his chair against the wall and enjoyed his cigar. "Hello, Dawson." It was more challenge than greeting.

"Larson. I think I know why you wanted to see me."

Larson's mouth twisted up on one side. "Oh, you *think* you know?"

"Yeah. It's about the cattle."

"Ahuh. The cattle you were to sell for me."

"I heard from one of the cattle buyers; Spencer it was. Some gal from the Bar C showed up and claimed they were hers. Somehow they got the Marshal in on it, an' he's holdin' up the beeves until it's cleared up."

"Yeah. The man you hired as trail boss got to talkin' to the... the gal. Prob'ly took a shine to her. He said a little too much."

"I kept away from it as best I could after hiring Simmons. He seemed a likely man for the job."

"Except he couldn't keep his mouth shut. Especially to a pretty female."

Dawson shrugged.

"So some Marshal got to investigatin', huh?"

"Yeah."

"He ask you any questions?"

"He didn't find me. I stayed a few miles away in Grantville like you told me after Simmons left."

Larson stood up slowly. "That Marshal might be on your trail without you knowin' it. He mighta even seen you headed this way."

Dawson smiled and shook his head. "Nope; I been around enough to when I'm bein' trailed."

"But not enough to keep from makin' mistakes."

Dawson shrugged again. "I'm only human."

"Yeah. Humans make mistakes. Humans die for their mistakes sometimes too; you know that?"

Dawson tensed and casually drew aside his coat to reveal the Remington hanging at his hip. "You gonna kill me, Larson?"

"No. You're my guest." He called over Dawson's shoulder: "Butch! Grady!" He then smiled to Dawson. "And while you're here I think you should see some of the sights." Butch and Grady came in. "Butch, you and Grady take Dawson here on the tour. Say, I've got an idea: why don't you show him that spot that Crandall liked so much?" He turned to Dawson. "It's a nice high spot. You can see quite a lot from there. Why, I'll bet you'll think you're even getting a glimpse of Eternity." With a jerk of his head Larson sent them on their way.

As he heard them ride off Larson leaned his chair back and enjoyed the rest of his cigar.

* * *

At noon Billy Holcomb rode in from his shift and when the others headed for the bunkhouse for some sleep he walked over to the main house. Kat was alone at the table, writing up some accounts. The sale of the cattle had stayed off the wolf for now, but she couldn't count on the Marshal clearing up the business of the brands in time to make up some of her other bills. The men had drawn their pay for the drive, but they knew that might be it for a spell.

She looked up as Billy entered. "Hey Billy. What's on your mind?"

Billy sat opposite her. "How much do you know about this Laredo?"

Her sigh was heavy and wearied. "That again? I know enough to trust him."

"Maybe. What do you know about him before he came here?"

"Nothin'. An' I don't need to know nothin' about it, either. Since he's been here he's done nothin' but help." Her green eyes bored into his. "An' if it's jealousy that's drivin' this, drop it. I ain't lookin' to go sparkin' an' spoonin' with the likes of him. Or the likes of you, for that matter."

"It ain't that," Billy lied. "But we're old friends, an' I jest wanna look out for ya."

"Much obliged; but I can look out for myself, as far as menfolk goes."

Billy stayed quiet a while and Kat went back to her figuring. Impatience and curiosity made her look up again. "What?"

"S'pose I knew somethin' about this Laredo; somethin' bad."

"Like what?"

"Jest s'pose. Should I tell him or you or the Sheriff?"

"How bad?"

"Bad as it gets."

Kat put her pencil down. Her fair face clouded. "You mean... like murder?"

Billy nodded.

"You're sayin' Laredo's a killer?"

"S'pose he was wanted somewheres for a killin'. What would you say?"

Kat considered a long moment. "I think I'd want to talk to him first; find out what it was about. Maybe whoever it was *needed* killin'."

Billy pursed is lips and nodded, mulling this over. "Maybe. I've known men like that. But I didn't kill 'em."

Kat was getting tired of this. "What's this about, Billy? You find out somethin' about Laredo or not?"

"Maybe." He started rolling a cigarette. "Didn't Bear call him Pete or something once?"

"Bear was wounded, prob'ly outta his mind with pain. Pete coulda been anybody he knew; don't have to be Laredo."

"You might be right." He stood up. "You might be right at that." He went out the door and started toward the bunkhouse.

Kat watched him go. When she returned to her figuring the numbers were a jumble. *What had Billy found out? Or what was it he thought he knew?*

Laredo was out riding somewhere. She might take a ride out, and she might find him. And if she found him she might ask him about it. And he might not give her an honest answer.

BOOK TITLE

* * *

Hammond sat in his room at the hotel, drumming his fingers on the writing desk. Things weren't going as promised at all. And he was sick of all those clandestine meetings. From now on he was dealing things in the open. That last telegram was also the last straw. He wasn't going to wait much longer.

This was Thursday. If he didn't hear anything in forty-eight hours, he was going to take matters in his own hands.

* * *

"Come with me for a couple of hours, will you Bear?" Laredo asked. With no cattle to mind and no immediate chores they had some time on their hands. "I want to show you something I came across and see if you come to the same conclusion about it I did."

"Sure."

Laredo led the way to the stretch of shale and the dark, thick ooze seeping from the cracks. They came down from their horses and squatted on either side of one of the cracks.

"Take a taste."

Bear stuck a gloved finger in the little pool that formed, sniffed it, and gave it a tentative lick. He told Laredo what he thought it was.

Laredo nodded. "That was my guess to." They stood up. "Bear, I think I have an idea now what this whole thing has been about."

CHAPTER EIGHTEEN

Kat heard two horsemen ride up and put her pencil down. She spun the cylinder of her revolver and let it sit easy and ready in its holster. Determination knitted her brows over the green fire of her eyes as she stepped out onto the porch. Laredo and Bear came down from saddles and started toward her.

"Kat!" Laredo called, "I think we've figgered out what's goin' on!"

"Don't take another step," Kat ordered.

Her tone froze them, as if her gaze were that of Medusa herself. Laredo and Bear exchanged glances before Laredo attempted to speak.

"But Kat — we got news for you."

"An' I just got news about you — Pete."

Laredo blanched beneath his sun-burnt hide.

"That's your real name, ain't it?" Kat challenged, "Pete? What's the rest of it? Pete What?"

Laredo stayed silent, but she could tell he was shaken. Bear looked even more anxious for his friend.

"Who'd you kill, Pete? Huh?" Kat was relentless. "Was it in a fair fight, or did you plug him in the back?"

Laredo stirred himself. "Who you been talkin' to, Kat? Who fed you this?"

"Never mind. I wanna hear it from you. Who was it, Pete? Is there maybe a wanted poster on you? Maybe even a reward?"

"Maybe." Laredo went on the defensive. "You gonna go to the Sheriff?"

"Maybe." Kat waited for a shoe that didn't drop. "Not that I expect much of him. But I thought I'd give you a chance to talk first. So what about it, Pete? Did you kill somebody? Is the law after you for it?"

"My business is private." Laredo slammed shut the vault.

Kat nodded. The staring match with Laredo came to a draw

so she turned to Bear. "What about you, Bear? You're the one called him Pete back when you got hurt. What do you know about this?"

"It's Laredo's business, like he said." Bear's easy-going manner was gone, though the drawl was still there. "If he ain't tellin', then I ain't neither."

Kat rested her right hand on her gun butt and dug her left into her jeans. She pulled out a few bills and set them on the porch rail. "That's a week's pay for both of you. You've got an hour to get off my land. Banty's pay's in there too. He's goin' with you."

"You'll be short-handed again," Laredo said. He knew it was a weak argument even before presenting it.

Kat shrugged. "There's no cattle to watch; an' that means no cattle to steal. I won't need more hands until we get word of the sale in Double Rock an' I got money to buy more stock."

"Then what?"

"I dunno, 'ceptin' I sure won't be hirin' you three back. Now git!" Her hand tightened around the butt.

Laredo signaled to Bear with a twitch of his head. They mounted and rode off.

Kat watched them go. Something salty and wet started down her cheek and she brushed it away with the back of her hand. Once they were out of sight she went back in the house.

* * *

Clem looked up as his visitor entered the newspaper office. He rose from his chair and came round the desk to meet him. "Hi. I'm Clem Grange, the editor. You're the man who was on the stage the other day, aren't you?"

Hammond came forward. "Yes. My name's Roger Hammond." He extended a hand with his business card in it. Clem took the card expecting to shake the hand but it was withdrawn before he could. "You newspapermen know about everything goes on in a town."

Clem smiled. "I'd like to think so. Keeps us in business."

"And I believe I can trust in your discretion."

Clem smiled again and added a nod. "Thanks for your

confidence. What can I do for you?"

"I'd like some information. How do I get to the Crandall ranch?"

"The Bar C?" Clem gave him directions. "You got some business with Kat Crandall?"

"Let's say for now I've heard about the place and might take a ride out there in a day or two. Here's where I count on your discretion to keep it quiet."

"Sure, Mr. Hammond. You can count on me."

"Thank you." Hammond touched his hat. "Good day to you, Grange." He went out the door like a man with purpose.

Clem looked at the card and his eyes narrowed with interest. This looked like a clue to Kat's troubles. He pocketed the card and stepped outside. Hammond was no longer on the street, and Clem went over to the telegraph office.

* * *

Laredo and Bear found Banty and when they were alone told him the news.

"You didn't tell her nothin'?" The little old man scolded him.

"No," Laredo said. "I can't let her be a part o' this."

"If anybody's got a right t' know, it's her!" Banty kept on. "I know yer sweet on her, Pete. Aw, don't gimme that look."

"It might be dangerous for her, Banty."

"It's dangerous for her already," Banty said. "Who you think told her? Who you think knows?"

Laredo shrugged.

"There's only one who's got reason," Banty pressed on, "an' you know who it is as well as I do."

"Yeah," Bear said. "She's known that Billy Holcomb since they was little. I bet he's the one told her."

"Sure," Laredo agreed, "but who did he know?"

"Want me to go fetch him so's we can find out?" Bear offered. The dark frown on his otherwise gentle face suggested how he might handle the questioning.

"No. 'Sides, he's in the bunkhouse an' that means goin' back on the ranch."

They rode in silence a ways until Laredo spoke.

"C'mon; I got somethin' I wanna show you."

He led the way to the place Kat had shown him where her father's body was found. As they drew closer he pulled up and his two companions stopped with him.

"What is it?" Banty asked, and then saw the dark form lying near the trail ahead, just below the high rocks.

The three rode up and dismounted, gathering around the corpse. It was a man of about forty in a business suit.

"Ever see him before?" Laredo asked the others and received two negative shakes of heads.

Banty checked him over. "No billfold or papers to put a name to him. Got a bump on the head, but that mighta come from the fall. Same with them bumps an' bruises." He rocked the head side to side and it lolled loose as a rag-doll's. "Neck's broken; prob'ly the fall."

Laredo nodded. "Interestin'. A might interestin'."

"This ain't what you wanted to show us," Bear said.

"No."

"An' what makes it interestin'?" the big man added.

"This body ain't what I wanted to show you, but this spot is. Kat showed it to me." He let them wait a moment, as they waited for his explanation. "This is where they found Kat's dad." He pointed to the corpse. "He was layin' right here."

* * *

Clem stopped in at the telegraph office. He wasn't expecting a wire but might pick up some news. "Howdy, Gabe."

"Howdy, Clem."

"How's business?"

"It comes an' goes. An' you know I can't talk about it."

Clem sat on the corner of Hayes' desk. "Sure Gabe, I know." He seemed to realize he was holding a business card in his hand and casually laid it on the table as if to see what it was.

Hayes tossed just as casual a glance at it, frowned with his mouth open a bit for a second, and slid it back to Clem. "Dropped yer card."

"Thanks." Clem put it in a pocket. "Stranger dropped by my

office earlier and left it." Hayes made no reply but Clem could tell one was itching to get out. "He came off the stage, and he's staying at the hotel."

"Ahuh. Lotsa folks git off stages an' stay in hotels."

Billy Holcomb entered the office and stopped when he heard Clem and Gabe talking.

"Seems to be some businessman from back east. Name of Hammond. Maybe he'll give you some business."

"How so?"

"Oh, he might need to send a wire or two back to his office." Again Hayes looked like he was about to speak. "Might even get one while he's here."

"You one o' them mind readers?" Hayes asked. "Durn if he didn't get a wire when he first come into town."

"Is that so?" Clem chuckled. "No Gabe, I don't read minds. Just a lucky guess, I suppose."

"Wal, I just 'member 'cause it come in same time he did."

"You always did provide good service, Gabe."

"I try."

"Anything new 'bout that Marshal what got shot?" Gabe asked.

"No; doc says he's wakin' up more often though. He says that means that coma is over with an' he's just restin'. Startin' to take some food — mostly soup and crackers — from the hotel."

"That's good news." Gabe looked up. "Got nothin' for you, Billy. You got somethin' for me?"

"No; just stopping by. I see you're busy."

"Oh, we're just gossippin' like a couple of housewives," Clem said with a grin. "Sit an' have a yarn with us."

"No. Thanks; maybe another time." He left in what seemed to Clem to be a bit of a hurry.

Bet he's headed over Doc's, he thought.

* * *

Billy started over toward Doc's and stopped.

Laredo and his pals were riding in. The little one, Banty, was riding double with Laredo because a body was draped over his horse, led by the big Bear. He didn't know who the body was but he didn't want to take a chance of the three seeing him. He turned between two buildings and watched around the corner until they took the body inside. He counted ten to be sure and went to his horse.

He had learned a lot inside a few minutes; and without even asking.

* * *

"Who is he?" Doc asked when the corpse was laid on a cot beside Marshal Conrad in the small sick ward in the back of Doc's office.

"Don't know; didn't have papers on him." Laredo smiled when he looked over to the other cot. "Say, Marshal. You look a lot better."

Conrad was sitting up propped by a stack of pillows and cushions. "I'm still weak; can't move much." But that deep, growling voice sounded healthy enough. "Least that's what Doc says. Can't remember just how I got shot an' ended up here. An' I guess I been noddin' off from time to time." He looked over to the other cot. "He a dead 'un?"

Laredo nodded. "My pals an' I found him out yonder a ways. He mighta fallen."

Conrad studied him. "Sounds like you doubt it."

"Or he mighta been pushed," Laredo added.

"Just as likely." The lawman in him rose to give him a brief shot of strength and he raised up on an elbow a bit for a better look. A grimace expressed the pain of the maneuver, but not groan. "Seems I know him; or at least I seen him somewheres."

Laredo and Bear slid the cot a bit closer to the Marshal and the un-wheeled frame scratched a complaint into tiled floor. Conrad took a good look at the face.

"You seen him?" Laredo asked.

"Yeah. Only once, but I remember faces. It's part o' the job."

"Do you know his name?"

Conrad frowned and nodded. "Called himself Dawson."

"Dawson? He's the one who was gonna sell Kat's stolen cattle."

The word "cattle" pulled a trigger on Conrad's memory. The

frown deepened as he mined his memory. Words dragged themselves out."Cattle. Stolen cattle. Those two men. Gunfight." The frown became a determined glare as he said. "I think I know where those cattle thieves are hidin'."

CHAPTER NINETEEN

Billy was making good time until he heard hoof-beats behind him. He turned off the road and hid his horse among the rocks above. Dismounting he drew his rifle from the boot and crouched where he had a good view of the road.

It was Clem Grange. What Billy had heard in the telegraph office Clem had heard too. From the direction Grange was headed Billy figured he was going to tell Kat, and that wouldn't do.

* * *

Clem felt something skim along the side of his head and the impact threw him from the saddle. He landed hard and took stock a moment. Everything moved, but his head felt like someone had set off a ton of blasting powder inside it. Blood streamed down the side of his face. He tried sitting up and his head spun like a child's top. He lay back down; that felt better.

* * *

"Jumpin' Jehoshaphat!" Banty exclaimed. "There's another one!"

A figure lay on the road ahead, but at least this one moved. And the horse was grazing nearby.

"Sure is a boomer crop o' bodies," Bear said.

"But this one's alive," Laredo said.

They rode over and sat beside him.

"It's Clem!" Bear brought his canteen and leaned Clem up enough for him to drink. "Easy there, pardner."

The water revived him a bit. "Wh—what happened?"

"Looks like somebody tried to scalp you with a bullet," Laredo said.

Banty was already coming with bandages. He pulled out a hip flask too.

Clem started to reach for the flask.

Banty held it away. "No, Clem; ain't for yer stomick. It's for yer head." He wet the wound with whiskey and Clem yelled out in pain.

"That hurts more than the wound!" he said.

"It'll kill what ails ya," Banty said. "A doc tol' me that oncet. Now hol' still while I bandage ya up."

The burning was subsiding. Clem nodded as he remembered. "Yeah. Read that somewhere myself. Alcohol's an antiseptic."

"I dunno 'bout that," Bear said, "but many a shot o' whiskey has taken care o' my pains."

Clem chuckled as he winced.

Banty did a good job; the bandage was tight and secure.

"Think you can ride?" Laredo asked.

"I can give it a try."

They helped him into the saddle. They tied him to his stirrup straps to make sure he didn't fall. He held on tight, his eyes shut and his head down.

"I can ride if somebody leads my horse," he said. "Not sure of my navigation with my head like this."

"Sure." Banty took the reins. "Where were you headed?"

"The Bar C. I've got some news Kat needs to hear."

The two looked at Laredo. All three had been barred from the ranch.

"Will this help find the varmints who rustled her cattle an' been tryin' to drive her outta business?" Laredo asked.

"I hope so."

"OK; the Bar C it is."

* * *

Kat was sitting in the rocking chair on the porch while Laredo was on the bench beside her enjoying a smoke.

"So Laredo has a past," Rawhide said. "Hell Kat, we all got a past. How d'you know I don't have a secret reason for hidin' my name behind Rawhide?"

"You've been with us too long for it to matter," Kat said. "My daddy trusted you so I trust you."

"But you don't trust Laredo?"

"Not anymore I don't."

Rawhide waited a moment. "You think Billy was tellin' the truth, that he thinks Laredo killed somebody?"

"You sound like you doubt it." Kat stopped rocking and studied him.

"Maybe he did, maybe he didn't. I don't know. An' I don't know where Billy got his information, an' neither do you."

Kat pondered that a moment.

"'Sides, seems to me Billy's got other motives fer bad-mouthin' Laredo."

"Like what?"

"You know he's allus been sweet on you."

Kat dismissed that with a sniff.

"He mighta come up with this just to get between you two."

"There ain't nothin' between me an' Laredo fer Billy to break up."

"You sure?"

Kat's face turned red as her hair.

Four riders approached and Rawhide shaded his eyes to see. "Talk about the Devil an' he comes a-ridin'."

Kat shot to her feet, her fists tight at her sides. "I told that varmint an' his crew to get off my range and stay off."

Rawhide looked closer. "That fourth one looks like he's hurt. Say, I think it's Clem Grange."

"Clem?" The anger eased a bit and her fingers unclenched. She stepped off the porch and Rawhide followed as the four pulled up.

Laredo and his pals dismounted and Bear helped Clem down. Clem swayed on his feet a little but steadied himself at the hitch rail.

Ignoring the other three Kat hurried over to him. "Clem! What happened? Who did this to you?"

"Can't say for sure. Somebody bushwhacked me; this thick skull of mine's the only thing saved me."

Kat came to the other side of the hitch rail and put an arm around his shoulder for support. "C'mon, let's get you inside."

As Kat helped Clem into the ranch house, Laredo and his friends glanced at each other as though asking whether to stay or go.

"Well," Rawhide said, "aren't you comin' inside?"

They exchanged one more glance and followed him in.

Clem was lying on a couch in the living room, his head propped with some cushions. Kat was kneeling by his side.

"Coffee'll be ready in a moment," she said. Turning to Laredo she asked, "Where did you find him?"

"On the road between town an' here," Laredo said. "The bullet just grazed him. Guess whoever shot him figgered he'd done the job."

Clem put a hand on Kat's shoulder. "I got something to tell you."

"It can wait, Clem."

"No it can't. There's this businessman in town; came off the last stage. Name's Hammond. He's an oil man from back east."

"An oil man?" Laredo said.

"Yeah. Says he's gonna ride out here, maybe tomorrow," Clem continued. "Seemed the impatient sort; don't know why he was gonna wait. He's been in town a couple of days already."

Kat sat back on her heels. "Why would an oil man wanna speak to me?"

"I think I know why, Kat," Laredo said. "An' I think it's why Larson has been tryin' to get you to give up."

Kat came to her feet and faced him. "I don't know what you're talkin' about — Pete. I'm much obliged to you for findin' Clem an' bringin' him here. Probl'ly saved his life, an' he's a good friend. But I said before I want you gone..."

"Even after I tell you what this whole thing is about?"

"I think you oughtta listen to him, Kat. This thing is startin' to make sense to me too; an' if Laredo he's going to say what I think he is, you oughtta listen."

The tempting, beckoning aroma of fresh brewed coffee decided her. They poured mugs of it and all but Clem sat around the table. After Laredo told Kat and Rawhide what he and Bear had found she was quiet.

"Oil; on my daddy's land," was all she could say.

"Makes sense now, don't it?" Clem said from the couch.

"Just about," Laredo said. He turned to Rawhide. "Is Billy around?"

Rawhide seemed to awaken from a daydream. "No, come to think of it I haven't seen him for a while. He might be most anywheres."

"Like maybe out dry-gulching newspaper editors?" Laredo asked with a glance toward Clem.

Clem gave a solemn smile and nodded.

* * *

Slim was on guard duty this afternoon. The sun was hot and turned the rocks that were his fortress of concealment into burning coals. There was a flat rock just beside him, and he bet himself he could put a fry pan on it and cook a meal. He was getting hungry anyway; the three sandwiches he had packed for himself before starting his shift were long gone. For that matter he hadn't been eating that good since working for Larson. And there were other things too.

There were those three men the other day, and Dawson the day before, who knew who else. And who knew who might be next.

He asked himself now why he had even sided with Larson in the first place. He never had anything against Kat. As to working for a female, if he was to work for one he'd rather it be Kat. Why, she most seemed like one of the boys anyhow.

A rider was coming and he got his binoculars. It was Billy Holcomb. What was he doing here? He seemed to know where he was riding, too.

Slim saw the other guard, to his left and closer to the trail, wave Billy on by. He'd heard Billy was working for Kat. Or was he? Lefty down below had waved him in as though expecting him.

If Kat thought Billy was working for her, but he was really a traitor, she ought to know about it.

Slim breathed a rare curse. He'd had enough. He gathered his gear and backed down from his perch. He had ridden in by a back trail which the other look-outs could not see, so his withdrawal would be unseen.

* * *

"Who do you think shot you, Clem?" Kat asked.

Sounds of an approaching rider interrupted his answer. Banty went to the door. "Some huge galoot I never saw before." The sound of heavy feet hit the porch. "Maybe you know him Kat?"

Banty stepped away to let the large newcomer enter. He stood just outside the threshold, hat in hand, a meek expression on his huge face.

"Miss Kat, kin I come in?"

Kat rose from the table and came half-way toward him. Her voice was firm. "Why are you here, Slim? You bringin' me a message from your boss Larson?"

Laredo drew his gun and the others followed. With four guns on him even the huge Slim cowered, taking a step back. He seemed a black silhouette against the red, setting sun, filling the frame of the doorway.

"No! Wait! I'm here on my own." He dropped his hat and raised his hands. "I don't mean to hurt nobody." With his left hand he slowly unbuckled his gunbelt, let it fall, and kicked it aside.

Kat relaxed a little. "I think it's all right. Lower your guns."

"Kin I come in now?" Slim asked after the guns were put away. "I got somethin' to tell you."

Kat had to chuckle. "You an' about everybody else today. Come on in an' pour yourself some joe."

The coffee did smell good, and Slim had only the water in his canteen all day. He poured a mug and took a sip.

"Sit down," Kat said, moving back to the table and setting an example, "and say what you have to say."

They all came to the table again. Clem made the experiment of sitting up and though it made his head ring he managed to remain upright.

"I've quit Larson. I'm tired o' all the killin'."

"Oh? Who's been killed, Slim?"

"Well, there was Hank an' the three men the other day..."

"What three men?" Laredo asked.

"I dunno who they were. Three men came snoopin' into the valley, an' the men on guard shot it out with 'em. Killed 'em."

"Who was on guard?" Kat asked. "Two of my former hands?"

"No ma'am. These were two that Larson hired later. He's got about twice as many now as he had."

"You sure there were three killed?" Laredo asked.

"That's what they said. Seems one mighta crawled off a ways, but they figgered he just died somewheres else an' they just didn't find him."

Kat turned to Laredo. "What are you talkin' about?"

"Remember Marshal Conrad from Double Rock?"

"Sure; he was going to look into the brand on those cattle we thought were mine. Why?"

"The boys an' me saw him earlier at Doc's, in town." He told about the Marshal being found by the stage driver a few days before.

"Yeah, I remember," Clem said. "That's when Hammond came to town, too."

"What had happened to him?" Kat asked.

"He'd been shot."

Kat gasped.

"Think he might be the one who crawled away," Laredo added.

"Then he made it," Slim said.

"Looks like."

"What was he doin' here?" Kat asked.

Laredo shook his head. "He weren't able to say. Seems his head's still kinda cloudy on some things."

"Were there other killin's, Slim?" Kat asked.

"Yes'm. Larson had some fella called Dawson thrown off a cliff. Same cliff where we found your pa."

Laredo swore. "Prob'ly thought he was bein' cute. Instead he made a big mistake."

"Dawson was the name of the man who was sellin' my stolen cattle," Kat said.

"That's right," Laredo nodded. "An' Conrad recognized him."

"Larson had him killed 'cause the sale didn't go right, I reckon," Slim said.

Kat had to agree; it was all making sense now. "Laredo, Clem, tell Slim all you've told me."

A while later, all the stories told, Laredo turned to Kat. "Well, have I got myself back in your good graces?"

"Maybe. There's still the thing about that name Pete, and about you bein' wanted for murder."

Laredo glanced at his saddle pals. "All right; I'll tell you the truth. But just to you; nobody else."

"Deal."

They went into Kat's bedroom and shut the door. A half hour later they came out.

"Men, we're ridin' into town," Kat said. "We've got an oilman to see."

CHAPTER TWENTY

There was a knock on Hammond's hotel room door. He wasn't expecting anybody. Maybe it was that newspaperman, wanting a story, or the telegrapher with a message. He took the papers he had been working on and stuffed them in the single, shallow drawer of the small writing desk and put on his coat. Arranging himself he opened the door and stepped back in surprise.

Clem stood at the head of what looked like a committee of the local Cattleman's Association. There was a tall, broad-shouldered fellow, a short wiry old man, a third who was big as a bear, and a fourth who looked like a boy at first before Clem stepped aside a bit and Hammond saw the rounded breasts formed beneath the plaid flannel.

"Mr. Hammond, you told me you wanted to ride out to the Bar C maybe tomorrow sometime," Clem said.

"Yes." Hammond scanned the group again warily.

"Well, some of the folks at the Bar C wanted to see you too; so we took the liberty of savin' you the trip."

Hammond's response was silent astonishment, ineffectively covered by an attempt at retaining dignity.

"May we come in?" Clem asked.

Hammond sort of shook his substantial mass and said "Of course; of course. Excuse my manners." He turned and welcomed them in with a sweeping gesture.

Clem introduced them all around. Hammond was particularly interested in Kat.

"So you are Miss Crandall?" he said.

"My friends call me Kat."

"Very well, Kat."

"I don't know yet if you're my friend or not, Mr. Hammond," Kat replied in a cool tone and a steady gaze locked on his eyes. "So don't presume on me an' I won't presume on you. Fair?"

"Certainly." He was uncomfortable at being bullied by a slim female but decided it was best to overlook it for now. He gestured to the single, hard-backed chair in the room. "May I offer you a seat?"

"Thanks." Kat straddled the chair, crossing her arms on its back.

To Hammond it was no different from some ruffian in a saloon. *Am I expected to do business with this — this hoyden?*

"We can talk here or at the ranch," Kat said, "your choice."

Hammond shrugged. "Since we're all here, why waste time? I apologize for the lack of accommodations," he added to the others.

"That's all right," Laredo said. "We don't mind standin'."

"Very well. Shall I have some coffee brought up? Or perhaps you gentlemen wish something stronger?"

"We're fine."

Hammond noted that: this Laredo person seemed to speak for them. He looked around for someplace to sit and chose the large chest at the foot of the bed. It wasn't comfortable but his legs were starting to shake.

Kat got right to the point."Mr. Hammond, a while back my daddy rode out to meet someone. He didn't tell me who it was or what it was about. But your comin' here and some things my foreman Laredo tells me he mighta rode out to see you. Is that right?"

Hammond cleared his throat. "Yes; yes, we were to meet. But I never saw him."

Kat didn't seem surprised. "Didn't that bother you?"

"Yes, of course. And I was going to try to see what happened; but then he sent his representative, a man called Larson, and I submitted my proposal to him."

Kat again wasn't surprised and the glances exchanged between her and the others mirrored the same confirmation of suspicions.

"Larson had no business meeting with you," Kat said. "He wasn't sent by my daddy, and had no authority to speak with you."

"Larson arranged to meet me at what he said was an old

line shack on the Crandall property."

"The shack we found, Kat," Laredo said.

"I know." Kat answered without turning to him. "What was your business with my father?"

Hammond took out one of his cards and offered it to her. "I represent one of the major oil companies back east. My firm had received a telegram from your father that a possible oil deposit had been found on your property. We replied that we were interested, and sent some men to confirm."

"I knew nothing about this."

"Larson dealt with them, I understand."

"Ahuh." Kat let that sound cover a heap of territory.

"Larson at first said he'd get back to us with your father's decision. Then we learned or your father's death. Larson has been handling things ever since, meeting me at that line shack, but he's been stalling me for months."

Kat stood up and gestured to Laredo. The room was too small for a private conference, but Kat wanted Hammond to hear anyway.

"This stinks of Larson," Kat said. "I'll bet he found the oil an' said nothin' to daddy about it. He prob'ly lured daddy to that spot, murdered him, and met with Hammond claiming to be his representative."

Hammond rose and drew himself up. "I had nothing to do with murder. I — I heard your father died in an accident."

"Accidents can be planned, Mr. Hammond," Kat said. "Especially if sombody's got a lot to gain from one."

"Like Larson, you mean," Hammond said.

"Yeah, like Larson." Kat strode over to face Hammond. "Larson's got no claim on any o' my daddy's land. I'm his only heir, so I own every stick o' timber, every blade o' grass, an' every grain o' dirt. I owned a couple thousand head o' cattle too, until Larson an' his men rustled 'em."

"You don't think I had anything to do with that, do you?" Hammond protested.

"I don't know," Kat challenged, "did you?"

"I assure you whatever Larson has done it was on his own responsibility."

Kat's "Ahuh" again spoke volumes of hidden meaning. "Mr.

Hammond, I'm gonna take you at your word; at least for now."

"I will do anything I can to help you. You must understand, the oil rights on your property will benefit my firm as well as you."

"Yep, I suppose it will." Kat stuck out her hand. "OK, Hammond, we got us a deal. Shake."

Hammond was used to only taking the hand of a woman, perhaps kissing it, so he wasn't prepared for the firm handshake he received.

Whatever happened next, he realized, might be out of his hands.

* * *

Slim met them at the Sheriff's office. He had gone ahead to make sure Stokes was present when they brought Hammond to them.

But first, as Kat had instructed him, he stopped at Doc's to see how Marshal Conrad was doing. The Marshal was sitting up in a chair rigged with wheels.

"I had Jackson the carpenter build it for me," Doc explained. "It's just a ordinary chair with some wheels attached but it serves the purpose."

"i come from Kat Crandall," Slim explained. "She wanted me to see how you're doin'."

"I'm doin' much better," Conrad said. "Thanks. Startin' to remember some more, too."

"Good. Kat an' the others are meetin' with somebody called Hammond, over the hotel. We're hopin' to get this whole thing over with soon."

"Oh? That's good news," Conrad said. "I even remembered how to get to the rustler's hide-out, though I'm in no shape to ride there myself just yet."

Slim paled a bit.

Conrad frowned. "What's the matter, son?"

"Nuthin'. Sure too bad if you can't lead 'em there."

"I can draw a map. That Laredo fella seems like he knows his business. If I draw a map for him he can take it from there."

"Yeah, I suppose he could," Slim agreed.

"They takin' this Hammond over to the Sheriff?" Conrad asked.

"Yeah; that's where I'm meeting them."

Conrad thought a moment. "From what I've heard tell of your Sheriff, he could watch a man while he's robbin' your bank an' claim he don't have enough evidence to after him."

Slim chuckled. "You're right about that."

"Maybe I oughtta come an' watch. Just as a by-stander, you understand."

"Might be a good idea," Doc said. "Slim, you're big enough an' ugly enough to push the Marshal over to the Sheriff's in this here chair. Go ahead."

Slim was unsure of the idea but he wanted to help Kat so he agreed. The hard part was getting the chair over the sill of the doorway. Then it rattled along the boards until they reached the Sheriff's office, and Slim had to lever the chair over the sill there again too. The whole way Conrad was complaining of Slim's "driving," and Slim was half tempted to shove the chair out in the street. But assaulting a U. S. Marshal probably held a mighty big penalty, so he managed to control himself.

"What's this comin' in?" Sheriff Stokes exclaimed as Slim rolled the Marshal into the office.

"I hear Kat Crandall has been complaining to you about rustlers an' some other goin's on around her ranch," Conrad began without ceremony. "That true?"

Stokes removed the ever-present cigar from his mouth. "Well, yeah."

"An' what have you done about it?"

"Well Marshal, you know well as I that there's procedures to these things. An' you gotta have evidence before you go after rustlers. 'Sides, I don't have no idea where they're at!"

"Well I do," Conrad said.

"An' so do I," Slim added, the words escaping him before he could catch them.

Before the two lawmen could question Slim's statement Kat, Laredo and Hamilton came to the door. Kat introduced Hammond to them.

"Mr. Hammond has an interesting story to tell."

Hammond told his story as he had said it at the hotel room.

"And that's the truth. Whatever Larson has done against this woman and her ranch, I assure you I had no part in it."

"That's a lie!" Slim said.

A thunderbolt might as well have struck them all.

Conrad broke the silence. "How do you know it's a lie, Slim?"

Slim hesitated. Like before he'd spoken on impulse and wished he hadn't.

"Slim," Kat said, "whatever you say I'm not gonna hold it against you." This calmed him a bit but he was still uneasy. Kat turned to the lawmen. "Until today Slim was one of Larson's gang. He's turned against him, and he can help us get Larson if we don't press charges."

"That might not be up to us," Stokes said. "The law doesn't take kindly to rustlers and murderers."

"Then why aren't those rustlers and murderers behind bars?" Marshal Conrad said. He jerked his head to the jail in the next room. "Behind *those* bars, for instance?" Conrad glared at Stokes a moment more before giving Slim a benevolent but stern gaze. "Go on, son. Tell us what you know."

"Well, I heard things. I mean, I didn't go to any o' them meetings Larson had. But if this Mr. Hammond's the one Larson was meetin' with, an' anything Larson said was right, this man is lyin'."

"I'm telling the truth, I say!" Hammond insisted, though his nerve was shaky. "And if this man is one of Larson's gang, Sheriff, I demand you lock him up. And I might even make a charge of my own: slander!"

"Who was payin' Larson, huh?" Slim shouted. "Huh? We was getting' paid, and paid pretty good too, an' Larson never said who he got the money from." He pointed a finger at Hammond. "But this Hammond feller says he's the one who was meetin' with Larson, so he's gotta be the one who was payin' him."

Hammond squirmed. "Some money exchanged hands at times."

"An' I'll bet you gave Larson that money to close down Miss Kat's ranch," Slim accused. "An' I'll bet you weren't particular about how he done it."

"All right!" Hammond exclaimed. "I was paying Larson to close down your ranch. He rustled your cattle to sell them and make back the money. Then we were going to use it toward buying your ranch when it went up for auction."

"Kat would never sell the Bar C!" Laredo said.

"If I couldn't make the next bank payments," Kat said, "I might have had no choice. The bank would foreclose and the ranch prob'ly woulda been put up for auction."

"Part of the deal was that after the sale Larson would be put in charge of the portion of the ranch to be used for cattle raising, as well as a share in the proceeds of the oil." Hammond sighed. Prison was sure now; but somehow it felt good to let it all be known now. "But I swear I didn't have anything to do with your father's death, Miss Crandall. You've got to believe me on that."

"There was other killin's," Slim said. "You might notta known about 'em but some folks got killed."

"I can think of two," Conrad said. "An' I barely escaped myself."

"An' there was that man Dawson we found too."

"Well Sheriff," Kat said, "you gonna swear out a warrant an' ride after Larson now?"

"No. I still don't have enough evidence."

Marshal Conrad made a comment about Stokes so-called "lack of evidence." We don't need to repeat it here.

"If you're not gonna act," Conrad said, I will. An' if you don't lock up Hammond, ah' he's not here when we get the rest of 'em, you're goin' in jail to take his place." To Kat he said, "We've got a posse to form."

"You can't ride like that," Kat said.

"I know it." He turned to Slim. "Slim, shove me on back to Doc's. I think he's got my belongin's there. I'm gonna deputize as many o' you as I got extra badges. Laredo, you seem a likely sort. You an' your pals gather up any more you want until we got us a posse."

Laredo grinned dangerously. "I'll be glad to, Marshal."

"An' I'll lead the way to the hide-out." To Kat he added, "Hate to tell you this, Miss Kat, but Billy is one o' Larson's gang. Just found out today when I saw him ride into the hideout without bein' stopped."

"That's all right, Slim," Kat said. "We suspected he might be a traitor."

"Well, it might mean killin'." Slim said it so quietly it was clear he didn't want to even think it. "I knows you two go way back."

Kat's eyes were hard. "If he's got it comin' ain't nothin' to be done to stop it. Same for all of 'em."

Slim nodded.

Kat put a hand on his arm. "I'm glad you're ridin' with us, Slim."

Slim grinned and reddened. "I'm glad too, ma'am."

CHAPTER TWENTY-ONE

Dobie tied his horse and climbed up to the rock. He was Slim's replacement for the next shift. He chuckled at the nickname, knowing Slim was everything else but. That's how you get nicknames: some are from where you hail from, or at least claim to, some describe some physical trait, some describe the opposite. Slim was of the last case.

Funny, Dobie thought as he reached the summit. *Where the hell has he gone?* There was no sign of Slim; all his gear was gone with him. Dobie hadn't seen his horse below, but it might have been tied somewhere else nearby.

He crouched behind the rocks, settled himself, clicked a round into his carbine and lifted head and shoulders a little over the ridge to study the road below. Nothing was going on. He glanced to his left; his buddy Red was in place, and they waved confirmation to each other.

Where the hell was Slim? Had he just left his post early, or what? There was more than one back trail to this post; maybe he had gone down the other and Dobie had missed him. He probably got tired of waiting, or hungry, or both and saw Red spell Bennett below and figured that was enough guard duty for now. *Fat lazy buzzard*, he thought. *Oh well, it's his butt not mine.* Besides, there was no way to send word back to Larson. And he was here now, and no one was coming.

They were safe.

Dobie chuckled at that. *Yeah, real safe.* He remembered the gun battle about a week before, when those three stumbled upon the valley. That was some excitement for a while; just like plugging Yanks in the War. Funny about that third guy, though. Sounded like he was the big one, the one that somehow crawled off. Larson sent out a couple of parties; you'd think he'd been found by now.

Dobie wondered what had happened to that big guy and then shrugged it out of his thoughts. He lit a cigarette and made himself comfortable. If anyone came riding up, and Dobie doubted anyone would, he'd hear them before seeing them.

Yeah; they were safe.

* * *

Larson spouted a few words and word combinations new to Billy, and he'd been around some.

"So the Marshal made it," was the first sentence Larson said not laced with epithets. "And he's at the Doc's?"

"Yeah. I thought you ought to know right away."

"Why didn't you put a bullet in his brain and finish the job? It's not like you ain't done it before, like that Simmons."

"Simmons was gonna blow the whole thing," Billy said. "That's why I did it."

"And this Marshal might do the same thing if he don't get dead quick."

"I was headed there to take care o' that but Laredo an' his buddies showed up first."

"Why? Tell me one of 'em was hurt; hurt bad."

Billy shook his head. "No, but they was carryin' somebody with 'em. Looked like a dead'un to me."

"Who was it?"

"Couldn't tell; didn't wanna get too close an' have 'em see me. He was in a suit though."

Larson grew pale. "In a suit? A big man, about fifty or so?"

"No, didn't look that old. An' tall, but just average size."

Larson spat out a name. "Dawson."

Billy turned a shade similar to his boss. "Dawson? The guy you hired to sell the cattle in Double Rock?"

"Who the hell you think I meant?" Larson fumed a moment, sitting and knotting his fists on his desk. "Shoulda figgered an' not had him killed like I killed Crandall."

This admission was news to Billy, but he concealed his surprise.

"Just 'cause the Marshal's alive don't mean nothin'," Billy said. "They say he's unconscious, that he don't remember nothin' about how he was shot and where."

Larson glared at him. "That don't mean he might start rememberin' at the wrong time."

"What're we gonna do?"

Larson thought a moment. "If the Marshal is as bad off as you say, he's not gonna be in any shape to lead a posse back here, even if he does remember. An' Stokes ain't gonna do nothin' neither.

"But we're gonna be ready just in case."

* * *

Banty had made a record riding to the ranch and back, bringing Rawhide and Dakota with him. He, Laredo, Bear, Kat, and Slim had all been deputized by Conrad. He had three deputy badges in his pockets and swore in Laredo, Kat and Bear. And when he was done that he went back to the Sheriff's office to be sure Hammond was locked up safe and secure.

There were almost three dozen men gathered now outside the Sheriff's office. Bear rolled him out to face them before mounting up.

"Men, you don't know me, most of you. I'm Bill Conrad, U.S. Marshal based in Double Rock." He tapped a thick finger on his badge. "This tin star gives me authority to enforce the law anywhere in the country. I've officially deputized some of you with badges; I'm about to swear in the rest of you.

"You're about to go up against a gang of rustlers, some of them real bad men. Some of you might not make it back. If anybody wants to back out now, I won't hold it against you. An' I don't think Kat Crandall or any o' her men'll hold it against you either." He sort of doubted that last statement, but let it lay.

As he had seen many times before the men glanced at each other, expecting, wondering, challenging someone to drop out. They all stood firm.

These are good men, Conrad thought.

"All right. Laredo is in charge, an' Slim is gonna show the way. Good luck to all of you."

Laredo put up his hand as a signal for all to be ready. They set their horses in a ragged formation, and with Slim on one side and Kat on the other they rode out. Conrad watched as they went.

Not for the first time he cursed this chair-on-wheels, wishing he was straddling a horse and riding off with them.

* * *

The posse reached a certain point and Slim said to Laredo, "Stop here."

Laredo raised his hand and everyone halted. "OK, we're stopped. Why?"

"If we go much further the look-outs will hear us. And if they know I'm gone Larson is sure to put as many men guarding the road as he can.

Laredo looked about. The road was narrow and bordered by rock on either side. He got his binoculars from his saddlebag and searched the skylines. The boulders ran on both sides as far as he could see. Snipers might be behind every rock. Laredo remembered hearing about a squad of Texas Rangers a few years back, about a half dozen, who were lured into an ambush in a dead end canyon not too much different from this. They had been guided by someone they trusted too, someone who betrayed them. All six were slaughtered; when other Rangers searched for them a couple months later they found that someone had dug graves and buried them. He didn't want that to happen to him. Not here; not with what he needed to accomplish.

"Are you takin' us the right way or not?" Kat asked, riding up.

"I'm takin' you the right way," Slim said, "but the *safe* way. They know I'm gone by now, an' I gotta play it safe for me too."

"So what're you plannin' to do?" Kat asked.

"I know another way, an' I don't think they'll be guardin' it. Least not as much as the main one."

Laredo and Kat exchanged glances. The others had been listening from around them and waited for their leaders' decision.

"We gotta trust you Slim," Laredo said. "You showed up

Hammond for what he was. An' you're prob'ly right about the gang aimin' for you." He searched the rocks for a hidden entrance and gave up. "Which way do we go?"

"Here." Slim rode his horse to a set of rocks that were almost like a giant's stepping stones, but manageable by a horse. Laredo followed, Kat behind him. The passage was only wide enough for single file, even more narrow than the road. Over the rocks and beyond was another path, rock and woods bordering it. Once everyone was over the step stones Slim called a halt again.

"This leads right up to the cabins where our hide-out is," Slim said. He pointed to a branch off the path that led into the trees. "We go in that way an' we'll be on him before he knows it."

Bear saw the branch of the path. "It looks like it'd be easy to guard." He faced Slim. Both were big, hard men. "This ain't a trap, is it?"

"No, I swear it."

"But they might be lookin' for you just the same, right?" Bear continued.

"Yeah, prob'ly." Slim gulped.

Bear said to Laredo, "How 'bout if Slim leads the way? If he's their friend they won't hurt him. If not, we'll know that too."

Slim's mass shuddered like a huge pudding. "Wait a minute..."

"I think it's a good idea," Kat said. She pulled up closer to him. "If you're on our side, Slim, this is your chance to prove it. If you really quit Larson's gang an' you're sidin' with us, you ride in first."

"An'... an' if they kill me?"

Kat laid a hand on his arm. "I'll avenge you."

Slim gazed down at her. She'd do it, too. "All right; I'll go first."

Laredo formed the line, placing his mount just behind Slim. When the posse was ready Laredo gave him the go-ahead.

Slim drew his gun and held it on his thigh as he guided his horse onto the hidden path. He heard the others behind him.

The path had some curves, and tree branches and brush

reached out and tickled at him and his horse as they went. Then the path straightened and the light of a wide clearing was seen ahead. Laredo and Kat, riding just a little behind Slim, saw a glimpse of it past him. Like the rest of those following they also had their guns at the ready.

Slim paused, nodded once back to Kat, and broke into the clearing. The others stayed back a moment or two.

Two or three were in the yard, and Slim saw Larson come out of the main house with someone that looked like Billy. He halted for a moment, a few yards beyond the trees, waiting for the moment they might see him.

The men in the yard were saddling their horses, probably to join the others on guard. Larson came out to talk to them, Billy following.

It was Billy who noticed the single, large rider who seemed to be making a target of himself. The size of the rider was unmistakable.

"Larson! That's Slim!" He drew his gun and fired.

The bullet sang past Slim's ear. He wasn't going to wait for the next one and kicked spur to his horse, turning him to the right.

The others drew their guns, their horses forgotten, and aimed their fire at Slim. It was obvious that Larson had ordered him shot on sight, maybe even put a bounty on him.

Slim knew about a moving target being harder to hit; he hoped that old adage was going to prove right.

But while he was avoiding their bullets a war cry sounded from the hidden path, and riders started coming at them. Some followed Slim, forming almost without thinking into the circle used by Indians in attacking. It probably saved some lives, because Slim's idea of a moving target was right.

The outlaws spent their ammo on the attackers, and hammers started to click on empty.

"Get inside!" Larson ordered.

The order startled one of the men, who stayed out and tried to reload. A rider charged at him, fired one shot, and the Larson man was out of the fight.

Larson and Billy had already huddled into the main house. One of the other men had managed to dive in with them before they shut the door.

"How many did you see?" Larson demanded as he hurriedly stuffed cartridges into his gun.

"A couple dozen," Billy said. "Kat don't have that many; an' Stokes sure didn't lead this."

"An' I don't see no shot-up Marshal, either," Larson said. "That ain't no posse; it's a lynch mob."

Billy had re-loaded and started firing out the window. "Don't make no difference if they're legal or not; shot or hanged, we'll be just as dead."

The gunfire outside started to increase; there were more than just the posse or mob or whatever now.

"The men've come!" Larson said. "Must've heard the shots!"

"Hope there's not more, comin' in the main trail if there's nobody guardin' it." He fired again, winging one in the shoulder.

Outside the outlaws clashed with the posse, bullets both missing and finding marks. Men fell from both sides, some just wounded, some done with this world.

Laredo and Kat had found cover behind a low wall, between the house and one of the other buildings. There was one small window they could see and both poured lead into it.

"It's useless," Laredo said. "We can't see in from here an' we're wastin' shells."

"An' they sure ain't comin' out as long as they think they're safe."

Laredo saw a clump of dry scrub nearby. "I got an idea. Cover me." He handed his gun to Kat and slid on the ground to the scrub bush. He got a hold of it and pulled. *Just like pullin' weeds,* he thought. *They don't come up when you want 'em to.* He took both hands and gave a harder yank. A good part of the bush came up. Not much, but it might be enough.

He stayed on the ground, dragging the dead bush with him until he was against the wooden cabin. He found a chink in the joining of logs and stuffed the brush in there. Striking a match he lit it. The smoke started to lead through the chink into the cabin. Laredo slid back the way he came.

"Smokin' 'em out?" Kat said when he got back.

"I know; oldest trick in the book. That's why it'll work."

He was right, in a way. The smoke didn't spread like he'd hoped; but the cabin itself started to catch fire.

Inside the outlaw who had managed to join them was coughing his head off. "That's it; I'm quittin'." He tossed his gun out the window and opened the door, holding up his hands." There was a shot and he arched backwards suddenly like a bent bow and fell to the ground.

Larson had shot him in the back.

But the smoke was getting to him and Billy now too.

Outside was chaos. Ammo spent, much of the fighting had become on foot and hand to hand. Those with knives had an advantage, unless in wrestling his opponent his knife got turned on him. Fists sometimes did as good a job as bullets, especially for some outlaws who were born bullies who had never faced someone who actually had the nerve to hit back. Such gave up rather than suffer more.

Banty's small stature, as it had always been, was misleading. He took on more than one rustler who was more than his size and got him down. Grady was one of them, and the fight seemed even for a good long time. Banty finally got Grady on his back and just beat his face in until Grady gave in.

Bear had sought Butch and found him. The two big men went after each other like a pair of grizzlies, and biting teeth and gouging fingers were part of their armory. They punched and pawed and clawed and rolled over much of the ground. Both

had faces that looked like raw meat, and blood flowed from several places.

Butch got Bear under him, grabbed his ears, and started pounding Bear's head against the ground. Bear got a similar hold and boxed both ears. Stunned, Bear rolled him off and sent a kick to Butch's head. The huge heavy boot even dug a dent into Butch's skull, but the big man shook himself to some level of consciousness.

But Bear wasn't done, and he dropped down on Butch like a mountain, hammering with both fists. Bear was like a madman, pummeling Butch until he lay very still, and even for a moment or two afterward. Finally he stopped, rose, staggered, and fell beside Butch, his battle fought and won.

BOOK TITLE

The cabin started to blaze around them, and one of the walls fell in. Choking on smoke, roasting from the flames, Larson and Billy fled from fiery death.

Laredo and Kat were waiting for them.

There was an exchange of gunfire, but no one had much ammo left. All four shot sparingly, from behind whatever protection they found, however inadequate.

"This one's mine," Laredo declared, gesturing to Larson.

Kat grinned. "Good; I got a score to settle with this one," her eyes on Billy. The two rustlers had chosen separate shelter.

Larson's gun clicked on empty.

Laredo rose from cover, his six-gun trained on Larson. Larson rose too, on unsteady legs, clutching his useless gun in a hand that dangled at his side. Now seeing him clearly for the first time, Larson stammered one word; a word of sudden but not quite full recognition.

"Y-you!"

Laredo came on, relentless, his gun rising to point at the center of Larson's forehead.

Larson couldn't move; his legs wouldn't obey his brain.

Laredo squeezed his trigger.

The hammer fell on an empty chamber.

A grim smile curled Laredo's lips. "You don't think I'd waste a bullet on you, do you?" He tossed the gun aside. "I need you alive." He balled his fists at his sides. "But first we're gonna have some fun."

Larson was more than ready, and determined to win. The gun dropped from his hand. He tossed dirt into Laredo's face for starters and sent a roundhouse blow that staggered him. Following up he punished him, left and right, body and head blows, and Laredo backed away for room. He managed to duck a blow and sent a straight shot into Larson's mid-section, doubling him over and setting him up for an uppercut. Larson went to the ground and half rose to his knees.

"Get up. I'm not done with you yet."

Larson stared at Laredo and the latter saw the wheels of recognition align themselves in the rustler's head, putting a name to the now known face. "Connors. You're Pete Connors."

"That's right, Larson; or should I call you Saunders?"

The name Saunders lit something inside Larson. He came to his feet swinging, and Laredo took a couple steps back to avoid the blows before charging in with two full punches to the jaw. Larson staggered and Laredo poured more on, pounding his body and hammering his brow. Larson retreated a moment and lunged at Laredo, sending him on his back. They grappled and rolled, neither getting solid punches in, but wearing each other out.

Kat emptied her gun and squatted behind the boulder where she had ensconced herself. Two more shots pinged overhead, scattering chips. Then she heard two clicks, and another, and she smiled.

Billy dropped the gun and looked about. There was a gun lying beside one of the men who had fallen, about twenty yards to his left. Kat had run out of bullets; all he had to do was sprint to that gun and get it, hoping there was at least one cartridge left.

He sprung from cover, ran, and was suddenly struck down.

Kat had seen him run, gave chase, and launched herself at him, bringing him down in a tackle.

She straddled his back, raining blows on his shoulders. He shoved himself up, spilling her off. They rose slowly, eying each other.

Billy was grinning. "You gonna beat me up, Kat?" He was backing away for room, running his fingers over his lips in anticipation.

"That's the idea, Billy," Kat said, stripping off her gloves and raising her fists. "Don't think I can do it?"

He laughed. "Just 'cause you gave me that black eye when we were twelve don't mean nothin'. I was a boy then; I'm a grown man now." He refused to assume a defensive posture, his hands remaining open at his sides.

"We can reload an' shoot it out," Kat said, "but you owe me this fight, Billy Holcomb, an' whether you defend yourself or not, I'm gonna collect."

The right she sent to his jaw rocked him, and the left staggered him. *She means business,* he thought, before her fist landed in his right eye. That really hurt! He blinked, and his eye was already glazing over. He tried to focus on her.

BOOK TITLE

She stood in a decent imitation of a boxer's stance, her fists raised and waiting. "C'mon," she taunted, "it's no fun this way. Forget I'm a female. Fight me." She waded in with three quick body blows and stepped back again.

Billy struggled for breath and his hands raised themselves and closed into fists. He had gotten into fights in his day, but he had never struck a lady, and he told her so.

"I'm not a lady," Kat said. "An' you should know that well enough." Her right again drilled into his mid-section, and instinct sent his left to her jaw. It spun her around and nearly took her off her feet.

Billy made a dive for the gun.

Laredo had Larson under him, but not for long. With an effort Larson threw him off and tried to run. Laredo swung a leg, tripping him, and he came to his feet as Larson picked himself up. Laredo's right sailed in a wide arc, crashing against Larson's chin, slamming him down and against a rock. Laredo stepped toward him and Larson kicked him square in the chest, toppling him as Larson with effort regained his feet.

Both men were tired, and Larson stood panting while Laredo forced himself up. Bruises were darkening their faces, blood seeped from nose and lips, and bodies screamed relief from their agony.

But like two tired bulls they closed again, locked together, fists thudding wherever they found targets. Laredo struck his head against Larson's and both skulls rang, but it broke them apart.

They stood panting, both wanting it over but neither wanting to give in.

"You can end this," Larson puffed, "but I know you won't."

Laredo shook his head. "You're no good — dead."

Larson grinned. "But you'd be good for me — dead."

"Ahuh. So I guess I'm gonna have to put you out without killing you."

Larson barked a laugh. "I wanna see ya try."

Laredo pulled as much strength together as he could and swung. Larson caught it on his arm and drove his fist into Laredo's stomach, bending him over and making his head a perfect target for a two-handed hammer blow from Larson. But in falling Laredo grabbed hold of Larson's legs, pulling him down with him. Again both were on the ground, scrambling for dominance, clawing and grasping.

As Billy dove for the gun Kat dove on him, landing hard on his back and wrapping an arm around his neck, pulling it back. They rolled, Billy keeping grip on the gun and lying on Kat, who swung a leg over his, holding him down. She grasped the wrist that held the gun and tried to turn it, but he was too strong for her. Even so, he was unable to bring the gun to bear on her, and while they struggled no progress was made by either.

He wrenched his arm free and brought the gun butt down on her leg. In reflex her leg moved and he partially wriggled free. But she grasped her own arm and hugged the headlock tighter, preventing him from entirely escaping. She tried turning, to get him under her, but the effort was useless. He began striking her arms, but her stubbornness kept the hold secure.

Billy finally twisted his own body, getting her on top and hoped the effort broke the hold, but she maintained it and straddled him. He shoved up onto his feet and she was forced to release him and back off.

He aimed the gun at her and fired.

She ducked, grabbing the gun arm with both hands, and shoving her shoulder into him, flipping him onto the ground. The gun went flying and both dove for it.

Already brutal, the fight between Laredo and Larson grew even more bloody. Both nearly spent, both determined to win, no quarter was given until one or the other was unconscious or dead.

Laredo at last got Larson on his back, straddled him, and grabbed handfuls of hair from the sides of his head, banging it against the stony ground until Larson's eyes fluttered closed. He bumped it viciously a few more times for good measure and sat back, exhausted.

Banty came up with some rope and started tying him up while Laredo was still sitting atop him. Laredo didn't rise until Banty had tied his ankles too.

Kat clutched the gun and hugged it to her, rolling and

aiming it with both hands. Billy had fallen just a few feet beside her, and half raised himself.

It was tense; Kat kept the gun trained on him, but didn't pull the trigger. Both were all but out of breath, but Billy managed to speak. A mocking smile curled his lips.

"You're not gonna kill me, are ya Kat? After all we meant to each other?"

She held the gun steady. Cold green fire glared on him.

"That was a swell fight. Bet you're just as hot other ways too, if you know what I mean."

The cold glare tightened.

"But I guess Laredo knows all about that, don't he?"

She thumbed back the hammer.

"Think maybe he'll share?"

She squeezed the trigger.

The hammer clicked on empty.

Billy's grin was now deadly. He started toward her.

She thumbed back the hammer and squeezed the trigger again.

The gun seemed to explode in her hand.

When the smoke cleared Billy was still grinning, his eyes still open and staring; but whatever he was staring at was not of this world. Above those eyes was a large, red, blossom where the .45 slug had entered.

She sagged back, the gun forgotten and her hands flat against the ground, trembling arms tried their best to hold her up.

Then other hands encircled those arms, and she was lifted, and she collapsed into Laredo's comforting embrace.

And no one there, including Kat herself, dared mention afterward the long, deep, powerful cry as she sobbed against his consoling chest.

EPILOGUE

Sheriff Stokes' jail had never been so full. In fact, folks around town didn't remember a time when there were more than two or three in the cells; and that was for the few times Stokes bothered to lock someone up for drunk and disorderly. The survivors of the gunfight, on the outlaw side, filled the two cells leaving no room to lie down. They complained to Stokes, and Stokes complained to Conrad since he had forced Stokes' hand in actually doing his duty for once.

"I got no pity for rustlers an' murderers," Conrad rumbled. He was healed enough to stand for short periods; or at least stubborn enough. "I sent a cable back to my deputies at Double Rock to send the Iron Wagon."

"Iron Wagon?" Stokes asked.

"Yeah. Kinda a mobile pokey," Conrad explained. "Heard Hickok uses something like it and stole his idea. We can store some o' them in it when it comes."

Conrad leaned on a heavy cane as he approached the cells. "Far as I'm concerned, justice would be stringin' you all up to the highest trees around. But this star says I enforce the law, which means all you buzzards get a trial."

Larson was the only one not in a cell. Manacled, chained, and cowed he was being held separately in a windowless basement, guarded by Laredo, Bear, and Banty in shifts. Conrad had proposed the plan to Laredo, who had agreed.

"So you're Pete Connors, huh?" Conrad had said to him.

Laredo had answered with a grim nod. "I am, Marshal. I owe too much to you to tell a lie now."

Conrad shoved the thanks aside. "You an' your friends saved my life, so I reckon I can do you a turn. Truth is, I thought I recognized you when we men in Double Rock, but a man can be mistaken about a face."

"I didn't do that robbery an' murder I'm accused of back in Laredo," Pete said. "But I couldn't prove it…"

"Until you found Larson, or Saunders, or whatever his name really is."

"That's right," Pete agreed. "What're you gonna do with him, Marshal?"

"A U. S. Marshal's got a lot of power, if he uses it right," Conrad said. "I think we can get a confession outta Saunders now, or at least prove he did it. That still means you're goin' back to Laredo and standin' trial." He peered closely at Pete. "I'll be at your side for the whole thing, son, an' you can count on me to back your play."

"That's fine with me, Marshal," Pete said. "You want me to ride with you to take Saunders to Laredo an' I'll do it, even if I gotta face the music to prove I'm innocent."

"That's about it, son. Soon as I'm well enough to ride that far we're leavin'. An' that's gonna be a lot sooner than doc thinks." Conrad steadied all his weight on the cane as he gripped Pete's shoulder. "I'm sure you'll be cleared." To Kat he added, "An' while you two were roundin' these varmints up I sent a telegram to the oil company Hammond so mis-represented. They're sendin' a man out soon as they can. Won't be here for 'bout a month they tell me, but I expect good news by then."

"Thanks, Marshal." Kat shook his hand and there was a brief gripping contest between them that brought grins to both of them.

"An' I also got news about the registry of that so-called Box O brand," Conrad added. "Ain't no such thing, so while we're in Laredo you go back to Double Rock an' look up them too cattle buyers. I'll write a note for you to show 'em before I go."

Kat thanked him again and looked like she was about to hug him this time but put an end to it by thrusting her hands in her jeans.

Conrad winked at Pete. "Strong woman you got there, Connors."

Pete grinned. "Yeah, I know."

Kat flamed. "Listen here Laredo, or Connors, or whatever your name is. I'm not your woman or anybody else's."

"O' course not, Kat; o' course not."

* * *

As he said, Conrad wasn't about to wait for the OK from any doctor. Soon as he could mount a horse he was ready to ride. They took it slow at first, and Connors (as we will call him from here on out) had to doctor and re-bandage his wounds a couple of times. Riding a horse even over good country can sometimes open a bad wound. But the two developed a friendship along the way.

Saunders, formerly known as Larson, was sullen and silent the whole way. Connors and Conrad were just as glad; neither wanted to talk to him. Just so *Saunders* talked and talked straight when the time came they were satisfied.

It was several days to Laredo but they got into town about an hour before sunset and took their prisoner straight to the Sheriff's office. Some passers-by on the street noticed Connors and murmured to each other. Connors eyed them warily.

"Don't let them get to you, son," Conrad said. "This here Saunders'll clear you an' these here folks'll have to find somebody new to gossip about." He hustled Saunders inside and Laredo followed.

Sheriff Duke Bradford was tall and lanky, his white hair and mustache belying a wiry strength and the energy of men half his age. When he saw Connors he nearly jumped from his chair, his gun already in hand.

"You can turn that gun over here, Sheriff," Conrad said, giving Saunders a shake. "If you wanna aim at somebody, aim it at Saunders here."

Bradford studied Conrad. He saw the Marshal's star, Saunders' hands manacled behind him, and the man he knew as Connors, wanted in his town for murder and robbery, apparently helping guard the prisoner.

"OK, you're a U. S. Marshal," Bradford said. "You better tell me what this is about, 'cause I been searchin' for this one... (he indicated Connors) for about five years now."

"I'm Marshal Bill Conrad, and I brought both men here. Now if you just lock Saunders up I'll explain what this is about."

Bradford secured Saunders in a cell and returned to his office. "Looks like we gotta palaver a bit. How about some coffee?"

Everyone agreed and Bradford pulled out a couple of tin mugs and poured a hot almost tarry fluid into each. Conrad wondered if it might have a use as railroad fuel, but wisely restrained the comment.

A half hour later Conrad and Connors had told their stories and Bradford had listened. Bradford remembered the case and even pulled out some notes he'd kept on the crime and the trial. When his two visitors were done he compared it with the notes and rubbed his bony chin.

"Yeah, I can see where it mighta been a frame-up. Come to think of it Saunders left town soon as Connors here was arrested, which didn't look suspicious at the time but sure does now."

"I was the bank's chief clerk," Connors said, "and one of the three people who knew the gold shipment was going to be there."

"So you were a likely suspect," Bradford nodded. "We all figgered that. An' you were found with an empty money sack with the bank's imprint."

"An' I had a quarrel with Landers, the bank president, that afternoon. I admitted to that in court. But I didn't kill him an' I didn't rob the bank."

"You said that money sack was planted."

"Yeah, an' I still say it."

"When you escaped jail we all figgered it was 'cause you were guilty."

"No, it's 'cause I wanted to find the skunk who set me up."

There was a rattle of the bars from inside. "Sheriff!"

The three men entered the jail. Saunders had run a tin plate along the bars.

"What is it, Saunders?" Bradford asked.

Saunders addressed Conrad first. "Marshal, if I stayed in Clear Springs I'd've been tried for rustlin', right?"

"Yep; an' for the murder of Tom Crandall too, if Kat has anything to say about it."

"You can count me in on that one too, Saunders," Connors said. "I'm backin' any play of Kat's."

Saunders chuckled. "Yeah, I figgered that. So that means the rope. An' if I confess to this, it means the rope too."

"Yeah," Conrad agreed, "but you'll also set an innocent man free."

Saunders leaned against the bars, clutching one in each hand. "Guess maybe I'll do somethin' right in my life, since it's about over either way." He turned to the Sheriff. "Sheriff, you got somebody to write what I say?"

"Sure. I can get Lawyer Dudley over here, to make it nice an' legal."

Saunders nodded his head. "It's the rope for me or a bullet if I try to escape. Well, you're only dead once."

* * *

The day Conrad and Collins left with their prisoner Kat rode with Rawhide and Banty back to Double Rock. Spencer and Marley were waiting, and Kat showed them the note from the Marshal.

Spencer and Marley looked at each other suspiciously. Kat grinned and winked at her two companions. She and Rawhide had seen this before on trips with Kat's father. Spencer and Marley were the best of friends; but that friendship went into a coma when it came to bargaining and business.

"Tell you what, Kat," Spencer said, "I'll offer this much a head." He wrote a figure on a notebook page and had to twist himself awkwardly so Marley couldn't look over his shoulder.

Kat took the bid. "Hmmm. Mighty interestin'."

Meanwhile Marley had scribbled some figuring on his own notebook and tore the page off and handed it to Kat. Spencer tried to steal a look and Marley crumpled the sheet in his hand.

Kat unrolled the paper. "Hmm. Mighty interestin'."

The two cattlemen stared at her open mouthed.

"What's so interestin'?" they asked, almost in unison.

Kat grinned. "You two gentlemen just quoted me the same offer." She scratched her head. "An' I'm plumb baffled which one o' you I'm gonna oblige."

The half-joking all-earnest squabbling between the two men finally ended when Banty broke in.

"Seems I remember a story in the Bible about a king called

Solomon. There was these two women who both laid claim to the same baby boy. Solomon's suggestion was to cut the child in half and divvy the parts up between 'em. Now, I don't recollect just how that story come out; hope it weren't the worse for the child. But mebbe we kin split the herd between you two, since it's all the same price an' we're all friends an' all."

Marley and Spencer looked at each other. Astonishment floated on both faces until both finally nodded.

"Deal."

* * *

As predicted, it was nearly a month before Howard Eldridge, representative of Hadley Oil, arrived in Clear Springs. He brought a crew of technicians with him and Bear and Kat took them to the site Connors had shown them. As they rode out another rider came to join them.

Bear shaded his eyes. "By gum if it ain't Laredo!"

Kat reined in her horse and looked.

It was Laredo. He waved his hat at them as he drew closer.

"Hi, Kat."

"Hi, Laredo."

There was silence for what seemed a month or so. Eldridge and the technicians were both curious and impatient.

"Laredo," Bear said, "these men are from the oil company. We were just about to show 'em what you found."

Connors, also known as Laredo, grinned at the men. "Then I'll show you myself. Follow me."

* * *

The technicians said it was potentially one of the richest strikes they had ever seen. Eldridge added, "I'll go back to town and wire my office. Once I receive their consent I'll have the papers drawn up. Miss Crandall, you are a very rich woman."

Kat stuck out her hand; Eldridge took it as he did a city lady's hand and was surprised at the manlike grip and shake she received.

"Mr. Eldridge, call me Kat."

Eldridge was taken aback again but smiled in embarrassment and said, "All right, Kat," and returned the handshake.

* * *

Kat and Laredo stood alone over the spot where giant towers and drilling rigs would soon grow from the soil.

"Guess now that you're name's cleared you'll be headed back to Laredo."

"No; Laredo's not my town anymore." He grinned. "But I don't mind you usin' it as my name."

Kat laughed. "You're right. You just don't look like a Pete Connors to me." He laughed with her. "So what are you plans?"

"Well, I'm sure even with the oil wells you'll still wanna run this ranch. An' that means you'll need a foreman an' some hands. I'd like to apply for the job, if you're willin.'"

"You're hired." She wasn't sure what the stir of excitement was that she felt. It was more than just his return and his desire to stay on.

"On one condition," he added.

She was puzzled. "What's that?"

"I wanna be partners."

"Partners?"

"Yeah. You an' me."

She stepped back, her hands loosely clenched at her side. "You sayin' this is your idea of a marriage proposal?"

"Yeah, plain an' simple."

She stared straight at him, her fists pressed tightly on her hips. Her green eyes were narrowed, boring into his. "Well all right. But don't you think just 'cause we're getting hitched that you can tame me."

Laredo put his arms around her. She resisted a bit, pummeling his chest for a moment before she gave up. He chuckled.

"Kat, I wouldn't even try."

BOOK TITLE

AUTHOR'S NOTE

I grew up watching the TV westerns of the 1950's and '60's. The first show I remember calling "my own" rather than something my parents watched was *Hopalong Cassidy*. There were a lot of westerns in those days, mostly written as children's shows but many were watched by adults as well. In the early and mid '50's these shows were on in the evening, but by the late '50's and early '60's many had moved to Saturday morning and afternoon.

At one time Saturdays included flying about the modern west with *Sky King* in his twin-engine *Songbird*, followed by Roy Rogers, also set in the post WW II west, then back to those "thrilling days of yesteryear" with *The Lone Ranger*. Later in the afternoon, according to memory, were *Annie Oakley* and *Wild Bill Hickok*, having adventures their historical counterparts surely never did.

So far my professional writing output has been three mysteries, two of which are still in print. This is my first western; and hopefully not my last. It's not the kind of western that has appeared on the screen since directors like Sergio Leone and Sam Peckinpah re-invigorated the genre in the '60's and '70's. Their westerns, and many that have followed, are raw and earthy and dusty; probably more like the real west may have been. This novel, however, is not in that vein.

The tone of this novel is intended to recall the old B westerns of the '30's and '40's, the kind that gave rise to nostalgic popular songs in the '70's like "Whatever happened to Randolph Scott? (...Whatever happened to Gene and Tex and Roy and Rex, the Durango Kid?" the song continues.) by the Statler Brothers, and "Hoppy, Gene, and Me" sung by Roy Rogers himself. It's intended also to recall that child of the B western, the old 30-minute western TV series: Roy and Gene followed Hoppy onto the small screen, along with *The Cisco Kid*, portrayed as he had been in B pictures by Duncan Renaldo. *The Lone Ranger* made the transition from radio to TV, just behind Hoppy; though William Boyd's series debuted in 1947, initially they were half hour cuts of some of his theatrical movies. *The Lone Ranger* was the first western especially filmed for TV, debuting in 1949.

The characters in this novel, therefore, have their originals in the old B movies and 50's TV series. Laredo is an amalgam of any of the drifters played in countless westerns by Hoot or Buck or Coop or Randy Scott or Duke, in his early B period. (And if you don't recognize the nicknames of these western movie greats, shame on you. Look them up.) Bear Ketchum, admittedly, has his counterpart in one of the most beloved characters of so-called "adult" westerns, Hoss Cartright. And Banty is largely inspired by Raymond Hatton, with a touch of Al "Fuzzy" St. John. (Again, if these names are strange to you look them up.)

Allison Katherine "Kat" Crandall is an amalgam of some of the many B western heroines who rode the range with Roy and Gene and the others; she especially has some Dale Evans, Gail Davis, and a good dose of Maureen O'Hara in her. I know, Ms O'Hara was never in a B western; but she held her own opposite Duke Wayne in several of his westerns, so she counts.

So don't look for the "real" west in this novel so much as a reflection of the "reel" west; which in some ways was also the west of Zane Grey and Max Brand and Luke Short.

So "return with us now to those thrilling days of yesteryear," and the story of Kat Crandall.

Stephen L. Brooks

June, 2014

Made in the USA
Columbia, SC
11 March 2019